Marion Lane and the
Deadly Rose

Also in this series
Marion Lane and the Midnight Murder

Marion Lane and the Deadly Rose

T.A. Willberg

ORION

First published in Great Britain in 2022 by Orion Fiction,
an imprint of The Orion Publishing Group Ltd
Carmelite House, 50 Victoria Embankment
London EC4Y ODZ

An Hachette UK Company

1 3 5 7 9 10 8 6 4 2

A CIP catalogue record for this book is
available from the British Library.

ISBN (Hardback) 978 1 4091 9668 6
ISBN (Export Trade Paperback) 978 1 4091 9669 3
ISBN (eBook) 978 1 4091 9671 6
ISBN (Audio) 978 1 4091 9672 3

Typeset by Born Group
Printed and bound in Great Britain by Clays Ltd, Elcograf S.p.A.

MIX
Paper from
responsible sources
FSC® C104740

books.co.uk

For Willie

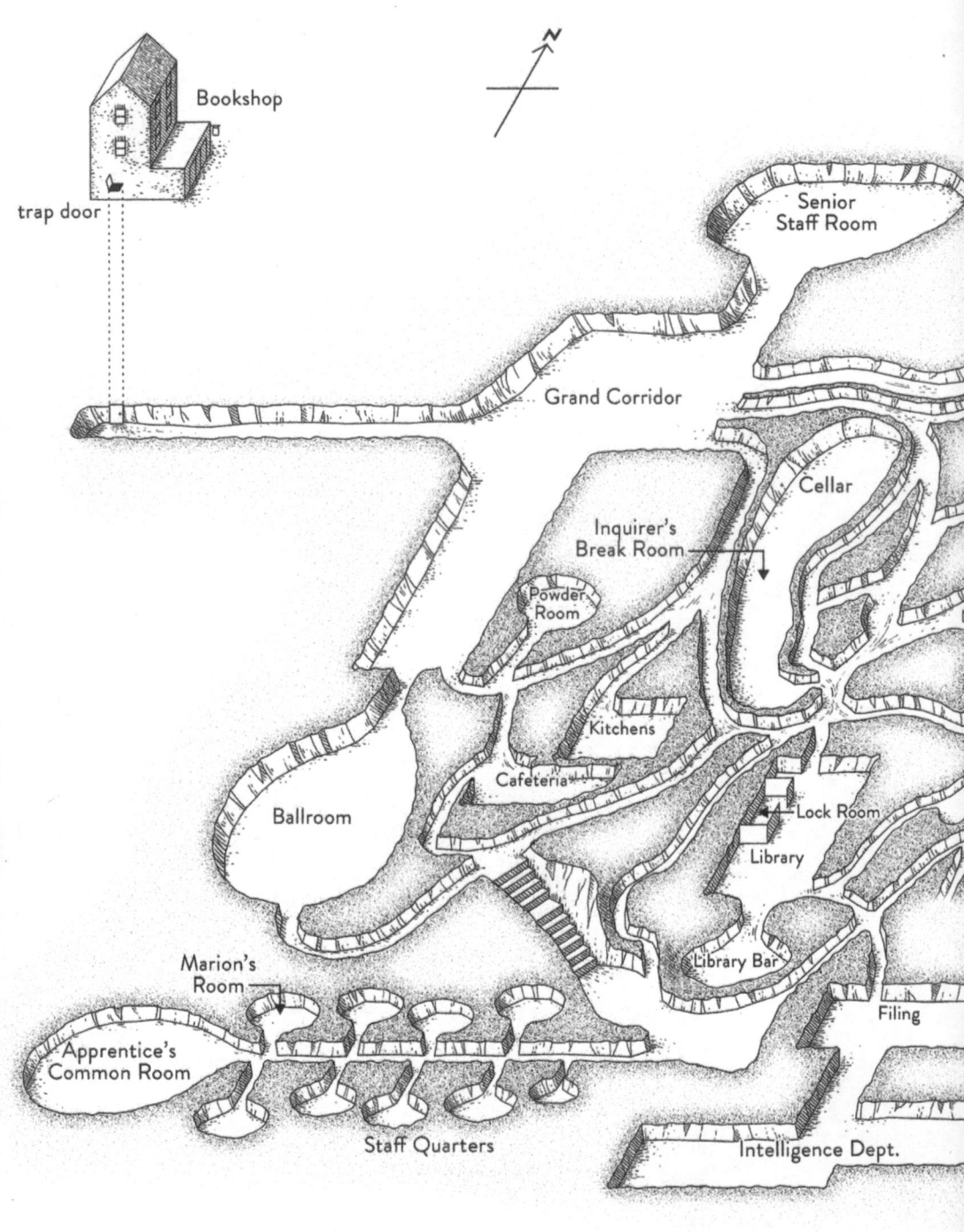

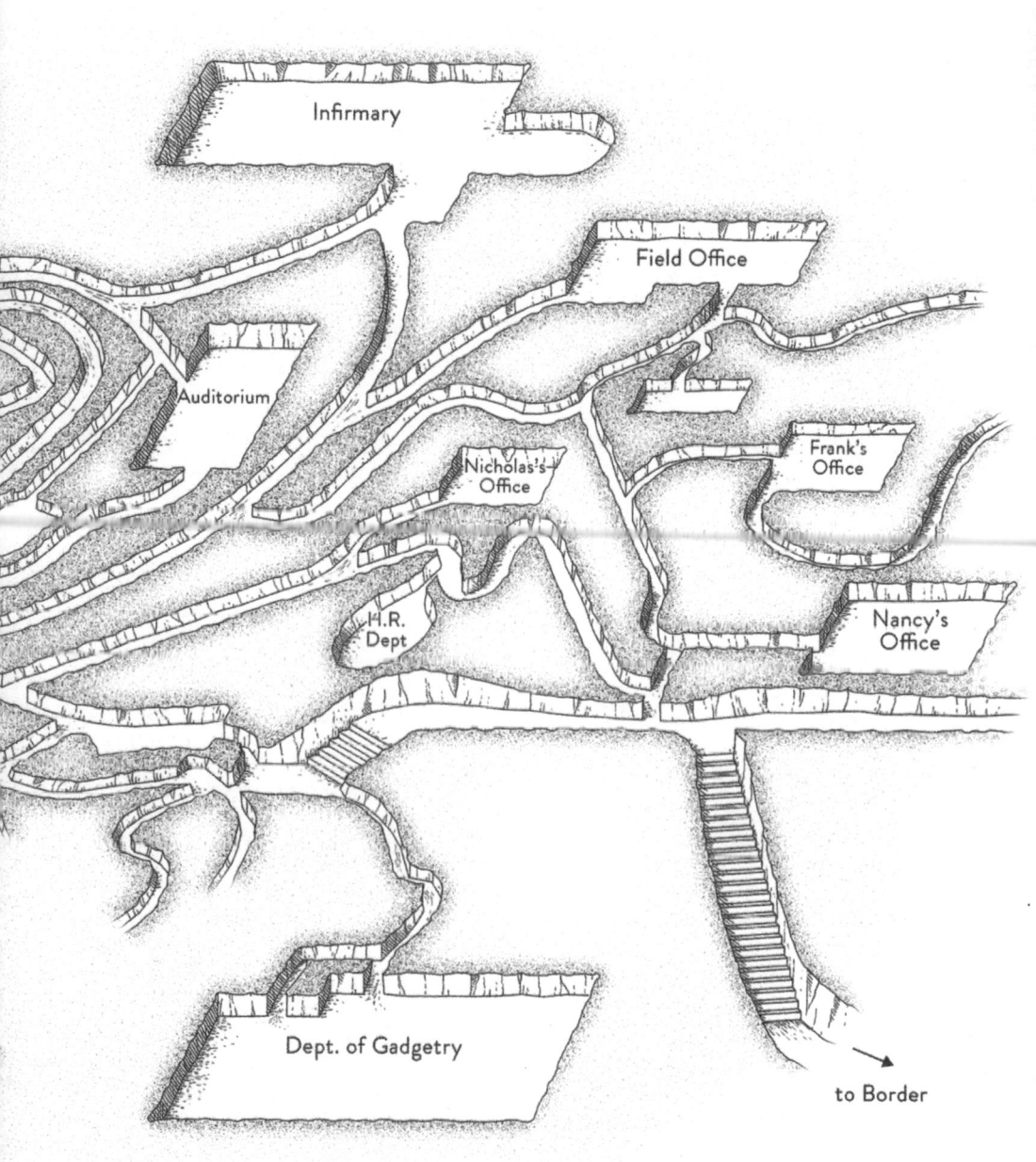

Infirmary

Field Office

Auditorium

Nicholas's Office

Frank's Office

Nancy's Office

H.R. Dept

Dept. of Gadgetry

to Border

I

Rendezvous

30 January 1959
Harrogate, England

Fraser Henley had fought against a blustering gale to arrive at the rendezvous point just in time. His fingers and toes were numb, flakes of snow melted on his coat sleeves, his shoulders, his neck. Everywhere. If it weren't that this meeting, and the opportunity it presented, was his only hope of living to see his twenty-eighth birthday, he certainly wouldn't have bothered.

He approached the entrance to the Old Bell Tavern, across the street from the pump room in Harrogate's centre. Heat and golden light streamed through the pub's windows. The sweet scent of ale filled the chilled air, for a moment drawing him back to the quiet, peaceful days of his former life, before he became entangled in the dark, sticky world of deceit and double-crossings and debts that must be repaid.

He checked his watch – five minutes past one in the morning. His contact was late, which wasn't a particularly comforting thought. He dug around in his coat pocket, pulling out a small chrome cigarette case and lighter. He didn't smoke, but a lit cigarette was his signal, a part of the plan. And if

1

there was one thing he'd come to learn about this wretched organisation to which he was chained, it was: you never strayed from the plan.

He lit up and took a long drag, exhaled the smoke into the icy air and peered warily at the street ahead. A part of him now hoped his contact wouldn't arrive at all. That way, Fraser would have a perfectly credible excuse to turn around and make a run for it. It certainly wouldn't be the first time he'd tried.

But where could he go?

He felt the wind cut through his coat, the cold sting his eyes. Everywhere he turned, he saw the edge of a coat tail slip behind a wall, a figure pull back from a windowsill. He heard their whispers on the breeze, felt their presence watching him always.

Wherever he ran, they would follow.

A shiver swept through him, rattling his teeth. He looked up and noticed something ghostly materialise at the top of the street — a stooped figure shifting from the darkness, moving swiftly towards him as though part of the wind itself.

Fraser's heart rate piqued as he saw the figure glide in and out of sight between the sheets of fog. But seconds later, it was right there in front of him: an elderly man, dressed in a dark grey trench coat down to his ankles, a chequered felt hat, a suitcase and polished ebony cane. He had a haggard appearance, deep furrows criss-crossing his brow. The muscles on the right side of his face were atrophied, giving him a permanent and threatening scowl. But even without this distinctive feature, Fraser would have recognised him anywhere — the man of his nightmares, the master of death.

He took a reflexive step backwards, recalling tales of the old man's past, rumours of his malice. He collected himself, realising that any hint of trepidation wouldn't be met with kindness or understanding. He inhaled a quick calming breath and spoke the line he'd practised ad nauseam the past few days. 'Fine weather for a smoke, eh?'

The old man frowned, turned his eyes skywards. The snow was falling faster and thicker than ever – vast sheets of it now layering the footpath like powdered sugar. 'Isn't it just?' he said with a grin, answering the secret signal. His English was clean, save for a hint of an accent.

They stared at each other knowingly, muted exchanges passing between them. Fraser knew he was only in this situation because he'd already made one stupid mistake, already deceived his deceiver, overplayed his hand. And in turn, the old man knew Fraser would do anything now for a chance at redemption.

'Fancy a chat?' the old man suggested, grinning maniacally. He turned around, calling out over his shoulder. 'Come along, follow me.'

Fraser hesitated, but only for a moment. It wasn't a request and he knew it.

The pair made their way around the back of the pub and into a narrow street lined with rubbish bins and scraps of waste. It was dark and mostly quiet, save for the hum of mixed voices from the pub and a peculiar mewling sound coming from somewhere near a large skip less than a yard off.

'By God!' Fraser said, unable to stop himself as he caught sight of the battered, nearly unrecognisable figure lying on the pavement to the left of the skip.

He jerked forwards, but the old man held out his cane, blocking the way.

'Now now, careful, young man, or you might end up the same.'

Fraser stopped, swayed on his feet. He was numb again, though not from the cold this time. 'Wha-what's going on?'

The old man pulled a crisp white handkerchief from his breast pocket and began polishing the head of his cane. 'I thought that might be obvious.' He fixed Fraser with those awful dark and harrowing eyes. 'We know what you did, you and your witless friend over there.' He gestured casually to the crumpled form, who was writhing and burbling, spluttering blood. 'You thought we wouldn't find out? You actually believed you could run away?'

'No,' Fraser blurted, a reflex. He didn't like to think of himself as a coward, but he realised now, he'd do anything to save himself, including betray his closest ally. 'It wasn't my idea,' he lied, glancing again at the body near the skip. It was moving, squirming, barely alive. How long had he been kept like this, half-conscious, in hopeless agony? And in those hours of pain and torment, what secrets had he revealed? 'I told him it was a stupid thing to do. I told him not to.' He turned back to the old man, unable to look his friend in the eye as he embellished the lie. 'I was going to turn him in. I just needed time to come up with a way—'

The old man interrupted. 'You were out of contact for five days. Did you not think that might look suspicious?'

'I wasn't thinking straight, everything happened so fast.' He breathed long and deep, drawing out whatever strength he had left. 'But I'm here now.'

The old man tapped his cane twice against the ground, a signal Fraser didn't understand. 'Does that mean you're still one of us, then?'

Fraser didn't falter this time. He was either one of them or he was dead. Easy choice. 'Of course.' He shifted his gaze to the left. Even in the alleyway's pale light, he could see the tapestry of contusions and swellings sprawled across his colleague's arms and legs. By God . . . even his *face*. But it was the distinctive mark singed into the left side of his chest that cemented Fraser's fear: a rose, pressed deep into the flesh with a branding iron, the old man's hallmark.

He looked away, unable to stomach it.

The old man, apparently satisfied that his message had been received, extracted a small leather satchel from his suitcase. 'Well, I'm very pleased to hear that. And I don't want you to worry, young man. There's no need for you to suffer the same fate as your colleague. So long as you do as you're told. And do it well, of course.'

Fraser took the satchel, extracted a file. He flipped it open. Pages fluttered in the wind, dislodging a letter held loose inside: an invitation printed on buttercream paper. The letter was addressed not to him, but to an alias he'd never used before. The Florist grinned as Fraser's troubled expression deepened.

'This is—'

He stopped, searching for the correct word, staring down at the envelope and considering what it represented: vindication, or a death sentence? He flipped through the file, a curriculum vitae containing a hazy photograph, a date of birth (not his own), personal history (completely fabricated) and list of talents (none of which he possessed).

'Everything is already set up,' the old man said, grinning still, a ghastly lopsided expression that turned Fraser's stomach once more. 'All you need to do is transform yourself into someone else, as you've done many times before. Take up this young man's identity, cast aside your own.'

Fraser ran his thumb over the photograph. Indeed, the face staring back at him was his own. But the eyes were cold and vacant, as though the soul inside had withered. And it would only get worse with time, he knew. Another metamorphosis, another untruth, another piece of his character stripped away, replaced with something alien.

He swallowed back the lump in his throat, folded the photograph and slipped it into his coat pocket. 'The application has been approved, I presume?' He'd been warned many months ago that this stage of the mission might be necessary, the hardest part, the most dangerous part. Only, he'd hoped to have vanished by then.

The old man, who'd been watching him with flickering eyes, now said: 'Partially. The final step is up to you. An interview. All you need to know for the time being is inside the file. The rest I shall explain as soon as we've established a reliable system of communication. Now,' he added with a note of misplaced levity, 'there's a train to London early tomorrow morning. You and I will be on it.'

Fraser decided not to ask any further questions. Frankly, the less he knew right now, the better. He forced his eyes to meet the old man's, who was still smiling at him with the air of someone awaiting his moment to deliver the punchline of some hideous joke.

'Simple enough, isn't it?'

'Yes,' Fraser answered with thinly veiled horror.

The old man clapped his hands together merrily. 'Wonderful, *wonderful!*'

Fraser turned back to the crumpled form behind the skip, bile rising in his throat as he allowed his brain to accept what his eyes were seeing – his once vibrant, healthy friend, now nothing more than a bag of crushed bones. 'What about—?'

'Ah, I'm glad you asked.' The old man leaned over his cane and extracted something else from his suitcase.

A Makarov pistol, Fraser realised with a start.

'Consider this your first . . . *trial.*' He handed Fraser the weapon.

In that moment, it was as if every thought in Fraser's head disappeared, clearing space for the only thing he needed to think about. He knew perfectly well what the old man was asking him to do and he knew just as well what would happen if he didn't. He looked at Eddie – his colleague, his friend, the man he'd spent six years training with, on assignments with, drinking and dancing and taking out girls. Those years had been such an adventure, even though in the back of their minds they'd both known that one day it might come to this if they were unlucky and foolish enough. They'd played with fire and now one of them had to burn.

'Your life or his,' the old man whispered, barely loud enough to hear above the swirling wind and the low drone of music drifting out from the pub's back window.

Fraser closed his eyes for a moment. He wished he were someplace else, in Prague with Eddie, back at home with his mum, at the bottom of the Thames, anywhere but here. He wished he could rewind the past six years, go back to the start and choose a different path. But underneath all that there was also something dark and vile cowering inside him. Something that reminded him why he was here in the first place. Self-preservation.

Your life or his.

He opened his eyes. The snowfall was lighter now, the wind softer. Dawn was coming – a new start, his only hope. He might be a coward, but he was a survivor, too.

He looked at Eddie – his swollen, bloodstained face fixed in an expression of agony, his mouth slightly parted, eyes wide and staring. The rose branding on his chest, testament of his betrayal, stark against his pale skin.

'You'd have done the same,' Fraser said as he pulled the trigger.

2

A Dark Day Dawns

9 February 1959
Fulham, London

Even though it was well past ten o'clock on a Thursday evening, the normally quiet and lifeless atmosphere of the Filing Department at Miss Brickett's Investigations and Inquiries was bustling more than it had in nearly a decade.

Here, concealed within a vast subterranean network of convoluted passageways, workstations, training chambers and grand halls, lay the 'post office' of Miss Brickett's, the clandestine private detective agency that served the City of London in a way no other could. Jutting out from the department's eastern-facing wall were the termini of hundreds of pneumatic tubes that climbed like tentacles upwards through miles of rock and brick to reach concealed postboxes dotted across London, through which Miss Brickett's received case requests and tip-offs.

Now, as the alert light blinked and its bell chimed, a letter appeared from one of the tubes and was collected, documented and sorted according to its contents. The Filing Department, on average, received around ten letters a week from the citizens of

London – those who knew of the Inquirers' existence and the location of the secret postboxes. But tonight alone, the agency had been overwhelmed with nearly two hundred hastily scribbled pleas for help. The requests had started pouring in around 5 p.m., just as Marion Lane, a second-year apprentice detective, had finished up her training duties and settled in the library bar with her colleague and best friend, foppishly handsome Bill Hobb. Marion adored Bill for uncountable reasons, but principally for his ceaseless inclination to protect her from physical strain or emotional turmoil. As if to affirm this once again, he pulled out a rickety bar stool and steadied it as she climbed up before hauling her overfilled haversack onto the counter (wincing with the effort). Bless him. But despite her build – flimsy as a willow branch – she was slightly more proficient at heavy lifting than Bill, though she'd never tell him so.

Unfortunately, they'd not managed even a sip of their selected drinks (wine for Marion, a pint of ale for Bill) before they were accosted by a short, robust lass with cropped hair, dressed in ill-fitting trousers rolled up to the ankles and a loose blouse. Maud Finkle burst into the bar, poured herself a whisky and announced: 'I need help.'

Only because she looked as if she were about to have a fit, Marion and Bill agreed to follow her through the library and down a set of stairs into the Filing Department.

'Blimey, what's going on here?' Bill asked, rolling up his sleeves in preparation as he noted the sky-high piles of unsorted letters scattered across the department floor. Bill was just the sort of person you'd call on in a crisis – quick-witted and invariably rational, always ready to help, albeit with a grunt and the occasional eye-roll.

Maud, normally utterly unflappable and indifferent, pointed to the ceiling and declared: 'The weather.'

Bill frowned, moving a hand through his dark hair. He passed Marion a questioning glance, who offered him a shrug.

Eventually, Maud elaborated. 'Thick fog, a real pea-souper. Zero visibility around London, jams everywhere.' She pressed a thumb into her eye. 'At least six people have already been injured in collisions. And there's looting, of course, and people struggling to get home. And since our sodding filing assistant decided February is a good month to take his annual leave, I've been stationed here all alone! The Met Office say it's already worse than the first day of the Great Smog.' She took a much-needed breath and tightened the belt of her cropped trousers (which were in no way compliant with the official agency uniform for women – pencil skirt and blouse – not that she ever seemed to care).

'Worse than the Great Smog?' Bill asked incredulously. 'You sure?'

The weather outside, whatever it happened to be, was generally of little concern to the employees of Miss Brickett's, sheltered below the earth in a perpetually sunless world.

A bell chimed from somewhere within the department. The yellow alert light flickered urgently and the lid of receiver box number eighteen – which was connected to a postbox hidden near the turnstile at Blackfriars tube station – clicked open to reveal a folded note.

Simultaneously, a group of five fully trained Miss Brickett's detectives (known as Inquirers) raced through the department and up the stairs towards the library, not giving Marion or the others a second glance. As was always the case when out in the field, the Inquirers were dressed inconspicuously in heavy grey overcoats and knee-high boots, each carrying a small leather briefcase, which Marion knew to contain a collection of Miss Brickett's curious and unique contraptions – light orbs, Vagor Compasses and reels of gleaming silver rope.

The bell chimed a second time.

'Someone get that, please!' Maud begged, waving her hand furiously as yet another letter popped from the end of receiver box number eighteen.

Marion jerked forwards. 'Right, yes.' She dashed to the receiver box, Bill hurrying behind her while Maud – who was particularly good at rapid, impassive decisions – took up position at the sorting station.

Marion picked up a newly delivered note and read its contents out loud.

> *'Dear people under there,*
> *I don't know what you're doing, but we need you. NOW.*
> *My neighbour's son wandered off just an hour before the fog started and hasn't come back. We live in Norwich Street.*
> *Please help.*
> *Jackie & Tom'*

'That'll be a category three,' Bill pronounced as Marion handed him the letter.

Category three meant the contents of the letter required immediate action and thus the letter was dropped into the Inquirers' inbox, where it would be collected by an available detective as soon as possible.

Click.

Another letter appeared. This time in receiver box twelve, which was connected to a pipe that extended almost five miles from a postbox outside Waterloo station, under the Thames and onwards towards Fulham.

Marion retrieved the letter and read it swiftly:

Hello down there,

I lost my wallet when someone bumped into me coming out of Euston station. It has all of my money in it. And a picture of my late wife. Please help. I'll wait by the station entrance. Am holding a black umbrella. I'm a man.

Thank you.

Marion handed the letter to Bill. 'Don't suppose we have time for this one?'

He showed the note to Maud, who simply rolled her eyes and pointed at the rubbish bin.

'Poor fellow,' Marion said, eyeing the crumpled letter and wondering if she should contest its swiftly decided upon fate.

She understood the Inquirers were incapable of assisting every individual who sent forth a request (especially on a night like this), but it always troubled her to imagine those desperate souls above ground, sending letters that would never be answered. For she knew, better than almost anyone, what it was like to feel unheard, disregarded.

'What if he waits there all night? We should at least tell him we're not coming.'

Maud flashed her an impatient glance. 'You're welcome to hop upstairs and help him, then. I'm sure it'll be easy finding a man with a black umbrella in this fog. Oh, and while you're at it,' she added, reading a new letter Bill had just handed her, 'have a look for Mrs Raleigh's lost "heirloom" brooch on Chester Avenue.'

At last, around three in the morning, there was a relatively long lull in the incoming stream of requests.

'Suppose we can leave?' Bill asked hopefully, stretching his arms behind his head.

Marion yawned. 'One of us has to stay in case something urgent comes in.'

'You're offering, then?' Maud asked, still in a foul mood though slightly less flustered.

'We all stay. Only fair,' Bill cut in assertively.

Maud mumbled something unsavoury, pulled a large silver hip flask from her bag, took a generous swig and handed it to Marion. She accepted, gratefully gulping down a mouthful of what she unfortunately discovered was straight vodka. She coughed and spluttered and didn't bother passing the flask to Bill, who hated vodka just a little more than she did. Maud looked at her and shrugged, snatched the flask back and took another long gulp.

Marion sighed, curled up into her chair. It was quiet now, save for the occasional patter of feet from the library above. Her eyes stung with fatigue, her neck ached. It had already been a long day of cleaning and fixing and assembling devices in the Gadgetry Department, followed by a two-hour shift in the agency kitchens. There, she'd assisted the head cook with lunch preparations, which she never got a chance to eat because by the time she'd finished, she was already late for her second stint in Gadgetry.

She loved her job more than anything. It was one year since she'd been recruited and introduced to this strange, twisted world to which she now felt – in every sense – tethered. And while the hours were long and the work occasionally irksome, there was nothing in the world Marion would rather be doing, no vocation or cause she'd rather be dedicated to. And, she realised as she glanced at Bill – who was flipping through yesterday's copy of *The Times* – and Maud – who was chuckling at a joke she'd just made under her breath – Miss Brickett's Investigations and Inquiries had not only given her a home, but also a family of sorts. Two things she'd lived most of her life without.

'Crikey, that's grim,' Bill said, lifting his face from behind *The Times*.

'What is?' Marion asked, unfurling herself and shuffling over.

Bill placed the newspaper on the desk between them and read the headline article out loud. '*Bizarre facts leaked as the investigation continues in the case of Eddie Hopper's heinous murder—*'

'Oh, I heard about this,' Maud piped up, wiping a trail of vodka from her chin. 'Poor sod was branded like a farm animal before he was shot.'

Marion looked at Bill for confirmation. He ignored Maud and continued reading.

'*The leaked coroner report of the body of a missing Londoner, who was found in a skip behind the Old Bell Tavern in Harrogate's town centre last week, has been released. According to an anonymous source, thirty-three-year-old Eddie Hopper was brutally beaten and his chest marked with a rose-shaped branding iron before receiving a fatal bullet to the temple. The barbarity of the case has shocked, mortified and intrigued the citizens of England, who have dubbed the perpetrator "the Florist". Scotland Yard has appealed to the public to remain vigilant and—*'

Maud snorted, cutting in again. 'Hah, well that's bound to come to us, then. *Remain vigilant* is Scotland Yard speak for *we haven't the foggiest who the killer is or where they are, so watch out, folks, you might be next.*'

Bill folded the newspaper and sighed, giving up.

'Seems about time. Anyway,' Maud went on, unrelenting, 'we haven't had a murder case in weeks and it's starting to get a bit dull around here. I'm tired of pushing papers and polishing gadgets. I want some *action*, something to get my blood pumping.'

Bill rolled his eyes. 'If you want something to get your blood pumping, sign up to join the tunnel maintenance team. I hear they're dealing with another rodent infestation near the field office.'

Maud muttered an insult into her hip flask as Marion turned to the door that led to the Intelligence Department – a hall lined with desks and cabinets and, usually, clacking typewriters. By now it was utterly empty, except for one lone Inquirer hunched over her desk, fast asleep. In some ways, she knew what Maud meant, about wanting to be an Inquirer in the field, trawling the foggy streets, searching for lost children, guiding the vulnerable home, interrupting the inevitable vandals who always emerged amid chaos and gloom. But she'd had more than her fair share of excitement and turmoil the year before. And, although it seemed in some ways to flow against the current of her person-ality, she now savoured the mundane, the unremarkable – so far as such things were possible at Miss Brickett's. Fortunately, nothing bizarre or unexpected had happened in the past nine months of her training and she'd been able to concentrate wholly on her career. She'd already been promoted to the position of assistant mechanic to Professor Uday Bal – her beloved colleague and head of the Gadgetry Department – and was just one step away from his first mechanic, the position she was hoping to earn at the end of her apprenticeship.

She'd also performed unexpectedly well on her first round of apprenticeship assessments – barring the one she'd been given in the middle of Michelle White's murder investigation. White was the agency's former filing assistant, killed by another employee whom Marion identified and brought to justice.

She rubbed the palm of her left hand, throbbing now as her memory flickered back to that fateful year and Michelle's killer, Edgar Swindlehurst, who'd poured acid over Marion's pinky finger, disfiguring it within seconds. Swindlehurst was gone now, locked away within the vast depths of the agency's underground prison, and yet his villainy still haunted her.

She blinked, turned to the department entrance where Nancy Brickett – the enigmatic agency founder – now stood, her trim figure sharply dressed in an ivory A-line skirt and white blouse. She gave the apprentices a short, businesslike smile, put on a pair of cat's eye spectacles – which only extenuated her astute appearance – and gave the department a quick scan; focusing on the noticeboard (now devoid of any light) and the pile of neatly sorted letters and envelopes.

'Very good,' she said as she sat down near the sorting station. 'You may leave. I'll monitor the receivers until morning.'

'Eh, you're sure?' Bill asked, more to Marion than to Nancy, who, as far as anyone knew, had never monitored the receiver boxes in all of her years.

'Thank you, Miss Brickett,' Marion intervened before Bill could say something stupid like, *Do you know how to sort incoming requests?*

They wished Nancy goodnight and, in something of a daze, the trio dragged themselves to their feet and stumbled from the department.

'You're staying here for the night?' Marion asked Bill and Maud as they made their way down a short corridor that led into the staff quarters several passageways south of the Filing Department. Marion was still the only second-year apprentice who held a permanent address at the agency, while Bill and Maud lived above ground.

'Common room, I suppose,' Bill yawned, stretching his neck from side to side.

'Unless you're offering up your bed?' Maud asked, perfectly serious.

Marion grunted. 'I'm not.'

'Fair enough. The common room it is, then.' Maud waved goodnight and lumbered off down the corridor, leaving Marion and Bill alone.

Immediately, Bill stiffened. He looked at the door to room number fifteen and Marion sensed what was coming next. He slipped his hands into his trouser pockets and fixed her with an expression that was a mix of concern, awkwardness and irritation.

'I heard you and Hugo are together now?'

Marion sighed inwardly. Bill had tried to bring this up on several occasions over the past week and, every time, Marion had changed the subject before he'd had a chance.

'It's just a rumour, Bill.'

He smiled in an odd, forced way. 'But I heard—'

Marion knew how this particular rumour went: she and Kenny Hugo (American detective and now Miss Brickett's junior Inquirer) had taken to the sheets last week after a long night in the library bar. Sweat, jagged breath, pumping blood, etcetera. But it wasn't true – Marion and Kenny hadn't so much as held hands. Unfortunately.

'Just a rumour,' she repeated with a snap.

Bill lifted his hands in a placatory gesture. 'Just asking.' He smiled again, the same feigned expression. There was another tense pause. 'And to be clear, I'm not jealous—'

'I know that!'

She really did. Yes, there *was* more to their friendship than banter and adventure and a shared distaste for hard spirits. But rather than love, it was something rooted in an understanding that they were here together in this strange underground world. Lost together, afraid together, so inseparable it sometimes frightened her. Which was why she knew Bill's curiosity about her 'relationship' with Kenny Hugo had nothing to do with jealously, but instead an odd fear that Marion would inevitably spend less time with him.

'Anyway,' he said, now sounding mighty awkward, 'just thought I'd get the news from the horse's mouth. If there was any. Which there isn't, obviously.'

This could have been the end of the conversation, but some fiendish mix of exhaustion and adrenaline made Marion want to draw out whatever Bill wasn't willing to say.

'You don't like him, though. Admit it.'

'Okay,' Bill said without missing a beat. 'You're right. He gets on my nerves.'

'Why?'

'Lots of reasons.' He paused, squared his jaw.

Marion crossed her arms. If she were being entirely honest, Kenny occasionally got on *her* nerves, too. Only . . . she *liked* it.

'He's loud,' Bill elaborated. 'He's arrogant. He thinks he knows everything about everything. And he thinks he's far too good for this place. Ex-New York City Private Detective Extraordinaire. Oh, and worst of all, he's no clue what football *really* is. I'm just tired of it.' He looked angry for a minute, then chuckled and waved his hands dismissively. 'You know what I mean.'

Marion shook with suppressed laughter. 'You're ridiculous!'

'But I'm right.' He laughed again, mimicking an American twang as he quoted one of Kenny's habitual phrases: *'Blazes, what is that thing?'*

'Okay, okay,' Marion said, jabbing him in ribs. 'That's enough. I'm off to bed.'

Bill smiled, genuinely this time, his dark eyes flecked with relief. 'Night, Mari. See you tomorrow.'

Marion waited until he'd disappeared, then stepped inside her room, dragged herself over to the washbasin and dowsed her face, armpits and chest in icy tap water. She looked up to examine her weary features in the mirror. Her eyes, normally cornflower-blue, were ribbed with broken capillaries and her eggshell skin had turned a concerning shade of grey. She really did need a good night's rest. But as she turned to her bed, something out of place caught her eye – an envelope, slipped under the door.

She walked over, crouched down. The envelope was stained with grubby brown blotches, yet tied with three delicate silk ribbons of red and gold. She untied the ribbons and removed the letter inside.

Marion,

Let me introduce myself as your partner, or perhaps informant is more apt. I believe we'll have much to offer one another in the coming months.

But I'll go first . . .

One of the new recruits is not to be trusted.

3

Algorithm of Blood

Marion woke what felt like minutes later, turning on the gas lamp beside her and drawing the duvet up over her shoulders. The low-roofed windowless room was cold and damp but decorated with fragments of comfort – framed photographs of her late parents and new friends, a side table scattered with an assortment of mismatched gadget parts and treasured tools. Opposite the bed was a small wooden chest she'd recently acquired, overflowing with a collection of ginger nuts, butterscotch gums, salted crisps and six tins of Ceylon tea leaves, a speciality her estranged grandmother – Dolores Hacksworth – had shipped over from America for Marion's twenty-fourth birthday. These, unfortunately, would have to be repurposed because, unlike so many of her countrymen, Marion Lane didn't drink tea.

It was a Friday and she lay in bed contemplating the day ahead. First, there was her meeting in the Intelligence Department, then a double shift in Gadgetry directly afterwards, followed by a three-hour case study session in the library after lunch. She realised just how fortunate she was to have a job she actually enjoyed and couldn't imagine what direction her life would have taken had she not been recruited last year. Would she have married that horrid furniture salesman Dolores had picked out for her, Mr Smithers of Smithers Furniture and Supplies? Or would she have followed her grandmother to America and taken up that clerical job on offer? She couldn't imagine either, so perhaps she'd have run away. Packed her bag (there was only one) and hopped on a train to Scotland. Or a ship to Ceylon to return those six unopened tins of tea.

She smiled at herself as she stretched and sat upright. Ceylon or Scotland would have been a grand affair, and yet she'd found all the adventure and mystique she could handle, right here, beneath the streets of London.

She turned to her bedside table and the folded scrap of paper there. Three ribbons of red and gold silk lay tangled on the floor and the shreds of the torn, grubby envelope beside them. It was a testament to how exhausted she'd been last night that, for a moment, she actually didn't know what she was looking at. She read the letter once more, though the curious message it contained was no clearer than it had been the first time. Her logical brain was screaming *prank*, another mindless quip courtesy of one of her colleagues.

But why was *she* the recipient of this strange piece of information – false or otherwise?

One of the new recruits is not to be trusted.

By 'new recruits', she presumed the letter was referring to the fresh batch of first-year apprentices due to start at the agency that week. She hadn't heard much about them yet. She didn't even know how many there were. But if the general chatter and whir of anticipation in the preceding days was anything to go by, she wasn't the only one at Miss Brickett's eagerly awaiting their arrival. And where excitement bloomed at the agency, so often did rumour and gossip.

She turned the letter over. It was blank on the other side and there was nothing else inside the envelope – no clue as to the sender's identity, no further information of any sort. It was certainly odd, but with no time to waste on the matter, she tucked it away under her pillow.

She applied a lick of burgundy gloss to her lips, slipped into her greyscale uniform, bundled her burnished hair into a low knot and started for the Intelligence Department.

Intelligence, the beating heart of Miss Brickett's Investigations and Inquiries – where cases were discussed, plans organised and secrets shared – was in fact a gloomy rectangular hall lined with office desks and perpetual clouds of tobacco smoke.

Today, on account of the thick smog still lurking in London's streets, many of the Inquirers who'd been called above ground last night hadn't yet returned from their expeditions and those who had – including senior Inquirer and head of the department, Aida Rakes – were hunched over stacks of unanswered letters and partially completed case files.

But Marion's focus was immediately drawn to a man seated at a desk somewhere in the middle of the hall. He was tall, obviously so even when slouched. He wore a collared shirt, crisp white and half tucked in under a black leather belt. His flaxen hair was slicked back into a perfect wave and even from such a distance, Marion could smell Kenny Hugo's musk and sandalwood cologne.

Self-consciously, she pulled the cuff of her left sleeve down over what remained of her fifth finger, smoothed her skirt over her thighs and threaded her way through the maze of desks towards him.

Kenny smiled as she approached. His deep hazel eyes flickered with interest, though Marion could never quite tell if this was because he was pleased to see her, or if his eyes just did that whenever they fell upon a member of the fairer sex.

'Heard you had a long night,' he said, pushing aside the case file he'd been working on.

'Not as long as yours. How was it up there?'

He leaned back in his chair, legs outstretched, ankles crossed, a pen behind his ear. 'Madness. Never seen anything like it. Nothing too serious happened, though, and the Met Office predict the fog will clear by tomorrow. All that about it being worse than fifty-two was a load of trash.'

'Ah, well I'm glad.'

'Yeah . . . ' He looked to his left.

Three desks over was junior Inquirer Kate Bailey, someone Marion had hardly ever interacted with but whom she now realised was very good-looking. Her hair was white-blonde, her eyes turquoise and shining. She looked like a doll, actually. Kenny and Kate exchanged smiles.

Marion raised her eyebrows. 'Your field partner last night, I presume?'

'She was.'

Kenny managed to tear his eyes from Kate and set them on Marion instead. His expression, as he did so, changed from obvious admiration to something more like curiosity.

'I heard Bailey's gunning for a promotion in Intelligence?' Marion said, repeating the rumour she'd heard over lunch a few days before.

'Yeah, that's the word,' Kenny said. 'She's hoping for Special Case Officer. She'd be brilliant at it.'

Beautiful and brilliant. Why, of course. Marion decided to change the subject. 'Did you happen to receive a letter this morning?'

'What's that?'

'A letter.'

Kenny looked befuddled. 'No. Should I have?'

'I don't know, that's why I'm asking. A letter was sent to my room last night.'

'How?'

Marion sighed. Kenny Hugo was intelligent, but sometimes he really did make it hard to believe.

'It was slipped under my door. Does it matter?' He continued to stare at her blankly, so she went on, thinking out loud. 'I was in my room briefly after six p.m. and there was nothing there then, and I was working in Filing until around three a.m., so it must have been sent sometime between six and three. It wasn't signed, so I was just wondering who it was from.'

Kenny turned quickly back to Kate. They exchanged another brief smile. 'Well? What did it say?'

Marion faltered. It seemed awfully odd to repeat what the letter had said, and Kenny would probably think it was a piece of rubbish and wonder why she was paying any attention to it (or, for that matter, telling him about it). He'd then suggest she find something else to occupy her thoughts and she'd snap at him for being rude. It just wasn't worth the energy.

'Nothing much,' she decided to say instead. 'Something about a meet-up.'

One corner of his mouth lifted in a smile. 'A meet-up? You've a secret admirer?'

Marion checked his features for any sign of jealousy. But no, he just looked as if he were having fun. 'That's definitely not it.'

He tilted his head to the side. 'Pity.'

Marion frowned and didn't say: *What's that supposed to mean?*

Kenny straightened up, pressing a hand into the small of his back with a groan. He seemed to have lost interest already in her letter and potential *secret admirer*. Not a good sign.

'What are you doing later? After work?'

'I . . . well, nothing, I suppose. Why?'

'Kate and I are heading to the Mayflower if you're interested? Around eight.'

Marion looked over at Kate, who was staring at them intensely, scowling even. 'You and Kate are going? Just the two of you?'

'Well, yeah. And you. If you decide to come. But anyone's welcome, really. Even Hobb.' Kenny sniggered at this, for whatever reason.

'Sorry, I can't.'

'Why?'

'Because I'm busy.'

'You just said you're not doing anything later.'

'Well, I am, I just remembered.' Marion looked at her watch, not really to check the time but rather to detach herself from Kenny's penetrating gaze. Why did he always look at her like that, as if he were trying to read further meaning into her expression? Perhaps they confused each other in equal measure. 'I'd better go,' she said. 'See you later.'

If Kenny sensed any hint of annoyance in her voice, he ignored it completely. He smiled, raised a hand in farewell and turned back to his typewriter. A second later, he called out after her.

'Oh, forgot to tell you . . . your meeting got moved.'

Marion walked back to his desk at a fast clip. 'Sorry?'

'You're supposed to have a case meeting now, with Aida Rakes?'

'Yes,' Marion said, making it sound like a question as she looked across the hall to where Miss Rakes was still slumped, now fast asleep.

'Well, it's not here.' He nodded over his shoulder to some vague direction. 'Frank's office.'

'Right, thank you,' she said impatiently, turning on her heels.

Feeling even a little worse than she had half an hour ago, Marion made her way from the Intelligence Department, through the adjoining Filing Department and up the staircase, across the library and onwards down several more corridors until she came to Frank's office. The door was already open and she stepped inside.

'In here,' came a voice from somewhere out of sight. 'Behind the wardrobe.'

Marion scanned the room, noticing that the large antique wardrobe she'd seen on all of her previous visits was no longer quite flush with the wall. She approached, peered around the back, where, much to her surprise, a corkscrew stairwell led upwards through the ceiling. 'Right,' she said to herself, manoeuvring her torso and limbs into the tight space, then up the stairwell, through the ceiling and onto a narrow landing that led to a brightly lit room.

'Ah, you got my message,' said a middle-aged man with tousled brown hair and grey eyes, dressed simply in a beige cardigan and matching chinos. Frank Stone was many things to Marion. High Council member, head of the Miss Brickett's apprenticeship programme, detective, tutor, counsellor and, most importantly, father figure.

Marion took in her surroundings – a concealed room, extravagantly furnished with red velvet wing chairs, a billiard table, card table and drinks cabinet, all pushed aside to make space for a work desk covered in office paraphernalia. In addition, a large corkboard had been erected on the wall opposite the hearth. Pinned to the board was an enormous map of England, over which lay a spiderweb of red string, tentacles of thread spinning out from a central point labelled: Harrogate. *Harrogate?* she thought to herself. Why did that ring a bell?

'I call it the Games Room. Do you like it?' Frank asked, practically fizzing with pride as he gestured to the space. 'It was an attic for years, but I had it refurbished recently into something a little more interesting. Allows me a bit of privacy now and then.'

'It's lovely,' Marion said, grinning at the delight on Frank's face. 'Only, I thought my meeting was with Aida Rakes. And in Intelligence?'

Frank's enthusiasm to show off the Games Room faded swiftly as he gave the corkboard a fleeting glance. 'Yes, there's been a change of plans. Miss Rakes has too much on her plate since the smog last night.' There was a short pause. The fire in the hearth crackled and fizzed, throwing a bronzed light across the room. 'I heard you had a busy night. Did you get any sleep?'

Marion, as usual feeling it necessary to convince Frank she was perfectly capable of anything, answered with an easy shrug. Frank had hired her one year ago and in doing so, changed her life. She'd never let him regret it.

'I don't sleep much, anyway.'

She turned to look at the corkboard and the collection of notes pinned to it. *Time of death? Motive? Isolated? Rose?* It was clearly a murder investigation, and a complex one at that. She pushed back her shoulders, straightened her spine, a spark of adrenaline coursing through her as she realised she was about to be assigned to yet another tangled case. Even though she was still just an apprentice, over the past year, Marion had found herself embroiled in many of the agency's most challenging inquiries, including last year's lead investigation into the whereabouts of a London arsonist known as the Scorch, who was finally brought to justice just before Christmas.

'What *is* all this?' she asked, gesturing to the corkboard and its web of string.

'A location algorithm. We received a rather unusual correspondence from Constable Redding last night.'

Marion nodded. Letters from Constable Redding of the Metropolitan Police, the agency's singular outside liaison, were seldom good news and almost always an indication that the case in question would be long and drawn-out.

'What's it about this time?' she asked.

'The investigation Scotland Yard is awash with at the moment. You've probably read about it in the papers.'

Marion blinked.

'The murder behind the Old Bell in Harrogate?' Frank prompted.

'Oh, *oh*,' she said, recalling *The Times* article Bill had read out to her last night. *Harrogate*, that was it. 'It sounded awful, from what I remember.'

'Quite so. The victim was badly beaten, then branded on the chest with a rose-shaped soldering iron.'

'Any idea why someone would do something like that?'

'I suppose you'd have to ask a criminal psychologist, but it's clearly not a simple murder investigation. A killer who makes his victims suffer like that . . . ' He trailed off.

'Sounds like the type of thing you see in gang violence. Do we have anything like it on record?'

'Not that I'm aware of.' He retrieved a slim file from his briefcase. 'Redding sent us a copy of the docket. He was assigned to the case two weeks ago, but I'm afraid he's now removed himself from the investigation entirely.' Marion gave him a questioning look, to which he responded with a shrug. 'Health reasons, apparently.'

'But if he's no longer involved in the investigation, why did he contact us?'

Frank stared into the middle distance. 'I'm not sure.' He shook his head, as though to untangle a thought. 'His letter seemed to imply that we should know more about the case than we do.'

They were silent for a moment. Footsteps clipped through a nearby corridor. A door clanged shut from somewhere further off.

'Anyway, it seems we're obliged to take on the case, and to do so with a certain amount of urgency.'

Marion watched Frank as he wrung his hands.

'Do we have any evidence from the crime scene? Fingerprints? Murder weapon?'

Frank consulted the case file, drew out a sheet of paper. 'Not according to the docket. Neither the pistol used to kill the victim, nor the iron used to mark his chest, have been located and there were no fingerprints anywhere on the body.' He moved over to the corkboard, fastened a sheet of paper to it, a list of some sort. 'In fact, we only have three leads of any use. The first,' he said, reading from the list, 'is the suspect – the Florist. We don't have a real name for him yet. Nor do we have any idea where he is.' His eyes swept over the red-string map. 'Which is why I've created this location algorithm of the first train from Harrogate to London the morning following the murder. Redding's docket suggests the victim died around two a.m.'

'How do they know that?'

'There were witnesses at the Old Bell who claimed to have heard a scuffle through the men's lavatory window some-time between midnight and two a.m. No one went outside to investigate, though one individual did peer through the window, where he saw an elderly man in a trench coat standing with a younger man, whom they now assume was the victim. The witness claims that the older man had a distinctive face, some sort of paralysis on the right side. Another witness claims to have seen the same man at the Harrogate train station the following morning.'

'And you assume he took the train to London from there, because?'

'We have evidence a ticket was purchased at the counter for the ten a.m. train to London for a Mr Smith, obviously an alias. The lady at the ticket counter described the exact same features – an elderly customer, a strange paralysis on the right side of his face. We then have another two possible sightings on the train around one p.m. in the dining cabin.' He jabbed a pen at the corkboard. 'Hence the algorithm. This is the Northern Rail route from Harrogate station to King's Cross. I've labelled all the stops along the way, including the changeovers. I wanted to create a map of all possible points of departure – the ones that are most likely – which would link back to anything in the suspect's case files. Problem is, thanks to our elusive docket, I don't have much to go on, other than the suspect's distinctive facial features.'

Marion mulled this over as Frank continued to stare at the corkboard, a hand rubbing the sparse stubble on his chin. 'How long is the journey from Harrogate to London?'

'Without delays, around four hours twenty minutes.' He pointed at a section of red string. 'Which means, if we trust the latter two witnesses, our suspect was still aboard the train after Peterborough station, the last stop before termination.'

'So, he got off at King's Cross?'

'Indeed. Thus, there's a possibility he's in London.'

This gave Marion another jolt of adrenaline, picturing the Florist as he wandered the streets of London unhindered. 'We should implement a reverse distribution. As you said, he has such a distinctive face, chances are high we'd have a hit.'

Frank looked surprised at the suggestion. 'We could, but it's a lot of work.'

A reverse distribution – where the agency put the pneumatic pipe system into reverse by rocketing tubes up instead of down – *was* a bucketload of work. As far as Marion knew, the technique had only been used a handful of times throughout Miss Brickett's history. And while it had proven itself to be effective on every occasion, it was collectively despised. Once implemented, anyone who opened the concealed postboxes to deposit a tip-off of their own would be met with a request or warning. In this case, Marion thought they could simply ask if anyone had seen an elderly man with a disfigured face.

'Yes, but it'll narrow our search, if nothing else,' she concluded confidently.

'I'll speak to Nancy and if she agrees, we can hopefully get it set up for Wednesday.'

'Yes, good.' She turned back to the list of items Frank had pinned to the board, her gaze fixing on number two. '*Old Sam.* Who's that?'

'As I mentioned, Redding has removed himself from the investigation. But apparently, he did so only after an interview with a "compromising witness", who knew both the killer and the victim, and used to work at a gentleman's club in Oxfordshire. The witness calls himself Old Sam.'

'Where is he now, Old Sam?'

'Redding claims he's disappeared.'

Marion raised an eyebrow. 'Meaning he's dead?'

'No, thankfully not.' Frank released a long breath. 'But Redding did say it would be in our best interests to track him down before Scotland Yard does.'

Marion let this idea work itself out in her mind. Redding had met with a witness he clearly thought held some weight in the Harrogate investigation and yet, instead of passing the shared information on to his colleagues at Scotland Yard, he'd removed himself from the case and passed it on to Miss Brickett's. She refocused. Frank was watching her closely, waiting for the penny to drop.

'So that must mean . . . ' she said with a note of hesitancy, 'Redding thinks Old Sam's witness statement would compromise—'

'Miss Brickett's,' Frank provided. 'Yes. I'm afraid so. I don't know exactly what we're dealing with here; Redding has been extremely vague and dismissive. He clearly wants to distance himself from the entire thing, especially anything to do with this witness of his.'

Marion studied the corkboard more carefully, forcing her weary brain to work. The maze of string made her queasy.

'You said Old Sam knew the Florist and the victim. What do we know about the latter?'

Frank read from the docket. 'Eddie James Hopper, thirty-three-year-old British national. Born and bred in London. Father a successful venture capitalist, mother a stay-at-home wife. No siblings. Hopper studied mechanical engineering at Oxford University and was a much liked, well-rounded student as far as his lecturers and colleagues were concerned.' He closed the case file and looked up. 'The only odd thing is that once Hopper qualified from Oxford in fifty-four, he vanished from public record. Until now. There was almost no account of him anywhere, except for when he applied for an identity document in fifty-seven. His parents say he moved out after graduation and lived in Oxfordshire alone, apparently unemployed. He hardly ever visited his family after that, lost contact with all of his friends and became a recluse.'

'So, he had a mechanical engineering degree but ended up unemployed?'

'He *told* everyone he was unemployed and yet, according to Redding, the young man spent most of his time smoking cigars at a highbrow gentleman's club called St Mark's.'

'Where he met Old Sam and, perhaps, the Florist.'

'Precisely.'

'We need to infiltrate that club, then,' Marion said immediately.

Frank nodded to himself, as though coming to some private decision. Marion waited, hoping he might say something more. When he didn't, she turned to item number three on Frank's list.

'What about the third lead?'

'The rose branding,' Frank clarified, jabbing the item with his pen. 'We need to understand what it *means*, what significance it carries, if there are any similar cases on record. According to the coroner's report, the mark was made while Mr Hopper was still alive, which suggests to me the Florist was sending a message of some sort, and perhaps any future victims a warning.' He took a step back, as though to view the corkboard from a distance. 'Three leads, three detectives. Perfect, isn't it?'

Marion was momentarily confused. 'Three detectives?'

'I'll be handling the second lead, finding Old Sam. I was hoping you and Hugo could join forces on the other two.' He tilted his head to the side as though realising something. 'You worked so well together last year, I just thought . . . but if you'd rather not—'

'No, you're right. We *do* work well together.' She cast her eyes to the floor, touched her blouse collar absently.

'But?'

'Nothing. It's just that we're . . . ' She trailed off, unsure how to finish.

'Ah, I see,' Frank said, offering a small smile.

'I don't understand,' she blurted, without catching his eye. It was the first time she'd even come close to admitting, to anyone, what she felt for Kenny Hugo and the vulnerability of it made her squirm. 'I thought we were growing closer last year. But now it feels as though we're back to where we started.'

'And you've told him how you feel?'

'He knows,' she answered, a cold snap to her voice. 'I don't need to spell it out for him, surely.'

Frank waited, watching as she fidgeted with her clothing, then finally pushed her hands into her skirt pockets. 'Did I ever tell you about your mother's eighteenth birthday?'

Marion looked up, her self-pity replaced with an overriding sense of expectation. Any chance she had to talk about her mother, who died when Marion was sixteen, she'd take.

'She'd just married your father,' Frank began, strolling over to the fire, 'and Alice and I were only friends – at least that's what we told ourselves.'

Marion nodded as Frank settled, warmed his hands by the hearth. She'd always suspected he and her mother had once been in love, even though she had no confirmation.

'I visited the morning of her birthday, which was just a week after the wedding,' he continued. 'I don't quite know what I did that for. I told myself I needed to pass on my congratulations, but really, I think I just wanted to see if anything had changed. Would she look at me differently, now that she was spoken for? But when she opened the door, I knew . . . ' His words petered out on a sigh. 'I told her I was leaving London for Dorset. She smiled and said she thought that was a wonderful idea. I smiled back and agreed, said I was looking forward to it.' He drew his focus back to Marion, a hint of wetness in his eyes. 'It was such an odd moment, almost as though we were both speaking a foreign language yet hoped the other would understand.

'Looking back, it seems so foolish. Why were we trying to conceal what we felt, when we were both certain the other felt the same? But we were so young and now, after all these years, I think I understand.' He smiled briefly, fading to a blankness, as though, just for a moment, all the life had been siphoned out of him. 'You see, my dear, some love, the deepest kind, takes time to come to the surface and be recognised for what it is. Unfortunately, we don't always *have* time.' He let out a breath, as did Marion, then glanced at the clock behind the drinks cabinet. 'We've wandered a bit off track, haven't we?'

He pulled out a sheepskin diary from his waistcoat and paged through, making notes while Marion let her mind fill with a maelstrom of emotions: regret, sadness, love. Her mother.

'. . . if I manage to get the reverse distribution set up,' Frank continued, Marion catching only half of what he said, 'we'll have a bit of time from now until then to decide what to do about infiltrating St Mark's.'

Marion nodded absently, her thoughts lagging.

'But in the meantime, I'm afraid I have something else to keep you busy. I suppose you've heard the news – three new recruits have been selected. I was wondering if you might help Jessica lead their orientation this evening.'

Marion's mind cleared at last, her heart beat a little faster. But was it excitement or trepidation?

One of the new recruits is not to be trusted.

4

Proctor, Longmore and Quinn

'Well, this is bound to be interesting,' said Jessica Meel, Marion's colleague and fellow second-year as they made their way to the auditorium later that evening for the new recruits' orientation tour.

Marion's day had already been a whirlwind of surprises, what with her case meeting in the concealed Games Room and assignment to the Harrogate murder. And although she was certainly eager to meet the new recruits, the feeling came with an obscure layer of misgiving, too. Which was why she was wholly relieved she wouldn't be giving the tour alone.

Even though she'd been wearing the same outfit all day, Jessica was still dressed immaculately in a perfectly pressed high-waisted skirt and boat-neck blouse – both of which accentuated her slim, tall physique – while her silken blonde hair, recently trimmed, was pinned back with quartz-encrusted clips. Speaking in her characteristic swift, spirited manner, she went on in the background.

'. . . you might not have a problem with Proctor or Longmore. But Quinn? I just don't see the two of you getting along.'

'You've met them already, then?'

'Just briefly this morning,' Jessica said pensively.

'Right, so who's Quinn and why won't we get along?'

'Ambrosia Clementine Quinn. She's just a bit, well, she's a bit like you, actually.'

Marion knitted her brows. 'Explain.'

A touch of pink bloomed on Jessica's cheeks. Whatever similarities Ambrosia Quinn and Marion shared, Jessica clearly thought they were undesirable.

'She *loves* gadgets. And she's desperate to please. Not that that's a bad thing, of course,' she added hastily, then slipped her arm through Marion's, fixing her with bright green eyes and flashing a smile that was like a gleam of sunshine. It was impossible to find offence in anything Jessica said when she said it with *that* look. 'Everyone wants to appease their superiors in a new job. It's perfectly natural. And you're not nearly as bad these days.'

If she really thought about it, Marion supposed Jessica had a point. She *had* always tried a little harder than everyone else to prove her worth at Miss Brickett's. She knew why, too. Because on some deep level, hidden far beneath her outward confidence and apparent aptitude, she still wasn't sure she deserved to be here, a part of this peculiar, extraordinary world.

'Oh! and Quinn has this ridiculously brilliant memory. It's really rather annoying. She'll probably be able to remember every screw and bolt she handles in the Gadgetry Department. Maybe that's why she was recruited.'

'Hmm,' Marion said, unconvinced as she considered the circumstances of her own recruitment.

She'd always assumed she'd been selected for her experience with mechanics, gained through six years working at an auto repair shop. And also, perhaps, because Frank had loved her mother and might have been doing her a favour. But the more

Marion came to understand this complex underground world, the more she began to wonder if there was another, far more simple and obvious reason why those who worked here had been chosen. Because whether you applied for the position or were plucked from obscurity, there was one criterion you absolutely had to fill.

She voiced her theory now for the first time. 'I suppose Quinn doesn't have much of a family.'

For, as far as Marion was aware, not a single employee at Miss Brickett's had a thoroughly constructed life outside the labyrinth's walls. Most were either orphans (like Marion), estranged from their families (like Jessica, whose father – a well-to-do businessman – lived between Dublin, Rome and Paris with alternating mistresses) or, at best, had the odd tie that could easily be cut. And it made sense, if you really thought about it – the fewer people there were on the outside to ask questions, the better.

A troubled, yet knowing, expression came over Jessica's face. 'Like the rest of us?'

Marion raised an eyebrow but said nothing more as the pair stepped inside the auditorium, empty save for three individuals standing near the podium. Jessica grabbed Marion's arm and leaped forwards with delight as she caught sight of the new recruits.

'Mari, this is Ambrosia Clementine Quinn.' She smiled at a thickset young woman with bronzed hair and freckled, waxy skin. 'Jerome Longmore.' She gestured to a solid, spirited-looking young man, who greeted her with smooth public-school vowels and an unsolicited recount of his day thus far. 'And Thomas Proctor,' she concluded, nodding at a tall young man with a wispy build and sleek white-blond hair.

Jessica pulled the new recruits into a welcoming embrace (ignoring Proctor as he attempted to circumvent the gesture with an awkward twist), while Marion shook hands with each and attempted to mirror Jessica's natural, easy warmth as she introduced herself. It wasn't that Marion didn't like the new recruits – how could she, knowing so little about them? But suspicion squirmed inside her as she stood there, watching them watching her.

One of the new recruits is not to be trusted.

Quinn seemed by far the most alert and inquisitive, her wide eyes scanning the room, absorbing every detail. In contrast, Proctor was staring at his feet, his white-blond fringe draped over his forehead. Marion might have marked him as simply withdrawn, but there was something a little more sinister about his posture, something she couldn't quite put her finger on. Finally, she turned to Longmore – shorter than Proctor, taller than Quinn and more gregarious (and talkative) than both. He sported a tangle of mousy brown hair that framed a featureless face, not entirely handsome or displeasing.

'These are yours,' Jessica chirped eagerly, rummaging around in her handbag before drawing out three basic agency maps. 'We'll be taking you on a quick tour this evening, just so you can get a feel for the place. I'm afraid it's rather easy to get lost down here, but you'll get your bearings after a few weeks if you stick to our rule of thumb.' She winked at Marion and together, they chimed: 'If a corridor isn't well lit, you shouldn't be in it.'

Longmore chuckled under his breath while Quinn and Proctor examined their maps in silence, their eyes tracing the infinite web of passageways and turns, stairwells, chambers and cul-de-sacs.

'What's this supposed to be? *The Border*?' demanded Proctor, pointing to a distinct label somewhere near the southern corner of the map.

'It's the edge of our premises,' Marion answered quickly. 'We're not permitted to go anywhere near it. Under any circumstances.'

Proctor looked up, his ghostly eyebrows raised. 'Oh yes? And why is that?'

Marion and Jessica exchanged a glance, each hoping the other would provide the necessary explanation. Last year, when Marion was a new recruit, the rumour had been that the Border was out of bounds simply owing to its ill-maintained corridors and convoluted layout. But, of course, she now knew the tunnels concealed two well-kept (and treacherous) agency secrets – a wartime laboratory, only recently boarded up, and the Holding Chambers: Miss Brickett's on-site prison, reserved for rogue Inquirers. Of course, she couldn't reveal either of these things.

'Because of the rats,' Jessica provided after a beat too long. 'Enormous rats. Legions of them. That's what we've been told, isn't it, Mari?'

Marion nodded vehemently. 'Absolutely. Rats everywhere. So, unless you fancy a touch of rabies . . . '

Quinn and Longmore stared at her, bewildered, while Proctor returned his focus to the map, scowling a little.

Marion cleared her throat to bridge the silence that had ensued. 'I suppose we should get started, then.'

The group of five, Marion in the lead, Jessica at the rear, led the recruits from the auditorium to the surrounding departments and chambers: the infirmary, the Grand Corridor, then southwards down the long stone staircase towards the Gadgetry Department. Marion's heart jittered with delight as she guided the recruits through the shadow-lined hall, filled with devices that gleamed, writhed and ticked, soared and slithered. Strangely, as she watched the recruits – Quinn in particular — gape at the shelves of gadgets and curious tools, she felt almost as though she were seeing the place for the first time. She also felt a note of tension as the recruits wandered past the workbenches, carelessly bumping into things. And when Longmore picked up a half-built Vagor Compass and flung it from hand to hand with utter indifference, she was forced to reveal a more cantankerous side of herself.

'Put that down, please!' she shrieked, whipping the gadget from his grasp before he could do any damage. She exhaled, ashamed of her outburst. 'Sorry, I just . . . gadgets are fragile and expensive. It's best not to throw them about.'

Proctor flinched, as though Marion's reaction had been directed at him, while Longmore shrugged, unperturbed, and Quinn marked something down in her notebook.

'No need to apologise, Mari, you're quite right,' Jessica said loyally. She turned her flaring green eyes on Longmore. 'The Gadgetry Department is the jewel in our crown. We're *all* protective over what goes on here.'

'You feel it too, then?' Marion asked Jessica as they led the recruits out of the department and back up the long stone staircase.

'Protective? Heavens, yes. I mean, we ought to. This place is our home.'

She glanced over her shoulder, as did Marion. The new recruits were several yards behind now, trailing up the staircase in a neat row. Proctor and Longmore appeared to waver between weary and bemused as they climbed the seemingly endless procession of steps, while Quinn stared fixedly ahead at Marion and Jessica, her notepad clutched under her arm, a pen twirling between her fingers.

'Anyway,' Jessica said under her breath, 'there's something I've been meaning to show you.' The night was growing old. The lamps that lined the staircase and corridors beyond would soon be turned down, casting the labyrinth into impossible gloom. Surreptitiously, Jessica opened her bag and removed a crumpled piece of paper. She handed it over. 'Found this plastered to the wall of the powder room this afternoon.'

Marion uncreased the paper. It appeared to be a poster of some sort, bearing a line of script that read: *ERPS. East Eight. 18. Every Fifth.* Marion cocked her head to the side, as though examining the peculiar script from a new angle might assist her in deciphering it. It didn't and she gave up, handing the poster back to Jessica.

'Any idea what it means?'

'It looks like some sort of advertisement, doesn't it?' Jessica remarked furtively, stuffing the poster back into her bag.

'Possibly,' Marion said, thinking back to the letter she'd received under her door the previous evening. Was there any connection? 'Or a code for something . . . ' She trailed off as they reached the top of the staircase, aware of Quinn, Longmore and Proctor right beside her and a prickling sensation crawling across her skin. The poster was interesting, but it would have to wait. 'Right,' she said to the recruits, attempting to sound nonplussed. 'I think we've done enough touring for the evening. Perhaps we should call it a night.'

Quinn consulted her map with a thoroughly displeased expression. 'But we've hardly seen anything yet. What about the ballroom, the staff quarters, the common room, the cafeteria, the kitchens—'

Marion glanced at Jessica, who sighed and conceded: 'We'll take you to the staff quarters and common room now, then up to the field office and library. Those are the only other important bits. The rest you'll get to know next week.'

Quinn shrugged and the party continued their tour with relative speed, arriving at their penultimate stop – a set that appeared to be a partially built two-storey house – with a little time to spare.

'This is the field office,' Marion announced, turning on the foyer lights, illuminating the full magnificence of the building – its ten differently shaped doors, its partially constructed ceiling and tapestry of mismatched windows. 'You'll spend a lot of time here, training for field assignments, learning how to bypass tripwires and evade security cameras.'

'It might seem grand,' Jessica added in earnest, stepping up to Marion's side, 'but it can be dangerous, too, if you're not paying attention.'

Marion smiled, recalling the first day she, Jessica and the others in her group had been shown the field office last year. Marion had been amazed, desperate to see beyond its walls and try her luck at the myriad ensnarements.

Now, as Quinn stared up at the peculiar building, hands clasped and resting under her chin in a prayer-like gesture, Marion could sense the same awe she'd felt a year ago.

'Can we go inside?' asked Quinn.

'I don't think so, not tonight,' Jessica declared without hesitation.

'But we have our first session here on Monday,' Quinn pressed, 'and I'd really rather know what I'm stepping into.'

Jessica was flustered now, glancing at Marion for assistance. 'There's absolutely no way I'm going to step inside there—'

'I'll take them,' Marion interrupted, turning to the second door on the left, a large teak one with five identical handles.

Jessica shook her head resolutely. 'How about I meet you in the library instead.'

'Me too,' Proctor chimed immediately, looking thoroughly relieved at the suggestion.

Marion glanced at Quinn and Longmore, ready to call off the idea if they appeared uncertain.

'I'm coming with you,' Quinn said, gesturing to Marion and already wide-eyed with excitement.

'And you, Longmore?' Marion asked.

He splayed his hands, obviously unbothered either way. 'Sure. Why not. This day could do with a little excitement.'

He looked ready to add something unnecessary and unrelated, no doubt an anecdote or drawn-out tale of some past-life experience, so Marion cut in swiftly.

'Follow me and do exactly as I do.' She pulled a set of gadgets from her bag: a lock pick, a penlight and pair of specialised binoculars. 'The first step is to get inside, obviously,' she explained. 'And with this particular door, that requires a little finesse . . . '

She turned the door's fourth handle twenty degrees clockwise while simultaneously inserting her lock pick in the keyhole. While the lock pick shimmied its way further inside, Marion coaxed the handle another ten degrees clockwise, then let it dial back to its resting position as the door clicked open.

She stepped over the threshold, trailed by Quinn and Longmore. The room beyond was designed to look like the atrium of a hotel, complete with reception desk, a waiting area, a lift at one end and a staircase at the other. Marion knew both the staircase and lift were rigged with several complex traps, though the ones along the staircase would be easiest to evade. She addressed the recruits as she pulled out her penlight and examined the way ahead.

'There's a tripwire across the fifth stair. It's nearly invisible, so you'll have to leap over the stair completely to be sure you avoid it. And if I remember correctly, two stairs after that there's a poison dart that'll come at you from the left. So make sure you're on your hands and knees when we get there.' She smiled at the recruits, hoping to reassure them, though after picturing what lay ahead, she was feeling a fraction less assured herself.

Marion, Quinn and Longmore emerged (thankfully unscathed) twenty minutes later from the corridor that cut through the field office.

Marion patted down her hair and straightened out her now thoroughly creased blouse. 'I suppose the only thing left to do is meet the rest of your colleagues. And here we are,' she added as a young man stepped through a door at the other end of the library, which led to the agency's bar.

Bill Hobb approached the trio, a wary grin on his face.

'Bill, this is Jerome Longmore and Ambrosia Quinn.'

'Welcome,' Bill said a little awkwardly, shaking hands with the recruits.

Longmore gave him the once-over, with slight contempt (probably because Bill didn't look anything like an aspiring private detective), then cast his eyes at the library bar entrance. A woman a little older than Marion, sallow skinned and important-looking, was striding over, her chin raised some- what higher than necessary as she gave each apprentice a cool, appraising glance. Amanda Shirley then cast her hawkish eyes on Marion.

'You're late. Everyone's waiting.'

Marion looked at the golden light spilling out from the bar, the throng of tightly packed bodies just beyond, hovering eagerly over the threshold.

'And drinking themselves into oblivion,' Bill added.

Amanda went on, eyes still fixed on Marion. 'Well? Are you going to introduce us?'

'Jerome, Ambrosia,' Marion said on a sigh, 'this is Amanda Shirley. Second-year apprentice.'

Amanda extended a bony hand as though she expected Longmore and Quinn to kiss it. 'And, more importantly, assistant case manager in the Intelligence Department. We're bound to have a lot to do with one another in the coming year.'

'Lucky you,' Bill murmured under his breath.

Longmore tilted his head to the side, examining Amanda with slightly more interest than he'd done with anyone else. 'Amanda Shirley,' he repeated, as though churning the name over in his mouth, testing its flavour.

'Time to go,' Marion said, pointing to the library bar behind her, now thrumming with chatter and an air of anticipation.

After another odd exchange of looks between Longmore and Amanda, the group followed Marion into the snug bar, filled as usual with the soft drone of a gramophone, the scent of woodsmoke and close to thirty Miss Brickett's employees – including Jessica and Proctor. All eyes fixed on Longmore and Quinn as they shuffled to the centre of the room.

'Let's welcome the buggers, come on!' boomed someone from a knot of third-years near the back, who were raising their pints to the bar at large.

There was a drumming of hands, a few hoots and whistles and a chorus of 'welcome' and 'good luck'.

Before anyone could settle into the celebration, however, Amanda pulled a small wooden box onto the bar counter and tapped it loudly with her fist, commanding the bar's attention. 'Shall we?' She cracked the box open to reveal three black velvet satchels tied with silk. The employees grinned knowingly at one another as Amanda turned to Marion. 'Marion, probably best if you do the honours this year.'

Marion stepped up to Amanda's side. She didn't much like what was coming next, but as a well-established Miss Brickett's tradition that would go ahead either way, she decided to play along. She untied one of the velvet satchels and laid out its contents. Inside was a set of five gadgets: a light orb, a tracking (Vagor) compass, a pocket watch fitted with a specialised alarm bell that could double as a Distracter, two pairs of Silent Film – silicone shoe coverings that muffled the sound of footfall. The last object, however, was nondescript – a simple brass ball no larger than a chicken egg.

As she explained how each gadget worked (barring the last), and what they could be used for, she noted Quinn's utter fascination, Longmore's near apathy and Proctor's timid angst. She was noticing a trend.

'Incredible!' Quinn gushed, examining each of her gadgets as if they were living creatures. 'These are all *ours*?'

Proctor eyed the gadgets less assuredly and from a distance. 'Who monitors all this?'

'All what?' Marion said.

'The gadgets, of course. You're just handing them over to us when we don't even know how to use them. What if they're dangerous?'

Marion stiffened. 'They're not. And I just explained how to use them. It's quite simple.'

Proctor turned away and muttered something, and although Marion only caught half of it, it made her skin crawl: '. . . they said the same about a Herald Stethoscope.'

'What the hell is this, then?' Longmore asked, holding up the fifth gadget – the small brass egg – and staring at it with an expression of slight annoyance.

An unidentified voice from the back of the bar answered with a chuckle. 'That's what you're here to find out, mate.'

The three recruits looked equally perplexed, though Proctor was distinctly nervous, too.

'I don't understand?' he said, holding the brass egg at arm's length as if it might explode in his grip at any moment.

Not far off from the truth, Marion thought.

'It's a puzzle,' she explained. 'If you can figure it out in time, you'll disarm the ignition switch and nothing will—'

'Ignition switch?' Proctor gasped, glaring at Marion.

'Are you having us on?' Longmore snapped.

Another voice called out from the knot of employees near the back: 'Either one of you figures it out, or we're all going up in flames.'

Several people laughed and in unison, the third-years sang: 'Tick-tock – three minutes to go!'

Proctor began to sweat, turning the egg over in his hands, rubbing it on his trouser leg as if this might reveal something, examining the contraption from every angle. Longmore's approach was no more astute though certainly more brutish, as he threw the gadget first against the wall, then the floor, then stamped on it several times. Quinn, however, did almost exactly what Marion had done last year when she'd encountered the challenge during her own initiation. Calmly, she sat down, placed the egg in front of her on the table and began to roll it back and forth, her fingers gliding meticulously over the brass surface. She stopped after thirty seconds – she must have felt the ridges already – then got to work shifting the moveable plates back and forth until she'd found a pattern.

Marion sighed. Jessica was right – Quinn had an affinity for gadgets, but more than that, she had an obvious *talent* for them, too.

'I think I have it,' Quinn said, standing up. 'Yes!' She shifted and shimmied the plates until the device opened up like a lotus flower.

Several employees clapped, but instead of joining in on the celebration, Quinn ripped Proctor's egg from his sweaty grip and disarmed it just as quickly as she'd done with her own. She was about to do the same with Longmore's, but it was too late. There was a fizzle, a wisp of bright green smoke and the egg burst alight with a sharp crack that reverberated through the bar, rattling the bottles of liquor behind the counter and the singular glass window that looked out onto the library.

Longmore cursed, Proctor shrieked and Quinn disappeared behind a stack of chairs.

Everyone else doubled over in fits of hysterics (except Jessica, who never found anything dangerous the least bit funny, and Marion, who felt distinctly guilty for putting the recruits through such unnecessary terror).

'It's okay,' she said, tapping Proctor on the shoulder then pulling Quinn up from the floor. 'It's just a Time Lighter. Nothing to worry about.' She picked up Longmore's flaming egg, still spewing wisps of harmless green smoke, and disarmed it swiftly. 'All fine. It's over.'

Neither Proctor nor Longmore looked in any way impressed by the prank.

'Ridiculous,' Longmore snapped, recovering his pride and downing a pint in one gulp.

Proctor took several long breaths, then turned to Marion with a strange look. She couldn't decide if it was fear or anger (or a bit of both), but moments later, as the others moved off, he pulled her aside and hissed in her ear – making it rather clear.

'That had better be the last time you play a trick on me.'

5

Monster by Moonlight

One of the new recruits is not to be trusted.

The warning rang clear in Marion's mind after her inter-action with Proctor in the library bar. And if she'd had any time to think it through, she might have realised that Proctor's behaviour at the initiation was the first real indication that her anonymous informer – the sender of the strange letter – should be taken seriously.

But the problem with keeping track of things at Miss Brickett's was that small concerns and minor misgivings quickly fell by the wayside and were forgotten. There was always something more urgent to deal with, such as the case of the Harrogate murder and the reverse distribution, which had been set up for the Wednesday following the recruits' orientation. As the public's replies began to stream in, Marion and Frank battled for the rest of the week to sort and read the nearly eighty-two apparent sightings of the old man with the lopsided face into 'plausible' and 'certainly a hoax'.

'I think it warrants investigation,' Frank announced after several minutes of staring at one of the only letters that held any merit – a tip-off from a young man who claimed he'd seen an individual fitting the Florist's description buying bread from his bakery at least three times in the past few days. 'Along with this,' Frank added, picking up another letter – a tip-off from a woman who said the Florist had almost certainly been using the telephone booth just a few streets away from the bakery. 'She lives in a flat that overlooks the booth,' Frank explained, 'and the last two Saturday nights at around ten, the Florist made a call.'

'Bug the telephone,' Marion blurted. Though as she said it, she realised it wouldn't work. Bugging a public telephone was of little use unless they knew exactly what the Florist sounded like and had time to wade through the hours of unimportant conversations from everyone else.

Frank wandered across the Games Room, hands in his pockets, his gaze distant. He turned around as he reached the billiard table, focusing on Marion. 'I'll have to send you out.'

All traces of exhaustion instantly extinguished for Marion. 'Send me out?'

Truthfully, she knew what it meant. *Send you out on your first field operation.* She'd expected that a field operation was looming; it was the most logical next step in her Inquirer training. Yet, the thought of trailing a killer like the Florist above ground turned her stomach.

'Not alone, of course,' he added, to Marion's relief, 'and only if you're willing. This will be a difficult one, but I believe you're more than ready.' He stopped, perhaps to check Marion for signs of distress. 'If it's too much—'

'No,' she said without thinking. 'Count me in.'

Frank placed a hand on her shoulder, gave her a look that conveyed trust with maybe a hint of uncertainty. 'Good, my dear. I'll have the stake-out set up for Saturday. And I'll let Hugo know. He'll be joining you.'

On Saturday afternoon, Marion and Kenny set off for Carriage Drive, a leafy street that ran along the northern boundary of Hyde Park in Central London. They were in Kenny's brown-and-white Hudson sedan (Marion didn't know he owned a car, but it had clearly been shipped over from the States, with its left-sided steering wheel). It smelled like him – musk, sandalwood, sweet sweat – and was scattered with a well-thumbed copy of *Men's Health* and several items of clothing. There were white loafers (of course), a black leather biker jacket (of course, *of course*) and – Marion noticed this one with a pinch of irritation and confusion – a brass-handled and elaborately embossed hairbrush. Kenny certainly owned a hairbrush (or several), but this seemed a little too frou-frou, even for him.

He caught her staring at it and looked embarrassed for a split second. But was he embarrassed she'd seen his lady hairbrush, or his lady's hairbrush? She decided she didn't want to know.

'Happy Valentine's Day, by the way,' Kenny said with a lopsided grin as they approached the bakery.

'Thanks.' She eyed the hairbrush again. 'I suppose this isn't what you had planned for tonight?'

'What? Backseat Bingo?' He laughed.

Marion blinked.

'Kidding. I didn't have plans.'

He offered her a wink, which was most confusing. Was he throwing her a line, or just trying to get under her skin?

'What about you? Has your secret admirer sent any more notes?'

She flinched, though tried not to show it. The letter in question was still tucked away in her room, still bewildering, still niggling at her subconscious. Why hadn't she thrown it away yet? Did she really believe it meant something?

'Don't be daft. I told you, it was just a work thing.'

Kenny didn't seem to hear or, more likely, didn't care. 'Now, this is what I'm talking about,' he said instead as they pulled up alongside the bakery where the Florist had been sighted, a few yards off from the entrance and as inconspicuous as possible. Mind you, this wasn't an easy feat in an American Hudson sedan with highly polished chrome hubcaps and a sticker on the boot that read *Daddy-O* in large red, white and blue lettering.

'What is?' Marion asked, frowning at him.

'The good, proper private detective work I signed up for. Sort of stuff I did back in New York.' He lit a cigarette and took a long drag, flicking the ash out of the window.

An elderly lady walking a small dog along the pavement glowered at them – at Kenny specifically – which suggested their cover was already blown.

Marion rolled her eyes. She hated herself for getting even a little excited by the idea of spending an entire day with Kenny Hugo, stalking the Florist. Had she forgotten what it was like to work with him, tolerating his idiot adages and tales of his past as a '*real* private detective'? Oh, what Bill would say if he were here now . . .

'If you love New York so much, why don't you just go back?'

Kenny let the cigarette dangle from the corner of his mouth. God, he was handsome.

'Can't.'

Marion turned her eyes back to the bakery – though there was nothing and no one to see. It was dusk and the place had been closed up hours ago.

'Why's that?'

Although she'd known Kenny for almost a year, and they'd experienced rather a lot together in that time, they hadn't ever talked about their private personal lives: their families, their upbringings. It just seemed as if there were always more pressing things to discuss. They had time now, though.

Kenny knocked his head back and slid down in his seat. Give him a hotdog and a bottle of Coca-Cola and he'd look exactly like an American copper on a stake-out, in the movies at least.

'I mean, I can, but I don't want to. Bad memories.' His normally frivolous tone turned sober.

For a while he just left it at that and Marion didn't press him. She knew what it was like, explaining the past, why some places haunted you. It was how she felt about the London above Miss Brickett's – the streets she'd walked with her mother, places where their memories endured, ghosts that never let her forget what she'd lost.

'Mama still lives there,' Kenny went on, 'and I do miss her. But it's difficult, after what happened.' He stopped, closed his eyes for a second. 'My sister and I were very close growing up. We were only eighteen months apart in age and so alike it sometimes made my head spin. We were thick as thieves, especially after Papa died and Mama became all quiet and withdrawn. We really leaned on each other, you know?'

Marion didn't know. She was an only child, but she supposed it would have made things easier if she'd had a sibling to lean on (rather than a vile grandmother) when her mother had died.

'Five years ago, Jenny married a lawyer from Boston and I knew right away he was a bad one.'

He looked at Marion and something flickered in his eyes – memories of an old pain, she presumed.

'You can tell with some people right away, can't you? You can *feel* it, like everyone has this energy they carry around with them and in some folks it just feels . . . heavy.'

Marion agreed with this decisively, several examples springing to mind. Thomas Proctor being the first. 'Oh, I know a few of those.'

'Anyway, I told Jenny what I thought of her man, obviously I did. But she didn't listen, didn't want to hear anything that contradicted her love for him. I think she knew it, though. I think she knew there was something black and rotten inside Lionel. The problem was, she wanted to be married so bad, she just pushed it aside . . . ' He trailed off. 'In the end, it ruined our relationship. There was nothing I could say about Lionel without it leading to a huge brawl that lasted days and sent everyone into a spin.

'I decided to change my approach, thinking it was the best way. I visited Jenny only when Lionel was out of town. I never asked her how things were going between them, or if she was happy. I mean, I knew she wasn't, but I didn't expect her to admit it, especially since I'd already said my piece.'

They were momentarily distracted as a red Mini Cooper pulled up alongside the bakery. An elderly man and a younger lady got out, collected something from the boot and drove off. Marion got a good look at the man with her binoculars. He didn't have a disfigured face. She sighed and waited for Kenny to continue.

'I tried my best to keep things tight between us,' he said, 'but it was inevitable that we drifted apart. I was always worried about saying something that would set her off. And all of our conversations seemed to lead back to Lionel eventually. I hated it.' His voice broke, the tiniest fissure in his composure. He cleared his throat and continued. 'I loved her so much, but I didn't know what to do to fix things. I should have tried harder, obviously.' He took another long drag, puffed the smoke out slowly, thoughtfully. It curled upwards in ribbons of grey, struck the windscreen and vanished. 'He killed her in the end. Shot her three times. Right in the face. Point-blank. When the police found her . . . there was nothing left.' He coughed lightly, hiding another break in his voice no doubt, then stared blankly ahead. 'I had to identify her body because Mama couldn't bear it. And I'll never be able to erase that sight from my memory. Never.'

'Oh, Kenny,' Marion said, her chest clenching. 'I'm so sorry. I can't imagine . . . '

'We didn't find out why he did it, either. The coward shot himself straight after. He never suffered, never had to answer our questions. I don't suppose it would have made much difference, but for some reason I've always wanted to know what they fought about that last night.'

Marion took his hand as the sun began to set across the park, the last streaks of light filtering through the windscreen, then dying out behind the bakery. 'Is that why you decided to become a detective?'

'I considered joining the force at first, but Mama begged me not to. I guess she thought it was too dangerous. She was the one who suggested private-eye work, thought it would be harmless.' He laughed ironically. 'Now look at me, trailing a madman in the middle of London.' He stubbed out his cigarette, raked his hands through his hair. 'Funny, huh? Death was the thing that brought us to Miss Brickett's, both of us.'

Marion let her memories spark − of her mother, her father, her old life at Willow Street. Death had been a shadow that followed her everywhere. But no, it wasn't what led her to Miss Brickett's.

'I don't think so, not for me,' she said, voicing the theory. 'I've always felt like an outsider. Different, you know? I remember sitting at my bedroom window every morning, watching the world pass by – children going off to school, men to work, women to the shops – and thinking how dull and pointless it all was. And yet no one seemed to notice, like they were walking around in the same dream, unconscious, and I was the only one awake.' She blinked, cast her eyes to the park boundary, where a bus had just pulled up, spilled its passengers onto the pavement – an indistinct knot of bodies that moved as one, hurrying home, the same blank expression on their faces. 'That's what drew me to Miss Brickett's, I think,' she went on as the passengers split up, disappeared. 'Purpose. Belonging. I wanted to fit in somewhere, I suppose. Feel like I was a part of something that made sense to me.' She shook her head, suddenly aware of how much she'd revealed, and suddenly uncomfortable about it. 'Sorry, you must think I'm—'

'I think you're incredible,' he said, cutting her off. He drew a breath, angled himself to face her. 'Look, Frank said something to me the other day that made me think. Lane, I want you to know . . the reason I haven't . . . it's just . . . what I feel for you isn't easy to explain, not even to myself.' He rubbed the back of his neck. 'If I told you I loved you like a sister, like Jenny, I know you wouldn't like it—'

Marion turned away, looked out of the window at the darkening sky, gold and pink turning black. She suspected, though she hoped she was wrong, that Frank had spoken to Kenny about *her*, about Kenny's feelings and how he should express them. The thought of it twisted her stomach into knots.

'You wouldn't like it,' he repeated, his voice cracked and flustered now, 'but only because you don't understand.' He reached for her hand, pulled it towards him. 'Lane, look at me.' He waited until she'd set her eyes on him. His face was contorted, screwed up as though he were about to implode.

'Love like that leaves no space for anything else. No jealousy. No ulterior motives. But it burns you up from the inside, too, because you know you can't live without it, though one day you might have to. You understand, don't you? That's why I can't, I don't . . . ' He turned to the bakery, his breathing ragged now. 'I lost Jenny. I can't go through that—'

'Kenny, please,' Marion said, unable to take it any longer. 'Let's just leave it, all right? We're here to work.' She stopped, then added as an ill-considered afterthought: 'And work is my priority.'

Kenny opened his mouth as though to argue, or perhaps agree, then inhaled sharply and straightened in his seat. Fortunately, there was no time for an awkward silence. 'Here we go, what's this?'

Marion turned to her right, to the bakery entrance. An elderly man with a cane and stooped posture appeared seemingly from nowhere and stood, one hand in his pocket, one on his cane, staring out across the greens of Hyde Park.

'Binoculars,' Kenny demanded.

Marion ignored him, taking the binoculars and pressing them to her eyes. Whatever had happened between them moments ago had dissolved completely and they were back to their usual bickering selves.

'It's him. Has to be,' she said immediately. 'Looks like he's waiting for something . . . someone.' She scanned the surrounding area, though there was no one else about.

'Could I have the darn binoculars?' Kenny hissed.

Marion handed them over, ignoring his tone. For several reasons, she was rather relieved the old man had decided to show himself just then.

'You're right, it looks like a rendezvous.'

'Brilliant,' she chided under her breath.

But it wasn't a rendezvous. The old man just stood there alone, shifting occasionally from foot to foot, staring out ahead of him, apparently at nothing. At one point, he looked directly at the Hudson, and while they were certainly too far off for him to see them sitting inside, it unnerved Marion. Even with Kenny by her side, she felt her nerves tingle with anticipation – she hadn't forgotten who they were trailing.

'He's moving,' Kenny said several minutes later. 'And *darn it*, he's going into the park!' He unclipped his seat belt, cracked his neck from side to side. 'We're going to have to follow him on foot.'

'Okay, but we have to be delicate about it,' Marion said urgently as she reached over to the back seat where Frank had packed a suitcase of essentials. 'We can't be seen. Not by the Florist, not by anyone.'

She hauled the suitcase onto her lap and took out a tracking compass (not that she thought they'd get close enough to be able to plant one on him), an assortment of surveillance devices, a Distractor (Marion's favourite gadget, a speaker disguised as a mechanical sunbird), two night coats and one coil of Twister Rope – just in case it came to that.

'Here, you'll have to keep this, I suppose.'

She handed Kenny the coil (because it was a Schedule 3 gadget, as an apprentice Inquirer, Marion wasn't permitted to handle it). She didn't know why she was bothering with rules and regulations right now, but old habits die hard. She looked up. The Florist was already halfway across the park and nearly out of sight.

'Come on, we've got to hurry!'

They leaped from the car and pulled on their night coats – dark grey ankle-length garments designed especially for this sort of mission, woven from strange silklike thread that rendered the wearer nearly invisible in poor light.

By the time they'd reached the south-western quarter of the park, a crescent moon had risen, bathing the landscape in a silvery blue. A small breeze picked up from the north and the lawn stretched out before them like a dark ocean. Marion pulled her coat tighter around her as the night air rippled past.

'Lighter on your feet,' she whispered to Kenny, who'd nearly given away their position several times as he crushed leaves and twigs underfoot. '*Glide*, don't walk.'

Kenny gave her a funny look and she was sure that if they'd been anywhere else more suited to having a debate, he'd have gone on about how being a *real* private detective required none of this 'gliding nonsense'. Regardless, several yards of gliding later, they stopped near the Serpentine. The Florist sat down on a park bench, his hands on his lap, his hat pulled down subtly over his eyes. He waited for a moment, unmoving.

Ten minutes of nothing later, Kenny stirred. Marion could sense his impatience.

'He's not going anywhere, Lane. And we can't loiter here all night, too suspicious.' He looked down at his night coat with a dissatisfied expression. 'Even in these things.'

Marion agreed, and yet the old man's body language – his subtly unrelaxed posture, the tension in his shoulders – told her he was waiting for something. 'He knows,' she whispered, fear trickling through her. 'He knows he's being watched.'

Kenny observed the old man more carefully, then gripped her by the arm. 'Well, let's beat it, then!'

Marion let him guide her back towards the car without complaint, but as they approached Carriage Drive, she turned around, pressed the binoculars to her face.

'I knew it! He was just waiting for us to leave.'

Kenny ripped the binoculars from Marion, but even from such a distance, she could see the Florist get to his feet and make his way along the lake's shoreline, moving in the opposite direction to Marion and Kenny.

'What the hell are you doing?' Kenny asked, incredulous as Marion started back for the lake.

'We have to follow him, Kenny. It's the whole reason we're out here. I'm not telling Frank we saw the killer and just let him go!'

She heard Kenny spitting insults at her from behind, but she didn't stop. The Florist had reached the end of the Serpentine, where it petered out and was replaced by a strip of reeds and overgrown grass. He turned slightly left, exiting the park at southern Carriage Drive. He crossed the street, came to a telephone booth and stepped inside.

For a moment, Marion was undecided. Whatever telephone call the Florist was about to make, it was sure to be invaluable intelligence, or he wouldn't have gone to such lengths to get to the booth unseen. She had a plan, a way to eavesdrop on the call. But it was high risk and she was convinced that if Frank was with her now, he'd forbid it. Thankfully, her partner tonight was a little easier to persuade.

'Give me your Herald Steth,' she said, holding out her hand expectantly while keeping her eyes right ahead.

'Sorry?'

'You heard me, just hand it over! Quickly!' She would have used her own if she'd had one, but since last year, Herald Stethoscopes – long brass listening tubes designed to pick up even the faintest sound through solid barriers – were classed alongside Twister Rope as Schedule 3 gadgets (potential to inflict harm with improper use).

Kenny seemed uncertain, but perhaps he'd known Marion long enough to realise that arguing with her might take all night. He handed over the stethoscope with a grunt. 'You're a stubborn woman, you know that?'

She ignored him and set about readying the stethoscope.

Kenny shook his head, defeated. 'Go round the back. I'll wait here and distract him if necessary.'

'Don't worry. I won't be seen.' She flashed him a confident smile then, stethoscope ready, marched ahead, aiming directly for the booth.

She could see the old man inside, the receiver to his ear already. She picked up her pace, turning left as she came to the front of the booth so that it might look as though she was simply on her way down the tight alleyway that split off from Carriage Drive. When she was out of the Florist's sight and certain there was no one around (or at least no one close enough to mark her as suspicious), she doubled back. Once in position behind the booth, she crouched down, pulled her night coat around her knees and pressed the stethoscope to her ear.

The first snatches of the old man's conversation were inaudible and nonsensical, but then the stethoscope acclimatised to the faint crackle of his voice.

'Very pleased to hear it,' the Florist said with the hint of an accent – Russian or Eastern European. 'And you're quite sure the system works? We can't afford any trouble with the main deal. Yes, yes. I can see that. No, possibly not.' A long pause. 'Well, then it appears you might not have killed poor Eddie in vain, after all.'

Marion pressed her ear more firmly against the listening end of the Herald Stethoscope as the Florist lowered his voice.

'Of course not . . . what do you mean, someone's suspicious? No, no, you passed the enigma.'

There was another long pause, punctuated by the occasional throat-clearing or incoherent mumble. And then, a voice from behind her shoulder.

She whipped around. Kenny was standing just to the left of the telephone box, facing two men who had stepped out from behind a line of trees across the street. Both were tall and burly, dressed in casual daywear despite the time of year – summer trousers and simple button-downs. And both were holding pistols at their side.

The men took a step forwards, closing the space between them and Kenny.

'Evening, boys,' Kenny said in a deadpan voice. 'Do we have a problem?'

Marion heard a click from inside the telephone box. The Florist put down the receiver.

'Blast!' she hissed under her breath. She moved an inch to her right, just enough to conceal herself behind the telephone box as the Florist stepped outside.

He paused at the door, so close Marion could hear him breathing.

'You tell us,' one of the burly men said, replying to Kenny.

'Not as far as I'm concerned,' Kenny chuckled, splaying his hands in a gesture of nonchalance. He pointed at the booth. 'Just waiting to use the telephone, if that's all right with you?'

Tap-Tap. Tap. Tap-Tap.

The Florist clipped his cane against the pavement, relaying some sort of Morse code signal to his burly guards.

A pause.

Marion held her breath. The silence throbbed, taut with apprehension.

A pistol was cocked, maybe two.

'Run!' Kenny's voice was shrill and sharp.

Marion dived left. Kenny sped after her. A shot was fired, ricocheting off the wall behind the telephone box.

The two burly men lurched forwards, but Marion and Kenny had already made it around the corner, into the neighbouring alleyway, and dived behind a parked car.

Footsteps followed them, stopping less than five yards away. A torchlight illuminated the dim alleyway, its beam searching up and down, left and right.

Kenny gave Marion a sidelong glance, then touched the hem of his night coat. She knew what he was thinking. The garments would do nothing to conceal them under the direct glare of a torchlight. They had to move.

Kenny slipped his hand into the suitcase, pulled out a small mechanical sunbird. He wound up a key hidden under the creature's wing, causing the bird to wriggle and squirm in his grasp. He gave Marion a hand signal. She nodded. Raised three fingers. Lowered one, then a second, and on the third, Kenny released the sunbird. It fluttered upwards, to the right, coming to rest on a nearby lamp post. Seconds later, there was a loud crack – something that might have been an engine backfiring, or perhaps a gunshot. The burly men turned to the noise, giving Marion and Kenny a split second to escape.

And, under the cover of dark, they slipped carefully back into the shadows.

6

Enigma

Marion swept up the spiral staircase to the Games Room above Frank's office. It was 8 p.m. on Monday evening and the surrounding corridors and chambers of Miss Brickett's were still, save for the clink of glasses from the library bar — the agency barman clearing up for the night — and the clip of footsteps as employees completed their final duties for the day.

She closed the door behind her and switched on the lights. The corkboard, work desk and filing cabinet that had filled the space the last time she was here had been removed, the billiard table repositioned in the centre of the room. A deck of cards, a dirty ashtray and two whisky glasses lay on the table near the drinks cabinet, as though a game had been recently interrupted and forgotten.

She strolled over to a chair by the hearth, settled down. No, not settled. How could she be after what happened at Hyde Park on Saturday? She'd been turning it over in her mind all weekend, wondering what she could have done differently, wondering if she'd blown their cover. Had the Florist seen her? Had he known the Inquirers were watching him? And if so, what did this mean for the investigation as a whole? She'd wanted her first field assignment to be a success, to return to the Games Room tonight with vital intelligence expertly gleaned from the Florist without his knowledge.

But despite her expectations, the expedition with Kenny to Hyde Park had been a failure. Not only had they nearly been shot and Kenny exposed (if not her, as well), but the whole thing had also done little to further the investigation. They'd gathered only three scraps of disjointed information from the telephone booth: the individual the Florist had called was Eddie Hopper's real killer (or so the old man had made it seem), the Florist was possibly of Russian or Eastern European descent, and something about an important 'deal' he and his contact were involved in.

The mention of a 'deal' was marginally interesting, suggesting the Florist and his contact (and perhaps Eddie Hopper) were involved in some shady enterprise that possibly turned sour. It had always been Marion's guess that Hopper's grim fate was punishment for a business-related blunder. But for now, this lead was just another dead end and the only other snatch of conversation Marion had picked up through the Herald Stethoscope was meaningless gibberish: someone was suspicious. Something about passing an enigma – whatever that meant.

She cocked her head to the side, pulled from her thoughts as she caught sight of a crumpled pile of paper lying among half-scorched pieces of wood in the fireplace. She got up, collected the papers from the grate. Some of them were singed at the edges, obviously thrown into dying flames, not quite hot enough to destroy them completely.

She frowned as she realised what they were – replicas of the poster Jessica had showed her, the one she'd found in the powder room: *ERPS. East Eight. 18. Every Fifth.*

There was a scrape as the door started to move. Marion shoved the papers back into the fireplace and dusted the ash from her hands just as Frank appeared. His eyes went to her, then the grate, the hearth. She bit her lip, not sure why she felt uncomfortable. Surely Frank wouldn't have minded her seeing the half-burned posters. Surely he'd be happy to explain what they were and why he'd been trying to get rid of them.

Curiosity, and perhaps a note of concern, crossed his features, then vanished, replaced by a smile. 'You're early. I should have guessed. Punctuality is your gift.'

'Hopefully not my *only* gift,' she teased, attempting to gain some composure.

'Do have a seat.'

Marion returned to the chair by the fireplace as Frank extracted a small metallic sunbird from his briefcase and placed it on the coffee table between them.

She let out a breath of relief. 'You retrieved it?'

The Distracter Kenny had set off on Saturday night was the reason they were able to escape the Florist and his men unscathed, but leaving the bizarre gizmo out in London for everyone to see (and perhaps steal) had been a risk.

'It was concealed rather well on a lamp post near the telephone booth. I don't think anyone would have noticed, but if they did, it obviously wasn't interesting enough to steal. We're in the clear.'

'Good, yes. And I suppose you've met with Kenny already?' she said, thinking of the whisky glasses, cigarette butts and unfinished game of cards on the table nearby.

The image of Frank and Kenny laughing over a nightcap caused her a childish twinge of jealousy. Marion had always been Frank's primary concern, his most trusted ally (or vice versa). And yet he'd never invited *her* for a private game of cards.

'Only this afternoon. He came to update me on his progress regarding the rose-branding lead. He's received word of a similar case recorded three years ago. Near Liverpool.'

'Similar?'

'A hotel maid was found dead in her quarters, the same marking on her chest. Apparently suicide, though I believe this was just a cover-up by the authorities. Hugo is trying to convince Constable Redding to gather further details on our behalf; unfortunately, he hasn't had much success. As you know, Redding is reluctant to involve himself in the investigation.' He lapsed into thought for a moment. 'Hugo also told me what happened at Hyde Park, about the bodyguards and the near escape.'

'Yes, sorry. We didn't realise the Florist had company until it was too late.'

Frank waved this off. 'Not to worry. Even if the Florist got a good look at Hugo, or you, he's going to assume you're with the police, which won't cause us any further trouble. Speak of the devil . . . '

Marion drew a breath as Kenny appeared – all suave and perfect hair, blue jeans and a crisp white shirt, sleeves rolled up to the elbows. He acknowledged Frank with a nod, Marion with a look that betrayed a modicum of uncertainty. It was the first time they'd seen each other since the stake-out, since he'd told her he loved her like a sister and she'd responded rather brusquely. Perhaps he was unsure now just what she thought of him, whether she was hurt, or put off altogether. Good. It was his turn to speculate.

'So pleased you popped by again,' Frank said to Kenny. 'Marion was just about to tell me what she heard through the Herald Stethoscope. Have a seat, Hugo.'

Marion passed Kenny a fleeting glance, then went on to relay everything she'd heard the Florist say through the Herald Stethoscope. 'Which means'– she added, after repeating the Florist's most chilling words: *Well, then it appears you might not have killed poor Eddie in vain, after all* – 'Whoever the Florist was calling from the booth is Hopper's *actual* killer,' Frank provided.

'Except, the Florist definitely had a part in the murder,' Kenny cut in, moving to the edge of his seat. 'Remember, we have witnesses who place him at the scene of the crime.' He stretched his legs out in front of him, clipping the coffee table with his brogues and not giving a damn about it. 'In other words, we now have *two* suspects.'

Frank twirled a gold ring around his middle finger, his lips moving silently as though he was running something through his mind. 'Remind me, Marion, what did the Florist say at the end?'

Marion frowned, trying to recall. It was the least interesting thing she'd overheard and yet, it had caught Frank's attention more than everything else. 'Well, I can't remember word for word, but it was something about someone being suspicious and *passing the enigma*. I didn't get to hear the rest.'

Frank looked past her to the hearth. The muscles in his jaw tightened. Marion glanced at Kenny, wondering if he understood something she didn't. But Kenny was oblivious, staring at the floor without any focus while he lit a cigarette.

She turned back to Frank. 'Does that mean something to you?'

Frank gestured to the fireplace and its crumpled papers. 'You've seen those, I presume?'

She shuffled in her seat. 'I didn't . . . I mean . . . Jessica showed me one a few days ago.'

'And I saw one in the break room this morning,' Kenny added, removing a fleck of ash from his tongue. 'What the blazes are they?'

'I don't know. I've been finding them all over the place. In the ballroom, in the library bar, in the corridors. I don't know who's distributing them, or what they mean, but in light of recent information . . . '

He finished the sentence in a mumble Marion couldn't make out. She watched as he rose from his seat, paced across the Persian rug, around the billiard table.

'I'm leaving for St Mark's first thing tomorrow. I need to find Old Sam. I don't know how long I'll be away, but in the meantime . . . ' He stopped, took a breath. 'Hugo, could you return to the telephone booth again this Saturday? I doubt the Florist will resurface there after your little altercation, but we'd do well to check. Any further information we can glean from these calls will be vital.'

'On it. No sweat,' Kenny said, tapping a finger to his forehead in salute before stubbing out his cigarette and flicking the butt into the hearth.

'And me?' Marion asked.

Frank gave her a look that she'd seen too many times to be fooled. He was trying to appear casual, to make her think that whatever he said next was said in passing, an afterthought.

'I'd like you to keep an eye on the new recruits for me. A close eye.'

'Keep an eye on them? In what sense?'

'I'm just concerned. There's something amiss at Miss Brickett's. These posters . . . I can't put my finger on it, but I'm certain it started with the arrival of the new recruits.'

The knot in Marion's stomach tightened, twisting in on itself. A memory stirred – *one of the new recruits is not to be trusted*. Did Frank know it, too? Had he received a similar warning?

'Or perhaps before,' he mused, mostly to himself. 'December, just after the recruitment test went out.'

He kneeled down beside the hearth, drew a box of matches from his trouser pocket, lit one and threw it onto the pile of posters lying in the grate. They caught alight, spawning a crimson blaze that cast a distorted shadow across his face.

7

The Liar's Eyeglass

One week had gone by since Frank left for St Mark's. One week of silence. Marion understood this was to be expected. Infiltrating the gentleman's club without raising suspicion would require utter immersion into Eddie Hopper's elite world. Frank, no doubt, had assumed another identity – a banker, a trader, a man with money and infinite connections. He'd have altered his appearance, modified his accent, cultivated a character that was easy to admire, easier to forget. Frank Stone was brilliant in the field, Marion knew. Still, it was hard to sit around and wait, to go about her routine work at the agency, all the while aware that he was out there somewhere in Oxfordshire, undercover but very much in danger.

In fact, it was impossible.

She was restless, consumed by thoughts that twisted then unravelled. Clues that were stark but incomprehensible. And while these flecks of information swirled chaotically through her mind, unordered and nonsensical, she decided to turn her attention to what Frank had asked of her. And thus her focus slowly began to shift, away from Frank, conspicuous in his absence, and towards the recruits.

But through the passing days, Longmore, Quinn and Proctor, as with all who came to work at Miss Brickett's, began a metamorphosis of sorts: a transmutation from the ordinary and unimaginative to those who accepted the bizarre and unbelievable as simply part of their existence. Things that, above ground, would be considered technically impossible — such as self-tangling coils of Twister Rope or soaring mechanical birds — were now regarded with vague interest and absolute acceptance. The new apprentices had also begun to acquire a sense of direction through the sunless labyrinth — whose corridors meandered into cul-de-sacs, short-cuts and endless detours. In turn, the labyrinth and everyone who worked there had come to know and trust the new apprentices.

Everyone except Marion.

In her eyes, Proctor was a darker, colder version of Bill — withdrawn, reticent, eyes cast permanently to the floor and an aura that suggested the depth of his character was hidden beneath fear and insecurity. He hardly spoke, but when he did — such as at the initiation in the library bar — it was with a vicious, biting tone, giving Marion the impression he was constantly defending himself, a growling hound chained and starved of attention. In addition, Proctor had been allocated a room in the staff quarters, which he shared with Longmore, and Marion had occasionally seen him roaming the corridor outside the common room late at night. Apparently, he was a sleepwalker, though he looked perfectly alert every time she'd bumped into him — wide-eyed and dubious — and she did wonder what he was doing alone and in the dark all those hours.

In contrast, Longmore was loud and gregarious, constantly blabbering on about anything and everything, charismatic and easy to like (if you fell for that sort of thing). He seemed to fit in immediately with several of the older apprentices, establishing a swift reputation among them as the 'most promising future Inquirer' on account of his tireless work ethic. But was his apparent confidence not a little overdone? How could a newcomer, someone so unacquainted to their surroundings, be simultaneously so at ease?

Then there was Quinn, who'd shown a penchant for the glistening gadgets of the Workshop, ones that were complex and evasive in particular. As she'd demonstrated the night of the initiation, she also had a natural talent for mechanics and within days had mastered almost all of the Gadgetry Department's assemblage procedures – something that had taken Marion close to a year to perfect. To Marion's credit, however, Quinn was far less adept at repairs than she was at production – no one knew how to put things back together as well as Marion did. And so, Marion and Quinn managed to work together without ever really needing to get along – Quinn assembling the new and shiny, Marion repairing the broken and worn. In fact, Marion might have even come to appreciate and respect Quinn, had it not been for the fact that she was forever writing things down in that notebook of hers.

What details was she recording? What secrets was she collecting?

On Tuesday afternoon, two weeks into Frank's expedition to St Mark's, Marion guided Quinn, Proctor and Longmore down the long stone staircase to the Gadgetry Department, where she was due to meet Professor Uday Bal – head of the department and principal engineer – about a new gadget he'd been commissioned to make. As ever, she kept the recruits within earshot as she watched them approach the gargoyle that guarded the entrance to the Workshop.

'What's the purpose of that thing, anyway?' demanded Longmore, frowning at the gargoyle, which had thankfully drawn his attention and put an end to a painfully long recital he'd been inflicting upon the group about his first few days as an apprentice.

'It guards the door, obviously,' Quinn answered before Marion had the chance.

Proctor took a subtle step backwards as Longmore touched the gargoyle's head. 'Guards it? How? All you have to do to get past is pull down the claw.'

'Left arm, actually,' Quinn corrected after consulting her notebook.

Longmore cast his eyes to the heavens as if Quinn were an imbecile. 'Well, it's not very—'

'Safe,' Proctor provided, speaking over him (which Marion now realised was the only way to get a word in around Longmore).

The two men stared at each other in a curious fashion while Quinn scribbled a quick line in her notebook.

'Let's just get inside, please. We're already late,' Marion interrupted, pushing all three aside, disarming the gargoyle and stepping past as it sank obediently into the floor.

Together, the four apprentices crossed the Workshop hall, where tall oval lamps fluttered in the perimeter, casting a dizzying pattern of light across the floor. In the farthest, darkest corner of the department, a door creaked on its hinges and, seconds later, a straggly figure appeared.

Professor Bal beckoned Marion over. As usual, his dark skin shimmered with sweat despite the relentless chill of the Workshop and his feeble frame seemed to wither beneath several layers of oversized attire. He smiled, removed his beloved green-chequered beret and, without a word, guided

Marion and the recruits to the workbench outside his office. Here, among an arrangement of tweezers, hammers and pliers, was a large section of drafting parchment covered by an elaborate pencil sketch. Marion traced her fingers over the paper, its gentle curvatures, lines and intricate dimensions.

'The new commission you'll be helping me with today,' the professor announced proudly, his accent perfectly English despite his Pakistani heritage.

'Goodness,' Marion said.

Ignoring Longmore and Quinn, who were still arguing over whether or not the gargoyle served a purpose, and Proctor, who was staring at Professor Bal in a fixed, unsettling manner, Marion sat down, drew the drafting paper closer to her. The professor, in response to the look of confusion on her face, handed her the magnifying glass he always carried on a chain around his neck. Now several times enlarged, Marion realised she was looking at what appeared to be a sort of magnifying glass itself, but with the addition of ten small gauges – each with its own needle and differing increments.

'It's called a Liar's Eyeglass,' the professor explained as Marion lifted her eyes from the sketch.

Longmore and Quinn fell silent in an instant and all three recruits now fixed their attention on the curious sketch in Marion's hand.

'A commission from Hanslope Park.'

Since her recruitment, Marion had witnessed an endless stream of orders come through the Factory – the agency's primary source of income – a facade warehouse in Clapham that claimed to sell and produce devices of espionage and subterfuge to MI5 and occasionally the CIA. But this supply chain was doubly deceptive, because MI5 believed that their brilliant contraptions were coming from the technical department at

Hanslope Park, and Hanslope – equally falsely – believed their orders were coming from the Factory in Clapham.

'It's a polygraph machine – a lie detector, I presume?'

The professor's eyes skirted from the sketch and back to Marion. 'It's modelled after an old design I made several years ago during the war. The British used them to weed out spies and traitors, but they went out of favour after forty-five, mostly because they're very difficult to use. I haven't produced one since.'

'How does it work?'

'The Glass detects alterations in a subject's eye – the size of the pupil, minute changes in colour, blink rate, even dilation and contraction of the ocular blood vessels.' He paused, waited for Marion to nod dully, then continued. 'All of which are strong indicators of whether someone is telling a falsehood or not. It requires a lot of practice, and perhaps a touch of talent to read its gauges, but if one masters it, the Glass is awfully accurate. Far more so than any other polygraph on the market.'

'I see.' Marion touched the drafting paper again. 'So, we have to make a hundred. Is there a due date?'

The professor's lips twitched nervously. 'Well yes, I'm afraid it's not going to be easy. We need it done by early April.'

'That's not impossible,' she said, trying to sound as if she meant it. 'I'll get started right away.'

She turned to her left. Quinn, of course, was writing something down in her notepad. Proctor was glancing furtively around the Workshop, his white-blond fringe pressed to his forehead with a layer of sweat while Longmore watched him with a strange expression. Marion took a breath and turned to the professor, who was fidgeting with his shirt buttons, craning his neck, trying to see what Quinn was scribbling down. Apart from the obvious problem that Quinn's quirk for recording everything was incredibly irksome, Marion wondered whether there was some other reason the professor seemed so put out by the habit.

'Perfect, thank you,' the professor said, drawing his eyes from Quinn at last. He patted Marion on the shoulder. 'I'm supposed to let these three help you' – he lowered his voice – 'but . . . just make sure they don't mess up anything.'

Five hours later, hampered by a blinding headache and aching everything, Marion put down her tools and stared at the jumble of metal pieces and springs on the workbench before her. During the arduous session, all she'd managed to do was break seven battery coils and melt an eighth. After the loss of half of one of her fingers, finicky, intricate work was more difficult. It had taken an extraordinary effort to learn a new way of holding and manoeuvring her tools, and even though she'd more or less mastered the art, it was evident to anyone who paid attention to her work that she still struggled.

'I can do it, if you'd like?' Quinn provided after observing Marion's attempt to thread a minuscule line of wiring into a battery coil for the third (unsuccessful) time.

'I've got it,' Marion assured her with a note of irritation, her hands shaking with concentration as she wound the thread of wire through the eye of a specially designed needle, then through the coil network. Just as she'd said it, the needle slipped. 'Blast!'

'What happened to you, anyway?' Longmore asked, looking at the stump on her left hand.

'An accident.'

'I thought it was a scuffle with a former employee,' Quinn piped up.

Marion glared at her. 'Do you have that written down in your notepad, too?'

Quinn flushed, crossed her arms. Proctor, who'd spent most of the session hunched over a Workshop manual, staring at it blankly, now straightened up, closed the manual and pushed it away as though it were contaminated.

'Edgar Swindlehurst?'

Quinn gave a short gasp. It didn't surprise Marion that the three recruits already knew about Swindlehurst. Michelle White's murder was without question the most talked about article of Miss Brickett's history.

'Don't believe everything you hear,' Marion said as the needle in her hand slipped yet again.

'Where is he now?' Proctor persisted, turning to Quinn as though she might be able to answer.

'In prison,' Marion provided – the truth, though perhaps not in its entirety. She used a cloth to wipe the dampness from her hands. Out of the corner of her eye, she noticed Longmore cock his head. 'Here,' she said to Quinn, handing her the needle and silver thread. 'Could you give it a try? I can't seem to manage.'

Temporarily distracted by the honour, Quinn twirled the wire thread through her fingers, marvelling at it as if she'd never seen something so incredible, then guided the thread through the lattice network with ease.

'Done!' she said, gleaming.

Marion smiled weakly, rubbed her palm, her injured hand. It was throbbing again. 'Well, I suppose you ought to do the rest. But not today.' She got up, stretched her neck, eager to leave the cloistered atmosphere.

Longmore looked at his watch, raised his eyebrows and muttered something vulgar about the time. Proctor leaped to his feet with more enthusiasm than he'd demonstrated all day, packed up his things and was gone in a flash.

Quinn was more reluctant, fussing with the contents of her bag, stalling. Once Longmore had left, she said: 'I know you're keeping an eye on us, by the way.'

'Sorry?' Marion kept her eyes fixed on the workbench.

'It's very obvious. You ought to be more subtle about it. Especially around those two. And,' she continued as Marion started to speak, 'if you spent less time watching us and more time keeping an eye on your own set of problems, you might realise what's going on right under your nose.'

This unnerved Marion, but before she could say so, Quinn had marched from the Workshop and was gone.

She looked at her watch. It was well past six in the evening and her stomach ached for sustenance, or maybe it was dread. She packed away her tools and cleaned the workbench, then crossed the hall to Professor Bal's office. The door was, as always, ajar.

The professor looked up from a heap of springs and screws laid out before him on his desk. 'Marion, you're still here? How did it go?'

'Oh, fine, I suppose.' She concealed her left hand in her right.

Bal smiled, pushed aside whatever it was he'd been working on and beckoned her inside. 'I've just been trying to wire the battery myself. Horrible task.' He chuckled to himself, then stopped as he glanced at her hand. 'It makes things difficult, doesn't it?'

She rubbed the mutilated stump, heat touching her cheeks. She hated it when her hand was mentioned, especially in the context of mechanics and what she could no longer do. She'd tried so hard to pretend the deformity wasn't there. She just wished everyone else would, too.

'I'm getting used to it.'

'There's no shame in struggle, Marion. Things are more difficult for you now, true, but you'll always be the best assistant I've ever had.' He got to his feet, pulled Marion into a tight embrace, his bony frame cutting into her own. When they released, he looked at her intently. 'There's something on your mind. What is it?'

'Just work,' she lied.

'Yes,' he said knowingly. 'It's been difficult, hasn't it? Especially with the financial situation.'

Marion frowned. 'What do you mean?'

'We're losing money, Marion.' He drew a piece of paper from the stack to his left, though he didn't show it to her. 'I didn't believe it at first, but someone's been assigned to look through our financial records . . . ' He paused. 'It's rather bad. And the worst part is, no one seems to know *how* it's happening. Everything seems in order and yet we're running at a loss—' He was interrupted by a light *tap-tap* on the office door.

'Excuse me, pardon the interruption.'

Marion and Bal turned around to see Quinn hovering on the threshold, a notepad clutched to her chest.

She looked directly at the professor. 'I forgot to mention something earlier and I thought I'd just pop back while you're still here.' She opened her notepad and began to page through.

The professor was immediately uncomfortable, even before Quinn said anything more.

'Forgive me, but when I was cleaning the shelves in the display cabinet yesterday evening, I couldn't help notice a discrepancy between the number of batteries stored there and the number listed on the parts inventory.'

Marion looked at Professor Bal, though he didn't seem able to speak. She decided to take over. 'You're keeping track of the number of batteries we store in the Workshop?'

'I keep track of everything.' Quinn paused for effect. 'It's how I'm able to be so precise.'

Eventually, Bal stirred from his trance. 'Thank you for pointing that out, Miss Quinn, but I updated the inventory list myself yesterday and everything was in perfect order.'

Quinn looked puzzled by this. 'What time yesterday?'

Bal began to fidget – first with his coat buttons, then a pen. 'I can't remember exactly. Around five.'

Quinn wrote this down in her notepad. 'Oh,' she said, frowning at something else she'd written a few pages back. 'Maybe—'

'Maybe what?' Marion said sharply, unable to stand the tension any longer.

Quinn snapped her notepad shut and smiled. 'Never mind. See you tomorrow.'

8

The Employee Rights
and Protection Society

Friday the thirteenth of March started much the same as any Friday at Miss Brickett's. A general fizz of anticipation carried through the corridors, eagerness for the weekend ahead. Apprentices were huddled together over unfinished assignments and last-minute shifts, discussing their plans with vigour – trips to the wintery countryside, to the theatre, group dinners above ground.

But for Marion, it wasn't a Friday like any other. While Kenny had returned to the telephone booth outside Hyde Park every Saturday evening since their stake-out, the Florist had seemingly vanished. And to make matters worse, Frank had been away at St Mark's for just over a month; his only correspondence since was a short telephone call where he stated: *the sun is out*, which apparently meant he was safe and things were going well. But had he tracked down Old Sam, Constable Redding's 'compromising witness'? Had he learned anything about Eddie Hopper and his connection to the Florist?

She wasn't just frustrated with the lack of information – she was disturbed by it. Yes, she was watching the new recruits, as Frank had insisted – especially Quinn, whose bizarre interest in the Gadgetry Department's inventory list continued, and it wasn't unusual for Marion to catch her hanging around the Workshop storage cabinet, counting things, recording things. But was that really the best use of her time, while the Florist stalked London undetected? Her friends didn't seem to think so.

'So, Frank's away on some top-secret assignment, and you and Kenny are just here . . . *waiting*?' Bill asked abruptly, halfway through the apprentice's weekly SpyCraft lecture, held in a teaching chamber west of the auditorium. He, Marion, Jessica and everyone's nemesis – David Eston – were seated together at the back of the chamber, an array of office equipment strewn around them. David and Bill, who'd despised one another when they met last year and even more so since, had been arguing about something Marion chose not to pay attention to. Somehow, it had led to a discussion about Frank's absence, and Marion and Kenny's assignment to the Harrogate murder.

She got the feeling Bill's question was more a jab at Kenny's self-proclaimed 'real detective' skills than her apparently redundant role in the investigation, but decided this wasn't the time to point that out.

Jessica pulled a vial of scent from her bag – her favourite: jasmine and pine – and dabbed a drop under her chin. 'Honestly, I wouldn't mind if I were you,' she said to Marion. 'Waiting around or not, spending all day with dreamboat Hugo's got to be the best sort of work I've ever heard of.'

'You got the hots for him as well now?' Bill piped up with a snigger.

'Darling, I'm only human,' Jessica said, throwing Marion a suggestive eye.

'To answer your question,' Marion said, as if she hadn't heard a word, 'I'm not waiting around. Neither is Kenny. We've been asked to keep an eye on things.'

She cast her gaze to the chamber entrance as Proctor, Longmore and Quinn stepped inside. SpyCraft — the practical and theoretical elements of detection and surveillance, how to lip-read, detect and plant bugs, decipher codes, analyse intelligence — was generally reserved for second- and third-year apprentices, although the first-years were allowed to observe the lectures if they had nothing else to do.

'You mean *them*?' Jessica asked, following Marion's gaze. 'Whatever for?'

Marion didn't answer. Her assignment to the Harrogate case and all the details surrounding it wasn't supposed to be a matter of casual agency debate. It was bad enough word had got out that the case was under investigation and that Marion and Kenny had been assigned. But that was as far as she dared let the rumour spread. No one knew she and Kenny had stalked the Florist above ground, nearly blowing their cover. And best it remained that way, especially after Frank had implied the investigation might be connected to something going on at Miss Brickett's.

She shrugged, focused on the faux typewriter Bill had handed her and began to examine it with a Wire Catcher — a compass-like device with ten gears in its centre, which spun in opposing directions when close enough to a bug or listening device.

Meanwhile, David, looking as uninterested as one could imagine, extricated a *Basic Workshop Manual* from his bag and opened it on page thirty-three: Wire Catcher Uses and Design. He looked from Marion to the manual and back again, contorting his chipped, hostile features into something that resembled the gargoyle outside the Gadgetry Department.

He picked at the sparse reddish-brown hair on his chin and, in his characteristically critical tone, said: 'It says here you're supposed to hold it at forty-five degrees.'

Marion ignored him (and Bill, who told David he'd like to see him do a better job). She gripped the Catcher with her good hand, then attempted to calibrate the gears with her left.

'Blast!' she hissed as the gadget slipped from her grasp, clipped the desk and landed with a clang on the floor.

Jessica made to pick it up, but Bill – having learned that Marion preferred as little help as possible when it came to handling gadgets with her damaged hand – mouthed: *'Leave it.'*

Marion noticed their exchange and smiled. 'Relax, you two. I'm not *that* sensitive.'

Bill raised his eyebrows incredulously and reached for the Catcher. 'So, can I do it, then?'

'No,' Marion said with a muffled laugh, seizing the gadget before Bill could touch it. 'Give me another chance at least.'

She ignored Bill's 'All-righty, then', and David's sneer and, after a third attempt, successfully managed to calibrate the gears. Then, with both Jessica and Bill leaning over her shoulder and David perusing the manual again, she began to glide the Catcher over the typewriter.

'Make sure you find every last transmitter hidden in the devices you've been given,' demanded Nancy Brickett, who was supervising the lecture in lieu of Frank. 'And remember, we've planted several different types of bugs in each device,' she added, peering at them intently – especially Marion. 'Some might even be invisible.'

'Didn't know we made invisible bugs,' Bill mused under his breath, now holding a penlight over the typewriter as Marion scanned it a second time.

'We don't.' Marion frowned as the Catcher began to rattle over the typewriter's paper guide. 'But we make *nearly* invisible ones like . . . this . . . ' She shimmied a pair of tweezers into the space between the guide and roller and pulled out a silvery wormlike contraption that would have been impossible to spot had it not been directly under the glare of Bill's penlight. She dropped the bug into the collection tray. 'Right, the typewriter's clean. I think. What's next?'

Jessica handed her a disconnected telephone. 'This one's bound to be riddled. Last time there were five just inside the handset.'

And, sure enough, as Marion scanned the earpiece, the Wire Catcher's gears began to spin. 'Might be one here. David, what does the manual say about—' She stopped, looked up. David was no longer seated at the table. 'Where did he go?'

'Oh, I knew he was one of them! Look,' Jessica said, gesturing to David and a group of four other apprentices now seated several tables off – all three new recruits and Amanda Shirley, who was handing out what looked like a small booklet to each of the others. Jessica bit her lip and spoke in a hurried breath. 'Amanda and the new recruits were sitting together like that at breakfast and David looked very much like he wanted to join. Seems like he has now, doesn't it?'

'Join what?' Marion asked, the Wire Catcher still jittery in her grasp.

'Well, that's the thing. I saw them this morning looking through that booklet, the one she's handing out right now. I caught a glimpse of the title, *The Truths*. I've no clue what it means,' she added in reply to Bill's look of bafflement. 'But when I tried to go over and ask them what in heaven's name they were doing, Amanda wouldn't even look me in the eye. Instead, she just handed me this . . . ' She scratched around in her bag, then pushed a sheet of paper across the table.

Something caught in Marion's throat. She put down the Wire Catcher and picked up the piece of paper, a poster. *ERPS. East Eight. 18. Every Fifth.*

Jessica hurried to cover the poster with her handbag as Nancy strolled past, her eyes sweeping the room. Once Nancy was out of earshot, Jessica continued: 'It's exactly the same as the one I showed you on the orientation tour. You remember?'

Marion nearly mentioned that she'd seen several more in the Games Room fireplace but resisted. 'Do we know what it means yet?'

'I might, actually.' Jessica threw another quick glance at Amanda, who was demonstrating (somewhat clumsily) to Proctor, Longmore, Quinn and David how to fix what seemed to be a small arrow-shaped badge to their lapels. 'I think it's a club of some sort. And I think they've been having meetings somewhere. That's what the posters must be for—'

'To recruit new members?' Marion said, catching on.

Jessica nodded, drummed her freshly manicured nails on the desk. 'Exactly. Which means, *East Eight* must be the location – somewhere in the eastern corridors, I presume – *18* could be the time, six o'clock, and—'

'*Every Fifth* is the date,' Marion interrupted again. 'The fifth of every month?'

'Just ignore them,' Bill interjected with a snort of irritation. 'Come on, they're a bunch of gits and we've other things to worry about today.' He picked up the Wire Catcher Marion had abandoned and drew it over the top of the telephone receiver. 'Especially since this session might be in our mid-year assessment.'

'Who said?' Jessica asked, distracted by the comment.

'One of the third-years. Apparently, they usually include a gadget practical and a repeat recruitment test in the mid-year assessment – you know, just to make sure we're as sharp as we were the day we started.'

'Recruitment test?' Marion asked, her interest shifting from Amanda to Bill.

Bill looked up from the Wire Catcher with a moan. 'You know, the test each batch of new recruits gets after they've been shortlisted but before their interview? I don't know what it was this year, but ours was the Trick Lock on the bookshop door. The one you neatly dismantled instead of—' He stopped short, remembering too late that Jessica didn't know this finer detail, the fact that Marion had dismantled (instead of disarmed) the Trick Lock during her recruitment test for Miss Brickett's last year. Fortunately, Jessica didn't appear to have noticed the slip and was instead concentrating on the Catcher in Bill's hand, which was rattling wildly once more, every one of its gears spinning so fast they were now a blur. 'Think I've got one!' he announced.

Thoroughly distracted, Marion used a screwdriver and a pair of tweezers to dismantle the telephone's earpiece (a procedure Bill and Jessica insisted they were useless at). Inside was a tiny gunmetal disc, one of Miss Brickett's most ordinary (but practical) bugs. She removed it with some difficulty, dropped it into a collection tray, reassembled the telephone and tried to refocus her attention on the assignment. But as the hour dragged on, the atmosphere in the chamber grew more cloistered.

Recruitment test, she repeated over and over in her mind. *Recruitment test.* Isn't that what Frank had said in the Games Room, just before he asked her to watch the new apprentices, just before he burned the pile of posters in the grate? *Enigma.* Connections sparked, her heart rate doubled.

She glanced over at Amanda and her sidekicks, who, having finished – or given up on – their assignment, were now chittering again, low and hurried, as though planning something.

After what seemed to be some sort of debate, they got to their feet in unison and marched purposely from the chamber.

Marion looked at her watch and muttered to herself. 'It's six o'clock . . . every fifth . . . the fifth of every month. No . . . *no!*' She shoved her tools into her bag, got up.

'Do I want to know?' Bill asked, watching her.

She looked at Jessica instead. '*Every fifth* doesn't mean the fifth of every month. It means the fifth day of every *week*.'

'Friday!' Jessica said, swinging a red velvet handbag over her shoulder.

Bill took a moment to piece together what was happening. When he did, he gave both women a resigned look and got to his feet. 'Let me guess. We're going to find the East Eight?'

'Right, it has to be down this way,' Marion said ten minutes later as she, Bill and Jessica (who, out of duty and interest, respectively, decided to accompany her) arrived at a previously barricaded corridor somewhere near the office of Rupert Nicholas – the agency's head of security. The rotten wooden slats that had once been used to dissuade anyone from entering this particular section of passageway – probably because it was ill-maintained and therefore treacherous, Jessica pointed out – had been cast aside by whoever had come this way before them. Amanda and the new recruits, clearly.

It hadn't been particularly easy to find the East Eight corridor, which was designated only by a poorly carved wooden sign at its entrance, illuminated by a single lamp. The way was quiet and poorly maintained – broken water pipes leaked from the walls, ventilation ducts in the ceiling creaked with neglect. The trio passed cautiously onwards, rounded a sharp bend and approached a cul-de-sac that ballooned out to reveal an extensive curved stone wall.

Jessica held up the guttering gas lamp she'd collected on the way. 'What in heaven's name?' She gestured to the left. Pinned to the wall and barely visible under the flickering light was a collection of posters, similar to the ones that had appeared all over the agency, only more *diverse*.

Marion ripped one from the wall and read it out loud: '*The Gadgetry Department is losing money. Do you know why? Vote for change, join the ERPS.*'

'ERPS. What does that stand for?' Bill asked, somewhat bemused.

'Here we are,' Jessica replied, pointing at a line of script below. 'The Employee Rights and Protection Society.' She removed the poster from the wall. '*Do you know what the agency does to rogue Inquirers? Why is this information kept a secret from us? What are the High Council hiding? Vote for change, join the ERPS.*'

'Blimey,' Bill said, a little more seriously this time. 'I wonder what—'

'*Shhh!*' Marion pressed a finger to her lips.

A door, which she hadn't noticed until then, opened and closed several feet away. Marion waited, then padded to the entrance. A small cardboard sign hung on the lintel with the words: *East Eight Chamber. ERPS meeting in progress.*

She turned to glance at the tunnel from where they'd come. In the distance, a light flickered once, then fizzled out.

'You know,' Bill reasoned in a whisper, 'this corridor is uncomfortably close to Nicholas' office. I think we should go back.'

'I agree,' Jessica breathed. 'I mean, we shouldn't hang around. Nicholas is going to want to know who's behind all those posters when he finds them and I don't think we should be anywhere near here when that happens.'

'Mari, come on,' Bill urged as something clanged beyond the door.

She gave the East Eight one last glance, ignoring a burning urge to know what was going on inside. But Bill was right. Rupert Nicholas' office was only a few corridors away and if he found them here, lingering near the wall of posters, they'd have a hard time convincing him they had nothing to do with any of it.

The Employee Rights and Protection Society must have been doing something right, because by the end of the following week, they were still around and what was more, their congregation had grown to ten members, including several senior Inquirers.

It was a tailspin to disaster, the apparent fluidity and ease with which the society had inserted itself into the fabric of the agency, setting roots, flourishing as if it had existed for months not merely weeks. Already the group had taken measures to distinguish themselves from the rest of Miss Brickett's, with the royal-blue arrow pin brooches they all wore in exactly the same position – two inches below their silver Inquirer or apprentice badges. Marion seldom saw a member sitting alone in the cafeteria or common room, but on the rare occasion that she did, engaging in conversation was nearly impossible. Once, she'd spotted Amanda huddled over a pile of documents in the library and had moseyed over as casually as possible. The second Amanda saw her coming, however, she jumped up, collected her papers and rushed off, leaving nothing behind but an ERPS recruitment poster.

And so the society blossomed, growing in membership and strengthening in fortitude. One by one, employees and apprentices were convinced to join, lured by the promise of security, benefits and community (and in some sense, curiosity).

'They're plotting a coup,' suggested Preston Dinn, fellow second-year, with flippant dramatics the following Friday afternoon as he, Marion, Bill, Jessica and Maud gathered for their own congregation of sorts – the traditional weekend drinks in the library bar.

'Sounds about right,' Maud added over her shoulder, cutting short the long-winded analysis she and Bill had been having on that night's football match.

'I don't understand it, though,' said Marion as she ordered a glass of wine from Harry, the agency barman, and flopped down on a stool at the counter. 'Why do Nancy and the council accept this rot? Surely it's against the bylaws and regulations.'

'Dream on, darling,' Jessica said, running a finger around the rim of her glass. 'There's nothing in the bylaws that says you can't start an organisation within Miss Brickett's, so long as it doesn't interfere with general agency procedures.'

Marion took a sip of her wine. It was good stuff and she let the lush fruity flavour wash over her tongue as she tried to forget her concerns about the ERPS.

The group fell into thoughtful silence, except Bill and Maud, who'd resumed their heated discussion on the finer points of Arsenal and Blackburn's forthcoming fixture. More drinks were poured and the sound of Elvis Presley's 'Blue Suede Shoes' drifted through the air as a gramophone turned noiselessly in the corner.

By seven o'clock, the Employee Rights and Protection Society, having adjourned their meeting minutes earlier, sauntered into the bar with an unmistakeable air of superiority. Like a torrent of dirty flood water, the group filled the bar with their chatter and inside jokes, and it was in this exact moment that Marion realised just how dangerous they'd become. It was impossible not to feel the pinch of exclusion, the ache to know what it was that made their gatherings so enjoyable. And she knew that the larger their group became, the stronger the pull would be for all those left on the outside. It was human instinct to want to belong – Marion knew that better than anyone – to feed off a collective confidence rather than manifest your own. She watched as they settled around a table they'd erected just for themselves, smiling and laughing and conspiring, their arrow pin brooches glimmering in the dim light, somehow obscuring the larger silver discs above them, the badges that had once unified all those who traversed the corridors of Miss Brickett's.

'I'd like to make an announcement,' Amanda said, getting to her feet and commanding the bar's attention with a charisma Marion had watched solidify over just a few short weeks. She sauntered over to the bar counter, clinked her wine glass with a fork and the chittering room fell instantly silent.

'Oh, here we go,' Maud muttered.

'It is my pleasure to announce that the High Council of Miss Brickett's Investigations and Inquiries has granted us, the Employee Rights and Protection Society, the honour of hosting a quiz night for the entire agency on Monday.'

The chittering started up again. Marion and Bill passed each other a questioning glance.

'The event will be completely funded and organised by our society,' Amanda went on, 'and is free and open for anyone who should wish to join. You can form teams of up to six and send your names in by the end of tonight.' She raised her glass and in perfect unison, the society members behind her did the same. 'We hope to see you there.'

'Sounds fun,' Maud said sarcastically.

'Bloody gits,' Bill declared.

'Let's participate,' Preston suggested, slipping one cigarette behind his ear while lighting a second. 'The five of us. Show them how it's done.'

'We'll come dead last,' Jessica added without missing a beat.

Maud agreed immediately. 'The five of us are about the least-educated group of people I've ever known.' She gestured at Bill. 'Except maybe you, Hobb.'

'And Mari,' Bill added loyally. 'She knows everything about mechanics.'

'That's not general knowledge,' Maud said resolutely.

'Actually,' said Preston, flicking ash onto the floor (which earned a small gasp from Jessica), 'I've brilliant general knowledge. Especially of geography.' He considered this for a moment. 'Well, *only* geography.'

Maud stared at him blankly for several drawn-out seconds. 'Since when?'

'Ages ago.'

'He does,' Marion chimed in.

'*How?*' Maud asked, her tone rising with disbelief. 'I thought you dropped out of school at fourteen?'

'Yeah.' Preston was smiling now, his tangled dreadlocks trailing down his back. 'Then I became a stevedore.'

'I know that.' Maud looked around at the others, perhaps searching for an explanation as to what being a stevedore had to do with a knowledge of geography. She turned back to Preston. 'Go on.'

Preston sighed softly. 'Well, I always wondered where the ships we unloaded had come from. So I saved up a few days' wages and bought myself an atlas.' He took a swig of beer. 'And then I studied it.'

'Well, there we go,' Marion said, smiling. 'Maybe we do have a chance.'

Maud looked off into the distance. 'It *would* be brilliant if we beat them at their own quiz, wouldn't it?'

Bill laughed, clinked tankards with Preston. 'I'm in.'

Jessica pursed her lips, turned to Marion. 'You started this.'

Marion chuckled, reached into her handbag for a chapstick. But as she did, she realised there was something there that hadn't been earlier – a sealed envelope, tied with ribbons of red and gold silk.

In an instant, the jovial atmosphere of the bar dissolved. She scanned the room – everyone seemed instantly suspicious, but that was certainly just her imagination. She excused herself.

Once sheltered behind a bookshelf in the adjoining library, she untied the ribbons, slipped a finger through the envelope sleeve and pulled out the letter inside. She recognised the thin, unsteady scrawl, the same person who had written the first note. Her mouth went dry.

Forgot about me? Thought you might have.

Well, I'm back.

Firstly, just to be clear, this information is meant exclusively for you, Marion. I'm afraid that if you mention our little correspondence to anyone – and yes, I will know if you do – it'll be the last you hear from me. And believe me, now that the ERPS has its claws firmly in Miss Brickett's, you'll need my information more than ever.

On that note, I'd keep an eye on things in Gadgetry.

Oh, and just to demonstrate my worth, the answer is string.

9

Magic Trick

Marion stood alone in the library, breath rattling in her chest. Several feet away, laughter and chatter drifted out from the bar, small talk and secrets shared between her colleagues, one of whom must have slipped the envelope into her bag just minutes ago.

She read and reread the letter, sweat beading above her lip. *Keep an eye on things in Gadgetry. The answer is string.*

She looked up, across the marble floor, the labyrinth of bookshelves still and silent in the dim light. It wasn't hard to imagine someone was hiding among them, watching her, listening, collecting information to lure her in. But why? And who?

She turned to the sound of a breath expelled, the swish of fabric. Her nerves buzzed. Someone was close.

'*Psst.* Over here!'

Everything inside her was tensing, ready for flight. 'What on earth?'

Kenny, dressed uncharacteristically blandly in grey flannel trousers and a black coat, a small suitcase at his feet, materialised from behind a bookshelf several feet away. He squinted, glancing around the library as though to make sure no one else was about, then beckoned her over.

'What are you doing?' he breathed as she approached.

'What am *I* doing?'

'You look antsy.' He took a step closer, fixed his gaze on the letter in her hand, the silk ribbons dangling from her fingers. 'What is that?'

She opened her mouth, then closed it — *if you mention our little correspondence to anyone . . .* 'Work notes,' she lied, whisking the letter from Kenny's reach before he could touch it, then shoving it back into her bag. She gave him a stern look, realising she hadn't seen him or heard from him in days. 'Where have you been all week?' Perhaps Bill had a point. Perhaps they were just sitting around waiting for Frank's return.

Kenny sighed impatiently. 'Picking up leads on the Florist. You might remember him . . . the murderer, branding iron. Ring a bell?' Marion rolled her eyes, but Kenny went on regardless. 'We had a potential sighting near Whitechapel three days ago, which I followed up with no luck.'

'So, he's still in London?'

'Looks that way. But that's not what I wanted to tell you.' He hesitated, lowered his voice. 'I had a telephone call from Frank this morning—'

'Is something wrong? You should have told me earlier. I told you to let me know if anything—'

'Cut the gas! Just *listen*. The call was in code, and very brief, but if I'm correct—'

'*If?*' Marion shrieked a little too loudly. 'What sort of code did he use? Repeat it to me – I'll know if—'

Kenny yanked her further behind the bookshelf. Someone dropped a glass in the bar. It shattered, laughter boomed, then silence.

'He's found him, Old Sam, Redding's "compromising witness". Problem is, Frank thinks someone's trailing him, so he couldn't risk telling me anything else.'

'What do you mean, trailing him?'

'I don't know exactly. I got the impression someone is tapping his calls, intercepting his letters.' He tilted his ear to his shoulder.

Marion heard it too, a breath, a sigh. Was it the agency librarian? Surely she should be off duty by now . . .

Marion waited for silence. 'But what if the person trailing him is the Florist?' she asked in a hurried whisper. 'Maybe he found out Frank is looking into him at St Mark's. Maybe he's gone there to . . . '

Kenny shook his head. 'You can't worry about that now.' He checked the time. 'Listen, Frank set up a rendezvous with you and Old Sam for tonight in half an hour. Do you know where letter case seventy-two is?'

Marion closed her eyes, her thoughts not yet caught up to what Kenny was suggesting. 'Letter case seventy-two,' she repeated. 'No, I don't. Not off by heart. I can look it up, though.' She looked down at his suitcase, then up again. Kenny's expression was troubled, far from his familiar relaxed countenance. 'And you'll be where in the meantime? We have to warn Frank in case—'

'Yes, Lane. I know. I'm going to Oxfordshire. Frank asked for my help in preparing an escape plan, should he need it.'

Marion pressed her fingers into her temples, stilling the panic.

'It's just a precaution. *Cool it.* Frank and I have everything under control. Now, are you able to find letter case seventy-two or not?' He faltered, muttered something she couldn't hear, his expression softened. 'If you're afraid to go . . . '

'No,' she snapped without consideration. 'Of course I'm not. If Frank thinks it's safe . . . I trust him.'

Kenny rubbed the back of his neck, uncertainty darkening his features. 'Yeah, all right. Don't forget, letter case seventy-two at—'

'Seven o'clock, yes. I've got it.'

'Take a light orb and when you get there, switch it on and off three times. Your contact will find you.'

'Mari, everything all right?' Bill called, appearing at the library bar entrance, his stance wide, dark eyes flaring – mostly at Kenny.

'Fine, yes,' Marion answered quickly as Bill hastened to her side.

Bill looked Kenny up and down, eyes settling on the suitcase. 'Going somewhere?'

Kenny, acting as though Bill wasn't there, addressed Marion. 'I'll see you later. Oh, and one last thing, Frank said you should take some money.'

'Money?' Marion asked.

Kenny shrugged, picked up his suitcase. 'That's what he said.'

'What's going on?' Bill pressed, stepping in front of Marion, his back to Kenny.

She gave him a pacifying smile. 'I just have to pop into Willow Street. Frank left something for me there.'

'Now?' He looked at his watch, eyes tight with concern. 'I'll come with you, then.'

Marion looked over his shoulder. Kenny was already gone. She forced herself to relax. 'No, really. It's fine.' She clutched her bag under her arm and started for the corridor. 'Back in a flash.'

After a quick rummage through the Filing Department's registry, Marion discovered that letter case seventy-two was hidden in the pavement on the corner of Great Russell Street and Montague Street, a well-used road that wrapped around the back of The British Museum in Bloomsbury. It was a considerable distance from the bookshop, even by bus, but she managed to get there on time.

Head down, shoulders hunched, she marched towards the location, the hood of her night coat pulled low over her eyes and a collection of gadgets stuffed inside her pockets: the light orb, a Distracter and a skeleton key. Her friends would still be at the library bar, sipping their drinks, dancing, laughing, warm and safe. Did one of them – her informer – know where she was? Perhaps she should have told Bill where she was going, at least. She wrapped her arms around herself and pushed the thought aside.

'This must be it,' she whispered moments later, tapping an oddly discoloured section of pavement with the toe of her boot.

She waited until a group of pedestrians had wandered past (and given her an odd look), then drew out her light orb and switched it on and off three times in quick succession.

There was a rustle in the line of bushes to her left, the gentle pad of bare feet, a movement in her periphery. She turned to the noise, but as she did, it moved, changing position with such speed, it was disorienting. Something tapped her on the hip.

'Hey! Get back here!' she yelled, catching sight of a figure dashing from her side. She shoved a hand into her coat pocket. Her Distracter was gone.

'*Whoa!*' gushed a small voice from several feet away, belonging to the small hand holding the metallic sunbird. 'So it's true. You *are* one of them!'

'Give that back!' Marion demanded, marching forwards, blood flushing to her cheeks. How had she – an Inquirer-in-training – managed to be pickpocketed by this child, who couldn't have been more than fourteen, dressed in a brown loosely fitting sweater, drawstring trousers and a tattered trilby hat?

The boy backed away, tipped his hat and gave her a crooked smile. 'How d'you do, miss? Old Sam's the name, pickpocketing's the game.'

'Yes, I can see that.' She stopped, gasped. 'Wait . . . Old Sam?' She stumbled over her words, finding it hard to believe that Constable Redding's "compromising witness" was just a little thief, after all.

'Right you are, miss,' the boy said easily, still gawking at the gadget, the street light reflected in his wide black eyes, glimmering with awe.

'Well, then . . . ' She gathered herself. 'Nice to meet you, I suppose.'

There was a long pause. The boy rattled the Distracter at his ear, perhaps hoping to hear something squeak within. Marion felt the night air close around her. Montague Street was empty, but she couldn't shake the sense that they were being watched. She'd better get this rendezvous over with.

'Tell me what you know.'

The boy ignored her, shook his head, tossed the sunbird from one hand to the next.

'We don't have time for games,' Marion urged. 'You agreed to come here. Tell me what you know.'

He gave her a mischievous grin, holding the Distracter aloft. 'Only if you let me keep it.'

Marion felt her hackles rise but caught herself before the emotion clouded her thoughts. She had no experience dealing with children, certainly not precocious ones. She looked him over, head to toe, his tattered outfit at odds with his confidence. He was penniless, that much was clear. But he was smart, industrious. He'd require something in exchange for his information, especially if he knew it was important.

'You can't have that one,' she said, subtly slipping her right hand into her pocket, finding the light orb. 'But how about this instead?' She released the catch that held the orb's cord, wrapping the end securely around her thumb. Then, in one brisk movement, she switched it on and launched it at the boy's head. 'Catch.'

Blinded and bewildered, the boy fumbled to catch the orb and in the process, allowed the Distracter to slip from his grasp. As if she'd rehearsed it several times over, Marion reeled the orb out of his hand and back towards her by its cord, then kicked the Distracter to her feet, leaving the boy empty-handed.

She'd expected him to retaliate, run at her, run away, curse. But instead, after a note of stunned silence, he gushed, 'Magic!'

Marion switched off the orb, wound up the cord. Warmed by the look of enchantment on Old Sam's face, she couldn't help but smile. 'Close enough. Now, tell me what you know and I really will give you something in exchange.' She dug her fingers into her purse and pulled out two pound notes.

The boy seemed to consider this for a long while, turning the proposition over in his head, eyeing the money. Obviously, he'd much rather have gained a shiny sunbird gadget or gleaming orb for his information, but perhaps he recognised the improbability of that now.

'Deal.' He touched the trilby, askew on his head. 'I work as a cleaner from time to time at St Mark's. That's how I came to meet your friend, Mr Gardner.'

Marion nodded. Donald Gardner – Frank's alias.

'I also knew those other men, the dead one and that one with the funny face.' He screwed up his features as though recalling something unpleasant. 'I've done lots of things for both of them, miss. Polished their shoes, carried their bags. They think I'm dim, like everyone else, so they're not careful what they say or do around me – think I'm no harm at all.' He suppressed a small laugh. 'But I watch and listen, see. *Everything*. And one day I saw that old man with the funny face do something very strange and I remembered it, just like I remember everything else.'

Marion glanced over her shoulder, a cool breeze tickling her there. Was that a figure hovering in the darkness beyond Great Russell Street, or just a shadow? She wondered how carefully Frank had thought this all through. If he believed his calls were being tapped and his letters intercepted, could he really assume it safe to send Constable Redding's compromising witness to meet Marion in the centre of London?

'Well?' she said impatiently, aware of her pulse throbbing in her neck. 'What did you see him do?'

Old Sam hesitated. Perhaps reconsidering whether two pounds was quite enough for what he was about to say. He chewed his lip, then blurted: 'I saw him post an envelope right into the ground.' He stamped his foot onto the pavement. 'To you people, the Inquirers.'

Marion's head reeled. She opened her mouth, her lips moving uselessly while Old Sam watched her with interest. 'Right,' she said at last, collecting her thoughts. 'And what was inside the envelope. Did you see?'

Old Sam nodded proudly. 'Money. Lots of it. And you know what, I saw him do it again a second time.'

Marion let the revelation brew in her mind. There was so much she wished to ask Old Sam. But a prickling in the nape of her neck told her they didn't have time. 'You met Constable Redding, too, didn't you?'

'Maybe.'

'You told him what you just told me.'

The boy didn't answer, instead drew a figure on the pavement with his bare toe.

'And then what happened?' Marion persisted, speaking hastily. 'You ran away?'

Old Sam crossed his arms, jutted out his chin. 'I wasn't

scared, if that's what you mean. I disappeared because the copper told me to. Asked me to keep away from the other coppers who'd be coming by soon enough, asking the same questions. The only person he said I could speak to was your friend, Mr Gardner.'

Marion nodded, the mystery of Constable Redding's odd behaviour finally making sense. Frank had assumed Redding's reluctance to embroil himself in the Harrogate murder was rooted in something sinister, while all along he'd been *protecting* the agency by removing himself from the case. He knew Miss Brickett's was somehow involved with the Florist, after learning what Old Sam had to say, and yet he'd given them a chance to sort the mess out before Scotland Yard got involved. For perhaps the first time in his career, Redding had demonstrated his loyalty to Miss Brickett's.

Marion focused her attention on the boy, ready to continue her interrogation. But something was wrong. His face paled. The muscles in his jaw twitched.

The boy cleared his throat, his eyes darting to the right, down Great Russell Street.

Movement. Not a shadow, after all.

'Pleasure to meet you, miss,' Old Sam said with forced confidence, tipping his hat, striding towards her, brisk, unsteady. 'Best you make a run for it,' he added in a whisper, sweeping past her.

Marion touched him on the hand, slipped the promised money into his pocket and watched him bolt into the line of trees from where he'd come.

She took a breath, turned, froze. A tall, burly man, recognisable as one of the Florist's watchdogs, was standing directly in front of her, right hand on his pocket. He closed the space between them, ran his tongue over his teeth.

Marion gave him a casual smile, a quick nod, then sidestepped him with lightning speed. He gripped her elbow, yanked her backwards and spat something foul in Russian.

Marion forced her posture to relax, drew back, looked the Russian in the eye. Had this been a field-training exercise, Frank would have instructed her to take control of the situation immediately. *Demonstrate confidence or utter bewilderment. Either way, you're not giving the perpetrator what they want.* Being short on confidence right then, she settled on the latter.

'May I help you?'

He said something else in Russian, then, realising this might not get him anywhere, switched to English. 'Why were you talking to him?'

Marion looked left and right, feigning confusion. 'Oh, that little boy?' She planted her hands on her hips, put on a disgruntled expression. 'We weren't talking. He stole money from my purse. I was trying to get it back.'

'Who are you? Police?'

'No, but I'll be inclined to call them if this goes on any longer.'

The Russian touched his right pocket again. No doubt he had a gun. He nodded at her coat. 'You armed?'

'You are, I think.'

'Take it off.'

'Pardon?'

The Russian wasn't falling for her game this time. He lurched forwards, swung an arm around her neck and pressed a pistol to her temple. 'Off! Now!'

Marion breathed, quick and shallow, shrugged off her coat. As it fell to the ground, the light orb and Distracter clanged against the pavement.

The Russian kicked the coat away, as though it were contaminated. He leaned in, his breath hot and wet in her ear. 'Come with me.' He removed his arm from around her neck and repositioned the pistol, pressing it into the small of her back. 'Move.'

Marion closed her eyes for a brief second, then started to shuffle forwards with useless tiny steps. A shiny grey Alfa Romeo was parked just around the corner, headlights on, back door open, engine fired up. She heard Frank's voice ring in her head: *Never let yourself be taken to a second location. If it's happening, fight.*

She took one more step forwards, balancing herself, counted to three. Now or never.

She spun round, curling her body like a spring as she brought a fist up and under, connecting with the Russian's elbow, then a knee to his groin. He wheezed, dropped the gun, stumbled backwards, clutching his nether regions.

Several yards away, the Alfa Romeo revved. Tyres screeched on the tarmac as it started to move, speeding directly towards her.

The Russian recovered, straightened up, swung a boot hard and fast at her stomach.

She stepped left, but not quite in time, and the boot caught her in the hip. She buckled and in a split second, the Russian had her pinned to the ground, hand on her throat.

The Romeo pulled up. Lights off. Engine cut.

Marion looked to her right. Her night coat, light orb and Distracter were lying just a foot away. She stretched her arm out, gasping for breath. The Russian was too busy strangling her to notice. She curled her fingers around the Distracter, looked up, her vision tunnelled.

With one last rush of breath, she let out a high-pitched scream, scooped up the Distracter and plunged its beak right into the Russian's hand. He bellowed, then drew back in agony as she ripped it free.

111

She rolled out from under him and scrambled to her feet.

The Alfa Romeo's door sprung open. Someone leaped out, yelling in Russian, charging towards her.

Time to go.

Ignoring the throbbing pain in her hip and raging thump of her heartbeat, Marion picked up her night coat, threw it over her shoulders and bolted.

10

Questions and Answers

'A kid?' Kenny said as Marion described her encounter with Old Sam behind The British Museum. 'And you think the Florist's cronies were following him?'

It was 5 p.m. the following Monday and the pair were alone in the Games Room, the first time they'd met since their respective expeditions above ground.

'How else could they've found us?' Marion asked hastily, picking her nails.

'So your cover's blown?'

'He thought I was with the police.'

'But they know your face.'

Marion shrugged. 'The least of our problems. They don't know who I am or who I'm working for. Though I'll wager that's what they were hoping to find out, had they managed to drag me into the car.'

Kenny considered this, a pen twirling between his fingers. 'What if Old Sam's bullshitting us? Maybe everything he told Frank was a lie. Maybe he's working with the Florist.'

'Doubt it. Why on earth would the Florist want us to know he was sending us money?' She winced as she shifted in her seat, her hip throbbing.

Kenny reached for her hand, then drew back when she looked away. 'You really should visit the infirmary,' he said, eyes fixed on her hip. 'It could be something serious.'

'It's just a bruise.'

Kenny shook his head. 'I'm really sorry. I didn't think you'd run into trouble like that. I should have gone with you.'

'Then we'd probably both be dead,' Marion said with a flick of her wrist, disregarding Kenny's frown. 'Now, tell me about Oxfordshire. Is Frank safe?'

Kenny chewed the end of his pen. 'I'm sure he is.'

'What do you mean, *you're sure*? I thought you said you went there to meet him!'

'I said I went there to set up the escape route. Frank insisted we couldn't risk meeting. Obviously we couldn't.'

Marion dropped her head into her hands. If Kenny hadn't seen or heard from Frank since his coded telephone call, could they really be sure he was . . .

Kenny touched her on the knee. 'Lane, relax. He's all right.'

'You don't know that!'

He seized her by the shoulders, lifted her upright (causing her to wince) and looked her directly in the eye. 'You said you trusted him. So *trust* him. Trust he knows how to look after himself. Trust he knows how to stay alive. He's been doing this job for a long time – long before you or me.' He let his words sink in, his fingers pressing tighter into her shoulder. 'Look,' he added as he released her. 'Let's not sit around and worry ourselves sick. Let's be useful.' He leaned back in his seat, folded his arms with an air of assertion. 'What do we know? The Florist is sending money to Miss Brickett's. Which means he's in cahoots with one of us, which explains why Redding removed himself from the case.'

For once, Kenny was right. She could drive herself senseless worrying about Frank. But it wouldn't do him, her or the investigation any good. She took a long breath. 'We have to follow the money trail here, inside Miss Brickett's. If we can find out where that money's gone, we can find out who the Florist is communicating with. And why.'

Kenny seemed to ponder this. 'Maybe the Florist knows we're investigating him and he's bribing someone here to drop the case, skew the evidence.'

'No, I don't think so,' Marion said immediately.

Though this was the most logical, probable explanation, something more twisted, more complex churned in her mind. She touched the bag on her lap, picturing the letter she still had, crumpled inside: *I'd keep an eye on things in Gadgetry.* Then at the fire grate, where flecks of ash remained, remnants of the ERPS's recruitment posters Frank had destroyed. She recalled the wall of propaganda Jessica, Bill and she had found inside the East Eight corridor just days ago. *The Gadgetry Department is losing money. Do you know why?* Could it all be a coincidence, a tangled web of happenings that had nothing to do with one another? Could she really trust her informer?

Kenny cocked his head to the side. 'Lane?'

'Gadgetry,' she said as she got up, clutching her hip, suddenly aware that they'd been sitting here in the Games Room too long, doing very little while an ally of the Florist wandered the agency corridors. 'We have to start in the Gadgetry Department. They're losing money and no one seems to know why. There's a leak somewhere and I'm starting to think the money going out is connected to what's coming in, to the Florist.'

Kenny didn't look entirely impressed with this line of investigation. 'Yeah, all right. What do you suggest? We analyse the department's financial records?'

'Maybe, although I doubt we'll find anything. Professor Bal told me the agency knows about the department's financial trouble and yet they don't understand it. I'm sure they've already scrutinised the records to no end. I need to have a look at things myself, but in the meantime, I suppose we'd better tell Nancy what Old Sam said.'

'Definitely. I'll head over to her office right away.'

There was a distant clang from the corridor outside Frank's office, followed by a rumbling chorus of voices. Singing, clapping, laughing, growing louder, louder.

'The quiz,' Kenny said, answering the look of bewilderment on Marion's face. 'It starts in ten minutes.'

Marion recalled the announcement Amanda had made in the library bar a few nights previously. She'd been somewhat excited by the idea of attending with her team – DimWit NitWit (Preston's choice of name) – but not now, not when Frank was stuck in Oxfordshire, relying on her to follow up on Old Sam's lead. She pushed past Kenny, onto the landing above the corkscrew stairwell. Outside the office, the chanting and applause had begun to fade.

'Lane, wait,' Kenny called after her. 'Where are you going?'

She gripped the balustrade, ready to descend. 'I just told you. To the Gadgetry Department.'

'Now? It'll be closed.'

'Professor Bal will still be there. He's been working late every night this week.'

'But the quiz—'

Marion turned around, gave him a sharp look. 'Oh yes, the quiz is certainly more pressing than a little murder investigation.'

He swept a hand down over his face. 'What I mean is, everyone's going to be there and it'll look odd if you're the only one who's not. Remember, we're trying to keep this whole investigation under wraps? Someone at Miss Brickett's is in communication with the Florist and the last thing we need is for word to get out that you've been sticking your nose where it doesn't belong. This isn't the time, Lane.'

She waited for the chanting chorus to fade completely down the corridor, then turned back to Kenny. 'I suppose that means you're attending, too.'

He hesitated, fighting something inside himself. 'Yeah, I mean, I promised Kate I would.'

Marion bit her lip, allowed her anger to build. She was glad for it. Anger was an easier emotion to control than hurt. Or rejection. Or whatever it was she should be feeling.

'I mean, I promised her I'd go because I'm on her team,' he explained, then let out a groan. 'I only joined her team because you lot never offered.'

Marion was purposely staring at the stairwell, her lips pressed tightly together.

'You're pissed at me. I get it.' He stepped in front of her, blocking her way. He touched her arm.

She forced herself to look right at him, jaw tight. 'Don't flatter yourself, Hugo. I couldn't give two wits whose team you're on.'

'Not about the quiz. About what I said at the stake-out.' He raked his fingers through his flaxen hair. 'I'm bad with words. I know. I'm sorry. I didn't mean—' He broke off, came closer.

His breath was on her lips. And despite all resistance, everything inside her swelled, bloomed, gushed. But just before she gave in, she sidestepped him and started down the stairwell.

'See you at the quiz, Hugo,' she said, not allowing herself to look back at his reaction.

'So, apart from sweet glory and rubbing the fact in their faces for the rest of time, what do we get if we win?' Maud asked Marion as they gathered around their assigned table in the common room, which was scattered with extra tables and chairs, overcrowded almost to the point of claustrophobia.

The fire was lit, crackling fiercely and spewing golden sparks onto the hearthrug. The mantlepiece above – which was usually packed with a teetering pile of board games and well-thumbed decks of cards – had been cleared to make space for a gleaming silver trophy, whose plaque read: *Miss Brickett's Quiz Night Champions, 1959.*

Marion, who'd decided not to tell Bill – or anyone – what had happened during her rendezvous above ground, shrugged inattentively and set herself down at one of four tables crammed into the compact space. A group of ERPS members sat a few tables away, including Amanda, Proctor, Longmore and Quinn. Brilliantly, they'd called themselves Team ERPS. Seated next to them was a group of five mismatched apprentices and Inquirers, including Kate and Kenny, who called themselves Team Intellectual Capital.

'That trophy, I suppose,' Marion said, answering Maud's question about what the winning team would receive. She inclined her head to the silver ornament on the mantlepiece.

Bill was looking at her curiously, scanning her body as though he knew some part of her was in pain. He leaned in and repeated the question he'd been asking her since she'd returned from her meeting with Old Sam on Friday night.

'You sure you're fine?'

She couldn't answer this. If Bill knew about her two previous expeditions above ground, both of which had almost ended in her abduction (or worse), he'd persuade her to remove herself from the investigation. But she couldn't, not when Frank was still in Oxfordshire and potentially on the run.

'And three hundred pounds,' Jessica cut in while examining her perfectly set bouffant hair in a pocket mirror.

'*Each?*' Maud asked, her eyebrows rocketing skywards.

Jessica clicked her tongue. 'No, darling, of course not. Three hundred pounds for the winning team.'

Maud turned to Preston. 'I hope you've been brushing up on all that geography you claim to know.'

He looked at her utterly unconcerned. 'No need, my friend. It's all in here.' He tapped the side of his head

Maud rolled her eyes and turned to Bill. 'And you, Hobb? You know your stuff, right?'

Bill, still somewhat distracted by whatever he assumed was going on with Marion, gave Maud a vague answer: 'Depends on the stuff.'

'Well, that settles it, then. We're never going to win.'

The table rambled on, Preston and Bill defending their intelligence, Maud looking increasingly annoyed. Marion had stopped listening. A reasonable sum of money, three hundred pounds, was being distributed to the winning team by the ERPS, but where did they get it from? She scanned the room, the throng of employees packed like sardines around her, tobacco smoke and hot breath stifling the air. Kenny was right. Nearly the entire agency was in attendance tonight, except the six members of the High Council – Frank (of course), Nancy, Delia Spragg, Barbara Simpkins, Professor Gillroth (who was on leave that week) and Rupert Nicholas. She wondered if Kenny had already told Nancy about Old Sam's revelations. Unlikely, since he'd come straight here from the Games Room.

She shifted in her seat, unsettled by the thought. But was she drawing connections where there were none, spinning out of sync like an uncalibrated Wire Catcher? The ERPS's three hundred pounds could have come from a multitude of innocent sources.

She shook the thought from her head, turned her focus back to the table. But the atmosphere had shifted among her friends.

'. . . Half, by my calculations,' Bill said. He turned to Marion, aware she hadn't been following. 'The ERPS. Half of Miss Brickett's are members now.' He began to list known members, including nearly all the third-year apprentices and three quarters of the junior Inquirers.

'What is wrong with everyone?' Marion said. 'Can't they see it's a load of tosh. Are they being paid to join or something?'

'Worse than that,' Maud corrected, reaching into her bag and drawing out a stack of crumpled papers. 'They're afraid *not* to.'

She smoothed the papers out on the table, each identical – a caricature depicting a row of young individuals (some of whom vaguely resembled the apprentices in Marion's year) standing in what appeared to be a prison cell, chained to each other with Twister Rope, Mr Nicholas hovering behind them, a large metallic snake curled at his feet. At the bottom of the page was a line of script: *The Truths, Part 1: Miss Brickett's Incarceration and Immolation.*

'What utter rot,' Jessica said, chewing a nail as she examined the poster more closely.

'*The Truths*,' Marion repeated, the phrase drudging up a memory. Her eyes skirted to the ERPS table, to David and the new recruits, stock-still and blank-faced as though they'd been drugged. 'The name of the booklet they carry with them everywhere.'

Maud nodded. 'Yeah, and from what I've heard, this is only the start of things . . . '

Just then, the common room lights dimmed. Mutterings of confusion rose and fell until all that was left was a soft snap and fizz of smouldering wood from the fireplace.

Amanda stepped into the gentle orange light cast by the flames. 'Welcome, everyone,' she announced, her voice shrill against the quiet. 'The ERPS and I have organised this, the first Miss Brickett's quiz night. I hope you'll enjoy it and I hope it'll be the first of many. There are twenty questions in total. If you know the answer to a question, please call out your team's name. Five points will be awarded for a correct answer. If you're wrong, another team will be able to answer for one point. At the end, we'll have a very difficult bonus question that, if guessed correctly the first time, holds thirty points. The winning team will receive this trophy . . . ' She pointed behind her to the mantlepiece. 'And three hundred pounds. Shall we get started?'

There was an ear-splitting ring of whoops and calls of excitement.

'First question . . . ' Amanda paused, allowing the room to settle. 'What was the name of the Duke of Wellington's warhorse used in the Battle of Waterloo?'

Maud puffed out her pockmarked cheeks. 'What the hell kind of question is that?'

Kate, of Intellectual Capital, called their team name almost instantly. 'Copenhagen,' she said easily.

Amanda passed Team ERPS a severe glance. They seemed to cower under the look. 'That is correct. Five points to Team Intellectual Capital.'

Team Intellectual Capital cheered. Kenny rubbed Kate affectionally on the back. Marion pretended not to notice.

'Next question,' Amanda continued. 'How many children did King Charles I have?'

Proctor, from Team ERPS, raised his hand, a smug look stretched across his face.

'Yes?' Amanda said encouragingly.

'Nine.'

'Absolutely correct! Five points to team ERPS. Next question. In what year was the Globe Theatre opened?'

'Oh, come on!' Maud cried, slamming her hand on the table.

Team ERPS, of course, raised their hand swiftly. 'Fifteen ninety-nine.'

'Correct!' cheered Amanda. 'Another five points to team ERPS.'

'This is a joke,' Preston said. 'Why did we even bother participating?'

In many respects, he was right. By ten o'clock, Team Intellectual Capital was at twenty-five points, Team ERPS was at thirty and team DimWit NitWit, having only got one question right – thanks to Bill, as it related to the history of Miss Brickett's – was at five.

But there was hope yet.

Maud looked almost delirious with excitement as Amanda read out the final question, worth thirty points in total.

'All right,' she said. 'The bonus question. Remember, it's only worth thirty points if answered correctly the first time. Otherwise, it's worth a single point. Here it is—'

Maud was perched on the edge of her seat, obviously hopeful, though that wasn't exactly how Marion felt. Even Preston looked a fraction anxious for the first time in his life.

Amanda took a dramatic breath. 'What are you afraid of if you suffer from linonophobia?'

The room went still for a moment, then the whispering and chattering began.

'Linonophobia, linonophobia?' Bill mused, repeating the word slowly and thoughtfully.

Team Intellectual Capital were huddled together, debating hurriedly among themselves, while Team ERPS appeared to be writing down a long list of possible answers.

'It'll be something bizarre,' Jessica breathed to the others. 'Something no one would likely be afraid of.'

'Like a table,' Maud suggested drolly, all the hope and excitement now lost.

Jessica rolled her eyes. 'Yes, Maud, like a table.'

The minutes ticked by and slowly, as if from the sludge of some long dead memory, an outlandish and improbable idea crawled into Marion's mind.

Something bizarre. Something no one would likely be afraid of.

She raised her hand. 'I think I know,' she said carefully, almost too softly to hear.

Everyone in the common room turned to face her.

'Mari?' Bill said, bewildered. 'What are you doing?'

She ignored him and turned to Amanda. 'String, the answer is string.' Her voice cracked like thunder in the bewildered silence.

Amanda's forehead creased in confusion. Maud, Preston, Jessica and Bill looked from Amanda to Marion and back again.

'That is . . . correct.'

There was a short interval of further silence, followed by a rapturous applause as Maud and Preston drummed their hands on the table and slapped Marion across the back.

'*Impossible*,' Amanda sneered under her breath as the cheers from Team DimWit died down.

'That means team DimWit NitWit has thirty-five points,' Amanda said, obviously in shock. She consulted her clipboard thoroughly, muttering to herself as she calculated (and probably recalculated) the final scores. 'Therefore . . . ' She paused again. 'They are the winners and the first title holders of the Miss Brickett's Quiz Night Champions.'

Bill seized Marion by the shoulders. His face was at first filled with glee, then incredulity. 'How the bloody hell did you know that?'

Marion didn't answer. Instead, she touched the crumpled letter in her bag and a clawing dread was finally set loose within her.

11

Fraser Henley's Second Kill

Curiously, the gargoyle that guarded the Gadgetry Department had already been disarmed and Fraser Henley easily stepped inside. Not that the gargoyle was a problem anyway – he'd learned weeks ago how ineffective it was.

He tensed his grip on the steel baton held at his side and glanced quickly around the eerie hall. But it was well past the witching hour and, despite the disarmed gargoyle, the department appeared to be deserted. He moved further in, observing the vague outlines of abandoned workbenches, drained cups of tea, plates covered in biscuit crumbs, half-assembled gadgets fashioned from bizarre materials and strange tools – evidence of another day's toil.

Fraser had never been inside the Workshop alone, certainly not at this grim hour, and he'd prefer not to again. The whole place – day or night, it hardly made a difference, since they were so far beneath the streets and sunlight – set his nerves on edge. As he'd felt so many times since his recruitment to Miss Brickett's, he was overcome with the urge to turn on his heels and run for it, up the long stone staircase, down the Grand Corridor, up through the bookshop and out into the open.

125

And yet, as with every other time he'd felt this way, Fraser was pinned down by the realisation that he had no choice. Like it or not, there was no alternative, no slipway or detour. He'd already sold his soul to the devil the day he shot Eddie Hopper outside the Old Bell Tavern.

But what else could he have done? Shot the Florist instead? Shot himself? Truthfully, he'd considered both. But he wasn't ready to die and killing the old man would only have amplified his troubles. The whole thing was an unfathomable pit of horror and once you'd jumped in – or been pushed – there was no way out, only down.

Had Fraser been pushed? No, perhaps not. He'd known exactly what he was getting into, even from the beginning, the day he'd met Eddie James Hopper outside St Mark's in Oxfordshire six years ago. Fraser was just a boy then, it seemed, foolish and naive and ripe for the picking. After so many years cloistered in his parents' flat in Manchester, taking odd jobs to pay the rent – doorman at the local hotel, milkman, then postman, then assistant at the scrapyard – he'd become desperate for a change, something wild and different and dangerous.

Well, he'd got the latter all right.

It had been a warm summer afternoon – he remembered it well. Fraser was out doing his postman rounds, when he saw Eddie emerge from the polished oak doors of the gentleman's club, trailed by a waft of expensive cologne and fellowship of highbrow men in tailored suits. Fraser recognised the glint in Eddie's eyes right away, the look that said *I've been places, I've seen things*. He was drawn to him, like a moth to a flame, as though Eddie were a deity calling him forth, reminding him that this was the pinnacle to which he aspired.

Looking back, it was serendipitous that the two men should meet. Eddie was educated and polished, bold and assured, the perfect antithesis to Fraser's character. And while Fraser was certainly not a member of the British upper crust, under the right conditions, he could be as intelligent and cunning as anyone who wiled away their afternoons over card games and politics. He was malleable. With sufficient motive and will-power, he could transform his character to suit his surroundings, rearranging himself to appear wise or dull, charismatic and alluring, or reticent and withdrawn. Yes, Fraser Henley could be anyone – a postman, a friend, a detective, a killer.

And so the two men's lives collided that day in Oxfordshire, their outer shells split apart, revealing a core that – despite their superficial differences – was uniformly foul and rotten. In time, Eddie came to trust Fraser, and soon their interactions moved from cafes and park benches to inside St Mark's. Fraser knew their rendezvous weren't merely social, though amid the fug of cigar smoke and rapport, it was easy to forget they were plotting to betray their country. But as the years rolled on and Fraser became more entangled in Eddie's devious world, he felt himself begin to recoil, regret. He knew what would happen once they'd completed their last assignment in Milton Keynes – the most treacherous yet – and were forced to defect to the East. It wasn't the life he'd imagined for himself. The idea of leaving Britain in exile terrified him. Taking up another life was unthinkable, especially one that would deposit him on foreign soil, rendering him a traitor to everyone he'd known. So yes, it was Fraser – not Eddie – who'd suggested the double-cross as a way out, knowing perfectly well that if it failed, they'd spend the rest of their lives on the run. Or worse.

Or *this*.

He shuddered, recalling that awful whimper Eddie had made as he took his final breath behind the Old Bell Tavern.

Fraser had tried to cast the memory from his mind, but it crept back every time he closed his eyes. He could still smell the blood – *God*, there had been so much of it. He could still feel the weight of the Makarov in his hand and hear the crack of the bullet as it whipped through the air.

He wasn't wicked or mad enough to believe it had been the right thing to do. No, it was and always would be as the old man had said – *his life or yours*.

Pushing the memory aside, Fraser made his way across the Workshop hall and onwards. The tall lamps dotted around the perimeter flickered when he brushed past, as though noting his presence, whispering to each other – *there's an intruder in our midst.*

He stopped halfway. Something moved at the edge of his vision, something indistinct, inhuman. Rivulets of sweat formed at the back of his neck, dripped down the furrow of his spine. He held his breath and peered into the darkness, catching only a glimpse of something that moved low and quick across the stone floor – he had an idea of what it was. He hoped he was wrong.

A strange sound reverberated in sync with the movement, metal scraped across stone.

Fraser waited, dead still in the near darkness, until the thing that moved disappeared back into the shadows. He wondered for a moment if he should give up and try again another night, but would he get the chance? Things at Miss Brickett's had been unravelling swiftly – what with the emergence of the ERPS and the rumour that Frank Stone had made it into St Mark's, where he'd coerced a witness to speak. Yes, Fraser was going to have to move things along rather more quickly. People were becoming suspicious – or the clever ones were, at least – and he feared it wouldn't be long before someone figured out exactly what was going on. In fact, someone already had – to a degree – which was why Fraser was here in the Gadgetry Department in the early hours of the morning, alert, ready, awaiting his chance to liquidate the problem before the Florist liquidated him.

He walked on, carefully and silently, still vaguely aware that someone else was in the vast hall, trailing behind him.

He reached Professor Bal's office unscathed. The door was unlocked, as promised. The room was empty, but a stick of incense still smouldered on the desk.

Perfect.

Fraser hurried, scratching through the desk drawers and filing cabinets like a creature possessed until he'd collected as much evidence as possible. He threw everything together in a pile, then placed the incense stick right in the middle. It took less than a second for the paper to catch and an exotic-scented flame to dance upwards.

Fraser waited until everything had been destroyed, then smothered the flame and started for the exit.

He paused halfway across the hall.

Something was behind him. Every fibre of his being could sense it. He turned around, just as someone stepped through the Workshop entrance ahead.

He squinted, straining his eyes. But the figure was vague and indistinguishable, standing there as still as a statue, staring into the darkness. He suspected it was the professor, for who else would be down here this early in the morning? But could they see him? Could they see anything at all?

The figure waited. Fraser waited. The air in the Workshop throbbed with the silence of held breath and indecision. The minutes ticked by. Nothing happened. Fraser began to sweat, so profusely that, at some point, he'd have to wipe his brow, but if he did, if he moved ever so slightly, he'd risk being seen.

Fraser blinked and his eyes refocused to the darkness. The figure in the doorway had vanished. He tensed. His lungs ached as he held his breath.

Footsteps.

Clip–clip–clip across the stone floor, coming nearer, nearer.

He took a step backwards, the steel baton cocked above his head. If necessary, he would use it.

The footsteps ceased, replaced by a groan, or perhaps a muffled yelp of shock.

Silence again.

Movement in the shadows. A whoosh of cold air touched Fraser on the cheek. It was right in front of him now.

He flinched.

There was a flash of gunmetal grey as he whirled the baton through the air. It came crashing down on something hard – bone? – which crunched and crumbled under the force. Someone screamed – long and terrible and desperate.

Fraser raced from the department, leaving behind the lifeless mess at his feet.

12

The Double Bluff

There was a violent thumping, beating, cracking.

Marion stirred in her sleep. Something was ripping in her chest, in her head, pressing the air from her lungs. Her hands stung, as if burned in hot oil. The skin bubbled and wept as amorphous shapes and twisting shadows haunted her thoughts like wraiths. She forced her eyes open and gasped for air, then touched the skin on her palm. It was cool and intact. Only a dream.

Rap-rap-rap.

She flicked on her bedside lamp and rubbed her eyes. The room was grey and still. But the sound hadn't been just a dream. It was coming from her bedroom door. Someone was knocking.

Rap-rap-rap.

'Yes?' Marion groaned, pulling herself from under the covers and lumbering to her feet.

Black spots danced in her vision as she rose too suddenly. Her head spun. Her hip throbbed. She took another breath, steadied herself, opened the door.

'Dammit, Lane! I've been knocking for nearly two minutes.'

Kenny was glaring at her, a lick of golden hair stuck to his forehead with sweat. He was out of breath and pallid, his usually serene features hollowed and tense.

Marion stared back – something was wrong. She wondered what time it was and how long she'd been asleep. It felt like only minutes since she'd crashed onto her bed, fully clothed, after the end of the quiz. Her team's win, beating the much-despised ERPS at the eleventh hour and at their own game, was all anyone talked about the whole night. And it was Marion, everyone seemed to agree, who deserved the most praise. She should have revelled in the opportunity, enjoyed the moment, yet all she could think about – amid the backslapping and hoots of congratulations – was that her win had come at a price only she was aware of: *Oh, and just to demonstrate my worth, the answer is string.* She swallowed hard. Kenny was twitching with unease. He wouldn't have woken her unless it was something serious, unless someone had . . .

Could it be Frank? Had the Florist tracked him down? Her entire body jolted at the thought.

'What?' she asked, her voice obscure, not quite her own.

Kenny shook his head and fixed her with a look that she was supposed to understand but didn't.

'It's Professor Bal—' he said at last.

A pause. Too long.

Professor Bal. Of course. *Stupid, stupid, stupid.* She'd meant to go down to Gadgetry last night, talk to the professor, follow the Florist's money trail and find out who he was corresponding with. Instead, she'd listened to Kenny and attended the quiz, enjoyed herself, celebrated, laughed.

Whatever had happened now, it would be her fault. She'd delayed things. Ignored her instincts.

'What's the matter?' she snapped again.

'He's . . . ' Kenny expelled a long breath. 'You'd better come and see for yourself.'

Marion tried not to panic as she followed Kenny from her room. She forced herself not to think. Not to surmise. Though every part of her was alert, ready. She expected the worst. That way, she might not be so shocked when it came – a mechanism of defence she'd used her whole life.

Her skin was cold and damp, her blouse sticking to her back, her chest.

They stepped inside the Workshop. A pile of splintered metal scales and springs lay strewn across the floor just outside Professor Bal's office. For a moment, she wasn't sure what she was looking at. Then she realised.

'Blimey, what's all this?'

Marion turned to see Bill dashing through the department doors and to her side, followed by a throng of apprentices and staff members – including ERPS members Proctor and Longmore, both apparently stunned at the sight. And Quinn, her notepad already open, a pen poised.

'What happened?' someone asked.

'Mari?' Bill said, mirroring her confusion.

'Where's the professor?' Marion asked, ignoring them all. She didn't care about Toby – the destroyed spy snake – or the crowd gathering around it.

Kenny nodded to his right, in the direction of the professor's office.

Marion let out a breath of relief. 'He's—' She wanted to say *alive*, but that would seem odd considering no one had suggested that he might not be. 'All right?'

Kenny frowned. 'Yeah, just a bit shaken, I think. He asked to speak with you.'

Marion nodded, pushed her way past Kenny and into Professor Bal's office. He was seated at his desk, his tattered green-grey beret folded in his lap. He looked up, his eyes sunken. Behind him on the desk was a pile of ash, still smoking.

'Professor?' Marion said, unable to formulate a full sentence or put together what she was looking at. 'What happened?'

Bal looked uneasy at the sudden multiplication in company – Kenny and Bill, who were hovering on the threshold. He turned his attention to Marion and spoke tentatively.

'I don't . . . someone was here this morning. Early, very early. I came down because I heard a noise—' He shook his head and dropped it into his hands.

Marion rushed to his side. She mouthed for Kenny and Bill to leave and close the door behind them. Marion turned back to the professor, squeezing his hands in hers. She gave him a moment to collect himself, then asked, 'Tell me, please.'

He pulled himself upright and took a series of steadying breaths. 'I don't know, really. I worked late last night, as I have been doing for weeks. You know why, of course. The new commission of Liar's Eyeglasses has been a disaster. I've been so short of time. I left at around two in the morning and went to my night rooms to get a bit of sleep. But I'd hardly settled down, when I realised someone was inside the Workshop. I had to go back—'

Marion stopped him. The professor's night rooms, which he occasionally made use of when he'd worked a long day or hoped to get an early start at the agency, were located at the top of the long stone staircase. There was no way he could have seen or heard anything happening in the department from there. But then she realised – the spy snake, designed to detect movement.

'Toby. You put him on patrol in the Workshop?'

The professor held up a brass pocket watch, which was paired to the snake and would have lit up when the creature's eyes sensed an intruder, alerting the professor. The snake and pocket watch had once belonged to the head of Miss Brickett's security, Mr Nicholas, but following a series of catastrophic events last year, both had been passed back to their designer and rightful owner, Professor Bal.

He lowered his voice as he replied, gesturing to the pile of ash. 'Everything is gone, Marion. All of this year's inventory lists, every record and note I made. Someone was here this morning. Someone knew I was going to figure it out and they did this to stop me. I'm certain of it.'

Marion couldn't keep the frustration from her voice. 'What are you talking about? Figure what out?'

'It's hard to explain. It was just a pattern I noticed, something in the way the inventory lists were filed.'

'But you're the one who files them, aren't you?'

The professor seemed suddenly ashamed. 'Yes, which is why no one believes me.' His gaze shifted to outside the office, to the pile of screws and scales. 'You see, Toby saw the person who did it, but I only saw a figure. I was in a state and to be honest, the only thing I'm certain of is that there *was* someone here. I ran over. The intruder got a shock, perhaps because they'd just seen me or perhaps because Toby was right there in front of them.

'The next bit happened in a blur, so quickly I can hardly . . . there was a crash of metal. I called out. The intruder dashed past me in the darkness and that was that. By the time I'd reached the light switch, all that was left around me was a mess of metal. Whoever it was smashed the snake to bits. Worst of all, Nancy and the others think it's my fault that the inventory lists were destroyed because I left a stick of incense burning.'

'They think it was an accident?' Marion asked incredulously, looking again at the pile of ash and yes, the stick of incense nearby.

The professor rose from his seat, slowly and unsteadily. 'No, worse than that. They think it was a set-up, orchestrated by me to prove a point I've been trying to make for weeks. They think I burned the lists but tried to make it look like someone else did.'

'That makes no sense. Why would—'

The professor interjected. 'I've been making a fuss lately, you see, telling the High Council that there's something going on here in Gadgetry that they need to investigate. They eventually agreed to an inquiry, which at first I was relieved about. But instead of finding out what was going on, they scrutinised my messy paperwork.

'I've always kept track of the inventory and orders in my own haphazard way. I know it's not perfect, but it's never been a problem, until now.' He placed his crumpled beret on the desk and poured himself a measure of some golden liquid from a crystal carafe. Marion had never seen him take even a sip of alcohol before. 'The facts of the matter are that the High Council believe I'm incompetent, negligent even, and that I destroyed the snake and set this whole thing up to make it look like I was right, that someone has been interfering.

'It's not a coincidence that I told them something like this was going to happen soon and now it has, but instead of confirming my predictions, it makes me look like a fraud. I'm done for, Marion. I just know it.' He looked at her as if he wanted to say something else. But before he could, the office door was pushed open and Frank stepped inside.

Marion started. Shock, then an overriding wave of relief. 'You're back. Oh, thank God!'

'Professor, Marion,' he said in greeting.

He was wearing a clean-cut deep-blue dinner jacket and matching trousers. He'd grown a thick moustache and his hair, which held an unnatural sheen, was parted neatly to one side. He looked nothing like the Frank Marion knew. Even the way he carried himself had changed, his normally unassuming demeanour warped by an air of self-possession. Clearly, he'd come straight from St Mark's in a hurry.

Frank gave Marion an impatient look. 'Apologies, Professor. Will you excuse us for a moment?'

The professor waved them off and Marion followed Frank across the Workshop, up the stone staircase. As they walked, he began to explain what he'd uncovered at St Mark's. And while the information was hurried and disjointed, Marion got the gist: the club was indeed frequented by the Florist, who went by several aliases (Gerald Temper being the latest) and was often seen with Eddie Hopper, conspiring over cigars and expensive liquor. Occasionally, the two men were joined by a third – a young gentleman, perhaps in his late-twenties. And while Frank had been unable to ascertain any details of the third man's appearance, it seemed likely he was the individual the Florist had telephoned from the booth outside Hyde Park, by default making him Eddie Hopper's killer.

'But did the Florist see you there?' Marion asked anxiously. 'Kenny said you thought you were being watched.'

'I certainly was. But I don't know by whom. Thanks to Hugo, I was able to disappear before my tail closed in. I heard about your altercation with the Russian. I'm sorry – I had no idea they were following Old Sam as well.'

'They learned nothing from me. It's fine. I'm fine.'

They'd reached Frank's office – the door was ajar. Across the room, the wardrobe that guarded the entrance to the spiral staircase had been pushed aside. Frank paused before they slipped behind it.

'One other thing, do you remember what I told you before I left for St Mark's? About the recruitment test?'

Marion pulled at her memories. So much had happened since then. 'Well, yes. But I've been trying to understand—'

'The enigma,' he interrupted, speaking more quickly than ever. 'You told me that was what you'd overheard the Florist say through the Herald Stethoscope and it floored me.' He placed a hand on the edge of the wardrobe as though to steady himself. 'You see, the enigma was the name of the recruitment test I sent out to my shortlist of potential first-year apprentices in late December. Similar to the Trick Lock test I gave the applicants the year before, including you, the enigma was a complex riddle and anyone who managed to solve it would find their way to a location in London where I'd hidden three interview invitation envelopes.' A rustle, perhaps of paper, drifted down from the Games Room. A clink of glasses. 'Both Proctor and Longmore passed the enigma, which is exactly what the Florist said.' He gave her a knowing look. 'Do you understand what I'm suggesting?'

Marion took a shaky breath. Whoever the Florist had been talking to that evening outside Hyde Park was, *is* . . .

'Proctor or Longmore,' she answered in a whisper.

'At first, I thought it couldn't be, or perhaps I only hoped it wasn't true. I resolved to push the theory from my mind until I had further evidence. Then I met Old Sam.'

Marion nodded hurriedly, connecting the dots. 'It adds up, of course.' Her limbs buzzed with adrenaline. 'But how do we know which of them?'

Frank placed a hand on her shoulder. 'I don't know yet. But there's more to it. I'll explain in a bit. Now, come on.' He ushered her up the stairwell. 'She's waiting.'

Marion flinched as she stepped inside the Games Room. Nancy was seated in a wingback near the hearth, her hands clasped in her lap, a stern glare in her eyes.

'What did the professor tell you?' she asked without preamble, pointing Marion to a chair opposite.

'That you all think he's lying,' she answered defensively, feeling the full magnitude of Bal's humiliation and destitution as if it were her own.

'That's exactly what he said? Word for word?'

'He said he told the High Council there was something going on with the inventory lists that bothered him and required further investigation, but no one believed him. And now the lists have been destroyed and you actually think it was sabotage on his part.'

Nancy pursed her lips. 'The High Council believes it was an act of sabotage by the professor, not us.'

'But,' Marion uttered, confused, 'you *are* the High Council?'

'What Nancy means,' Frank explained swiftly, 'is that she and I believe the professor. Unfortunately, there are some individuals on the council who are convinced otherwise. Who have been swayed.'

Marion ran the four remaining council members through her mind: Professor Gillroth, the agency's oldest member and a man who held a wealth of secrets, some of which were undoubtedly sinister. Barbara Simpkins, the agency librarian, a fickle drunk who could certainly be swayed with minimal persuasion. Delia Spragg, the agency tailor, a frumpish woman of little notoriety and, of course, Rupert Nicholas, head of security, whom Marion believed would revel in any opportunity to stir drama and mistrust throughout Miss Brickett's.

'But that's ridiculous. It makes no sense,' Marion retaliated, addressing Nancy though not assured of her own conviction. 'Why would anyone jump to a conclusion as convoluted as that?'

'There's no need to raise your voice, Miss Lane,' Nancy said, lowering hers. 'We've just told you – *we* believe the professor. Someone obviously destroyed the inventory lists to conceal evidence the professor was close to uncovering. Under normal circumstances, I'd have said this to our employees and insisted we investigate the matter. The problem is, since a few weeks back, Frank and I have been the target of several conspiracy theories. And lies. You might have heard about that absurd publication doing the rounds, *The Truths*?'

Marion's memory flooded with the caricature Maud had showed her last night – agency employees chained and imprisoned. Miss Brickett's Incarceration and Immolation. 'The posters,' she answered. 'There was one of you, too?'

'Several. And they seem to have struck a nerve, sparked some ungodly groupthink among our employees and High Council members, which has put Frank and me in a rather ineffectual position. I might be the head of this agency, but I only have as much power as my subordinates grant me.'

'So, what you're actually saying is, you've been overrun by the ERPS?' Marion asked, hoping her summation of the situation was more an exaggeration.

'Perhaps not entirely, not yet,' Frank said with forced optimism. 'But indeed, something dark and elaborate is brewing.'

'Then we must identify and extricate the new recruit, the man who's been communicating with the Florist,' Marion proposed. 'Whoever he really is, he must be at the core of all this.'

Nancy got to her feet, made an impatient gesture. 'It's not that simple, Miss Lane. Both Mr Longmore and Mr Proctor passed the enigma without fault. Both have perfect records and nothing in their personal files to suggest they aren't who they say they are. We're dealing with a professional turncoat, not the Florist's errand boy. And even if we knew who he was, there wouldn't be much I could do about it until I've disentangled the mess the ERPS has put me in.'

'Yes, it's an unfortunate predicament,' Frank elaborated awkwardly, twisting his hands. 'The point is, we need to stop the ERPS. And to do that, we must understand exactly what's going on in their meetings, what their ultimate goal is. But every time I've tried to isolate and question a member, they dash off as though their life depends on it. Clearly, they've been instructed not to speak to anyone on the outside.' He took a break, twisted the ring on his finger anxiously. 'I'm sorry to do this, Marion. I've already put you in danger one too many times. The problem is, neither Nancy nor I would be permitted to join and there isn't anyone else we could think of for the task. No one we trust, anyway.' He gave her a pained look. 'I need you to become a member of the ERPS.'

13

The Truths, Part 2

Marion and Bill sat alone around the fireplace in the common room. Coals glowed in the grate – amber eyes, peering out, watching. The room was cold but tonight there was something else in the air – a tension that pulled on Marion's nerves like an astringent.

It was sometime in the early evening the following Thursday. Marion had spent the better half of an hour explaining to Bill what Frank had told her in the Games Room about the warring members of the High Council and Nancy and Frank's failing grip on the agency as a whole. She couldn't tell him the finer details, of course, about Proctor and Longmore and their probable connection to the Florist, though she did explain what Frank had asked of her at the end. She expected Bill's reaction to be dubious at best, but he was looking at her now with an expression so unfamiliar to his soft features. It was unmistakeable anger.

'Frank asked you to join the ERPS and you're actually considering it?' he asked, flicking off a spark that had leaped from the fire and onto Marion's sleeve.

'Of course I am. That's why I'm telling you.'

Bill pointed out that if Frank and Nancy's suspicions were accurate and the ERPS had corrupted the High Council, then they were putting Marion directly in the line of danger by asking her to join the organisation as a mole. Thank heavens he had no idea how much danger they'd already put her in.

'If the ERPS are so corrupt, what do you think they'll do when they realise you're there to eavesdrop on them? If you're right and they already set Professor Bal up like that . . . ' He trailed off.

Marion tried to brush his concerns aside, but really it was this notion that had been turning her stomach all afternoon. She wondered how easy it would be to convince the ERPS that she was there for genuine reasons. After everything she'd done to show her defiance to the organisation, not to mention humiliating them by snatching the quiz-night victory from under their noses, surely they'd be immediately suspicious of her request join. Her only hope was that they were too enamoured of their own importance to question this new, albeit peculiar, addition to their fray.

But there was another problem, even worse than the first.

Frank had specifically requested that Marion tell only as many people the truth behind her ERPS membership as necessary. He'd stated, logically, that the more people who knew the truth, the more likely it was that her mission would fail.

'We don't really know who's working with them and who's not,' he'd reminded her once Nancy had left the meeting, 'or who might claim to be against them one day and a member the next. We need to make people believe you're a part of them, truly and wholly, if this plan is to work.'

And even now, even before she was a member, Marion knew what this would mean. Her friends – Maud, Jessica, Preston – would find it hard to accept that she'd suddenly decided to join the very organisation they'd collectively sworn to dismantle. She'd become an outcast to the group of confidants she'd relied on for support. And what if Bill felt that way, too, even though he knew the truth?

'I don't know what you expect me to say, Bill. If the ERPS are a front for something more sinister, we have to act quickly and figure out what it is.'

Bill ignored this, reached into his haversack. 'You've heard what's coming next?'

Marion frowned, her eyes fixed on the folded poster Bill had retrieved.

He handed it over as he said: 'Every non-member is getting one, apparently. Unsurprisingly, Professor Bal's was first.'

Marion clasped her throat. The poster was a caricature of Professor Bal, crudely drawn to accentuate his spindly frame and oversized clothes, an enormous magnifying glass held over his face, disfiguring him. Beneath was a line that read: *The Truths, Part 2: a secret carried from the slums of Pakistan to the rotting soul of London. Illegal immigrant hired as head of Gadgetry to avoid deportation.*

'And here's the other thing,' he added as Marion crushed the poster in her hand, bit back the rage clawing up her throat. 'Once you're a member, that's it. You won't be able to leave.' He moved to the edge of his seat. 'Have you seen Ambrosia lately?'

'What? No. Why?'

'She was one of them – you know that, of course. But word is, she told them she was leaving and the next morning, she arrived at work to find all of her things destroyed. Her books burned. Her notes. Personal and irreplaceable items. Everything. She received a threat, too, an ultimatum stating she'd better return to the organisation or she'd regret it. So, of course, she's back with them now – doesn't have much choice.'

The fire popped and crackled, spewing black smoke into the chimney and a fleck of coal onto the hearthrug.

'They're not just a pest,' Bill persisted, stamping out the spark with the toe of his shoe. 'They're dangerous. I understand why Frank wants someone on the inside. I understand what he's trying to do. What I don't understand is why it always has to be you.'

'Always?'

He turned away, shook his head, muttering something.

Marion's chest tightened with every second Bill froze her out. She knew he was protecting her, as he always did. Most of the time she loved him for it, but sometimes, like now, she wished he'd just take her side instead – guide her rather than shield.

'If you have something to say—'

'You know what I have to say,' he answered without making eye contact. 'I don't think this is your problem. I don't think Frank was right to ask this of you. Why not Kenny? Why not someone else? This investigation's already taken a toll on you. I'm not an idiot, you know. I can see it.'

'Frank doesn't trust anyone else enough,' she said. Her cheeks burned. Was it true? Did Frank really trust no one else at Miss Brickett's, or was there another reason he'd asked her to do his bidding? 'It's not fun for me, you know that? I'm not doing this because I want to.'

Now he looked at her, but his expression no longer betrayed anger. It was worse than that. Disappointment.

'No, of course not. You're doing it to please Frank.'

Marion drew a breath, hot and sharp. 'What's that supposed to mean?'

'Come on, Mari.'

'No, tell me. Say it.'

Bill clenched his jaw.

'*Say it,*' she repeated.

'All right.' His voice was hard and quick. 'I think you've been Frank's skivvy since day one. Doing his dirty work, his dangerous work. You'll do anything for him, no matter the cost, no matter how dangerous. And he knows it. He's using you now just like he used you last year to clear his name.'

'I can't believe you—' She breathed, forcing herself not to cry. 'Frank didn't *use* me last year. I chose to help him. And, by the way, so did you.'

'No. I chose to help *you*. Nothing I did last year was for Frank. Everything I do is for—' His voice broke, he inhaled stiffly. 'Look, I've been on your side since the beginning, Mari, and I always will be. That's why I have to say this, even though you don't want to hear it.' He paused in preparation, softening the edges to his voice. 'Frank is using you. Maybe not intentionally, maybe he doesn't even realise. But it doesn't matter. I know you think you're a Miss Brickett's apprentice only because he pleaded with the High Council to have you recruited, because he knew Alice and had made some promise to her to keep you safe. But I don't think that's true. You deserve to be here. You're a brilliant mechanic, a brilliant detective. You've proved your worth more than any of us over and over again. It's enough now. You don't owe Frank, or this place, anything. Remember that.' He stood up so quickly, he lost his balance for a beat.

Marion felt another surge of emotion, frustration and regret and fear and something else she didn't recognise.

Bill turned to leave, then turned back around. For a moment he seemed like his old, gentle self, but then the bitterness returned. 'And another thing – it's not just Frank. If Kenny didn't agree with this little infiltration into the ERPS, I bet you'd have reconsidered.'

'Kenny doesn't know,' she snapped, not quite sure this was the truth. She hadn't seen him for nearly forty-eight hours.

'Right, well, I'll wager he won't try to stop you.'

Ignoring the twisting in her gut, Marion left the common room shortly after Bill, crossed the corridor and paused outside room fifteen. She was furious, searing with indignation. But she had to prove, to herself at least, Bill was wrong.

She rapped against the door.

There was no answer, but she could hear something. Was it panting? Groaning?

A few more seconds and the door cracked open a slither.

'Lane?' Kenny stared at her, a towel wrapped around his waist, moisture clinging to the bare skin on his chest, his torso. He was clearly surprised to see her, though he didn't look particularly happy about it. He raked his fingers through his damp hair — freshly applied cologne mixing with the scent of soap and shampoo. 'Something wrong?'

'I . . . no. I just wanted to have a word,' she said.

'About?'

'Did Frank tell you what he asked me to do?' She lowered her voice. 'Concerning the ERPS?'

Kenny was distracted, clearly. 'Eh, no. But I'm meeting him tomorrow morning. Look, this isn't a great time. Do you mind if we talk later?' He glanced over his shoulder.

Someone muttered something from beyond. He flashed them a quick smile, turned back to Marion.

'Oh, *oh*,' she said, cheeks burning.

She could see Kenny's bed through the crack in the door. She could see the crumpled sheets. And she could see the outline of someone tangled inside them — she needn't guess who.

Kenny closed the door softly behind him, pulled the towel further up his waist and whispered. 'What's going on? You in trouble?' His eyes had lost their usual gleam, or perhaps it was just that Marion no longer noticed. 'If you need me, I'll get dressed and we can—'

'No. I'm fine. I just wanted to tell you . . . I mean, I wanted to ask whether you'd heard about—' She waved her hands dismissively. 'Never mind. It can wait.' She bit her lip, pictured Kate Bailey, covered only by sheets that smelled of sandalwood and musk. 'I'm fine,' she repeated, keeping the catch from her voice as she turned to leave.

14

The Warrant

On Friday, the night of the ERPS recruitment dinner, Marion found herself alone in her room. Of course she was alone. Bill didn't want anything to do with her now that she'd decided to follow Frank's instruction. She hadn't told Jessica or the others what she was about to do, and Kenny was similarly oblivious – not that Marion had seen him since their awkward encounter.

But none of that mattered, she repeated incessantly to herself, while the ERPS marched through the corridors of Miss Brickett's, sparking madness and mistrust, luring employees into their den.

She examined herself in the mirror above the washbasin, catching the reflection of a pile of ERPS posters on her bedside table. The society's propaganda publication, *The Truths*, had grown to astronomical proportions over the past days. More posters revealing highly classified agency information or 'alternative opinions' were distributed by hand, some of which implied that Miss Brickett's lack of general security and employee screening was the reason Michelle White had been murdered last year. In addition, primitive and sometimes obscene cartoon depictions of non-ERPS employees had been plastered along the Grand Corridor day after day, accompanied by the tagline 'Whose secrets are next?', subtly implying that if you didn't want yours displayed, you'd better hurry along and join the society.

Last night it had been Frank's turn and a caricature of him was distributed, depicting a cartoon of his likeness attached to an arrangement of strings like a marionette, Nancy standing behind him playing puppeteer. This morning it had been Marion's — a nude childlike cartoon of her sitting on Frank's lap, their hands cuffed together.

She hoped Bill hadn't seen it yet — she suspected, ironically, he'd find a lot of truth in it.

She pulled on a pair of capri trousers and a white cardigan, curled her hair into a low knot, took a breath, and steeled herself for a night of feigned enthusiasm and extreme self-control.

'Marion?' Amanda said as she greeted her at the entrance to the East Eight Chamber, the door pulled half-open, her body perched defensively in the gap.

There was a hint of surprise in her tone, which Marion had expected. But there was also a note of something that sounded bizarrely like relief.

'You're here for the dinner?'

'Yes,' Marion said flatly, pushing her hands into her pockets.

'But . . . ' Amanda looked over her shoulder, then lowered her voice. 'This is a *recruitment* dinner. If you're here tonight, we assume you mean to join us. And if you join, you won't . . . you *can't* leave.'

'I know that.'

Amanda swallowed, rubbed her throat.

Were those dark circles beneath her eyes, broken capillaries under her skin? It looked very much like she hadn't slept in days.

'All right. What are you going to tell them? You need a good reason to explain your sudden change of heart.'

Marion didn't understand what was going on. Amanda had been front and centre of the ERPS's recruitment tactics ever since their formation, so it was believable that she wanted Marion to join, even that she might assist her in the process. But there was fear in her voice now, desperation, as though she were concerned Marion might not be accepted. Why?

'Well,' Marion said, clearing the unease from her throat, 'I've realised you lot were right about some things.'

Amanda made an impatient gesture with her hands. 'Yes? Such as?'

This was easy. There was only one thing the ERPS had brought up in their endless rally of propaganda that Amanda, or anyone else, might believe Marion would side with.

'Mostly your suggestion that the agency ought to heighten security. I can see how we need it, especially after Michelle's death last year. I felt the consequences of that more than almost anyone. And I know the agency could have done more to protect Michelle, and all of us.' She sighed; it wasn't forced this time. 'But, you see, I got more involved in Michelle's case last year than I really wanted.

'And when you lot came round, suggesting all these changes, all these things the High Council have done without our best interests at heart, well, I didn't want to be a part of it. I didn't want to be involved. But I suppose I realise now that if we don't do something to protect ourselves, and stand up for what we believe is right and fair as employees, we might not get another chance.' She let her words settle. A chill coursed through her as she realised nothing she'd said was actually a lie.

Amanda studied her for a moment, then checked again over her shoulder. Music, or something close to it – a low purr, like drums rattling – had started up inside.

'Good, yes, all right.' She stepped aside awkwardly. 'Say that to the others. It might work.'

She ushered Marion inside, through a short corridor with an undulated ceiling, across a gravel-lined floor and into a tunnel mouth, which opened into a much larger, grander space. The chamber was furnished with a collection of elaborate royal-blue banners bearing the society's name along with the slogan 'to reform, improve and remain' in large gold lettering. The music, or rattling, was louder here, pulsing out from a set of hidden speakers and filling the air with an odd vibration that set Marion's nerves alight.

'I'd never even heard about this chamber until now,' Marion said conversationally, taking in her surroundings. 'How did you come upon it?'

Amanda muttered something incoherent.

'What's that?'

'Harry,' she spat out in a hurry. 'Harry, the barman, suggested the location. I don't know why.'

They'd arrived at the entrance to the chamber's atrium, a small archway that led into a room Marion could only just make out, filled with tables and chairs arranged to seat five at each. Amanda gripped Marion by the arm so hard she winced.

'Before we go inside, I need to ask you something—'

'Miss Lane. How wonderful to see you, dear!'

Marion started as Delia Spragg, High Council member and agency tailor, materialised at Amanda's shoulder. Her grey hair was pinned behind her ears, and she was dressed in a red wool cardigan and black skirt – both of which were far too tight for her well-cushioned physique. Her dull brown eyes swept over Marion, then Amanda. There was a difficult silence, during which Amanda stared unblinking at Marion, something pleading in her eyes.

'Eh, you too, Mrs Spragg,' Marion said, breaking the tension. 'I didn't realise you were a member.'

Spragg gave her a surreptitious smile. 'Member?' She laughed shrilly, wet her lips. 'Well now, come along, the meeting's about to start.'

She guided Marion, Amanda trailing behind, into the atrium and up to a table where Proctor and Longmore were seated. The sight of them gave Marion an immediate pang of discomfort.

'Do take a seat.' She gestured to the unoccupied chair between the two men as Amanda rushed off to a table near the back where Quinn, looking weary and pale, was seated. 'Have something to drink. Relax, enjoy yourself.' Spragg clasped her hands against her chest. 'We're so pleased to have you with us, truly.'

Marion bit her tongue, poured herself a glass of wine and watched Spragg scuttle off back to the atrium, where she welcomed in fellow High Council members, Miss Simpkins and Rupert Nicholas. So Frank was right. The ERPS *had* swayed at least half of the High Council and, by the look of the congested chamber, *more* than half of the lower-level employees.

'I thought you were adamantly oblivious to the failings of Miss Brickett's?' Proctor cut in, pulling her from her thoughts. 'Have you suddenly seen the light?'

'Give it a rest, Proctor,' Longmore snapped on Marion's other side. He leaned in, whispered, 'He's like this with everyone who joins. Doesn't trust a soul.'

Clever man, Marion thought.

She placed her glass carefully on the table. Proctor was still staring at her with those odd, searching eyes. He was everything

Marion disliked in a colleague – furtive, difficult to read. And *strange*. Was *he* the Florist's ally? She thought back to the three occasions when she'd bumped into him wandering the corridor outside the staff quarters late at night, once on a Saturday. It certainly added up, since the Florist had been telephoning his contact at 10 p.m. every Saturday from Hyde Park.

She turned to Longmore. He was grinning curiously at her, his once nondescript features somehow more striking now – his fawn hair tinged with gold under the chamber light, confidence lengthening his posture. He stretched his hands behind his head and, unsurprisingly, started blabbering about his plans for the upcoming weekend.

Nancy said the Florist's co-conspirator wouldn't be an amateur, but rather a professional liar, a well-primed trickster, someone who could configure themselves with ease. Longmore was certainly confident enough to pull that off. But could it be? Could *he* be the spy?

She pushed the warring theories from her mind. For now, all she had to do was convince the ERPS she was a loyal new member. She gave Proctor a thoughtful look and answered his question.

'As I said to Amanda earlier, I must admit, I was sceptical of the ERPS at first. But seeing your recent accomplishments, I thought it only sensible to delve a little further.'

'Sounds well-thought-out,' Proctor said suspiciously, raising his eyebrows.

Longmore grunted. 'Why don't you tell us why you joined, Proctor?'

The two men glowered at one another. Spragg had returned to the table, perhaps sensing the wrath brewing between the recruits and hoping to stifle it.

'To keep an eye on things.' Proctor answered Longmore's question with a sneer, Marion observing them both intently.

'That's interesting,' Longmore said facetiously, 'because keeping an eye on things is my reason for joining, too.'

Marion looked at Spragg, wondering if she understood what the two men were talking about, but the old woman appeared impervious, albeit a little flustered.

'Well?' Longmore challenged, pushing back his shoulders. 'Tell us, Thomas. What sort of things have you been keeping an eye on?'

For reasons unknown to Marion, this statement caused Proctor to bristle. He picked up a beer bottle from the table. Longmore was on his feet in seconds. The two men faced off. Proctor raised the beer bottle and in one brilliant swoop, brought it crashing down on the table. Shards of glass flew everywhere. Spragg jumped up to break the pair apart, but almost as quickly as it had started, the feud was over. The men didn't say another word to each other and moved off to opposite corners of the chamber as if nothing had happened.

'Well, that was a bit much, wasn't it?' Spragg said in a slightly higher pitch, smoothing the tablecloth before her. 'But I'm actually rather pleased to have you alone for a moment, dear.' She produced a slim booklet from her bag and slid it across the table, its title glaring: *The Truths*. 'Now that you're one of us,' she said, opening the booklet to its first page, 'you deserve your own copy. I realise some of what you read in here will be hard to accept, but as they say, the truth sets us free.'

Marion pulled the booklet towards her, stared down at the opening page, which contained a faded clipping from *The Telegraph*, dated 20 April 1958: '*Body of brutally murdered woman identified as spinster Michelle Gertrude White.*' She paused to look up at Spragg, who was smiling sorrowfully, then returned her focus to the booklet and read on: '. . . *police are asking the public for any information on the relatives of the victim, who appears to have been stabbed in the throat, her partially decomposed body dumped in the Thames.'*

Spragg clicked her tongue sympathetically as Marion finished. 'Terrible, isn't it? And yes, I have to admit, I was a member of the High Council when the decision was made to drop poor Michelle's body into the river, but what could I have done? Nancy didn't allow us much say in the matter. But it scared me, I'll tell you that. I had to help wrap the body, then we dragged it up through the bookshop in the middle of the night, hauled it into Frank's car and . . . well, you can guess the rest.'

She stared thoughtfully across the chamber as Marion processed what she'd just read, and heard, bile churning in her stomach.

'You know, dear, you and I have a lot in common.' She giggled at the look of disbelief on Marion's face. 'Oh yes, I was recruited for my mechanical skills, just like you. My father owned a tyre factory before the war and taught me absolutely everything about cars.' She turned her eyes to the distance, drew a handkerchief from her bag. 'He and my brother died in France, two weeks apart, and I was left to manage the factory with my ailing mother. We couldn't manage, of course, and were forced to sell. If it hadn't been for Miss Brickett's, I'm not sure where I'd have ended up.'

Marion followed Spragg's gaze as it swept over the faces of the ERPS, each so familiar – apprentices and employees, most of whom shared a common history of abandonment and destitution.

'That's why I'm doing this,' Spragg went on, tilting her face towards Marion. 'We have so much to fight for here. We cannot let the lies control us any longer. You've done a valiant thing joining us, dear. Together, we'll put things right. Mark my words.' She patted Marion on the shoulder and wandered off, leaving the booklet behind.

Soon, a food table was opened, offering only boiled eggs, toast and a few cuts of cold beef. Marion didn't have an appetite but served herself a plate anyway. She settled back at her table, her mind whirling. Yes, she'd wondered what had happened to Michelle White's body after the murder last year. Yes, she'd assumed the High Council would have had to get rid of it somehow. But casting it into the Thames, to rot and swell and be picked apart by fish and maggots . . .

'It's the same every time,' Proctor said, settling down next to Marion, staring at his plate of food. 'Keeps us modest, apparently.'

Marion forced a forkful of egg and toast down her throat. 'Right, makes sense,' she lied, her mind still filled with flashing images, gushing grey waters, a body wrapped in cloth. She pushed aside her plate and took a breath.

Proctor lifted his head, glanced around. Longmore was standing a few yards off, chatting to Amanda. Marion tried to interpret the way he was looking at them, but it seemed an unusual mix of jealousy and interest. After a while, he turned back to Marion.

'By the way, now that you're one of us, you might do your friends a favour and encourage them to join, too. Before it's too late.'

'What's that supposed to mean?'

Proctor shook his head, got to his feet.

She rose after him, gripped his forearm. 'Answer me.'

He glowered at her as he ripped himself free. 'Just a warning. Take it or leave it.'

Marion faltered. Unable to find a reply, she let him leave. She turned to the back of the chamber. Amanda and Longmore were still facing one another, though now apparently having a debate of some sort.

Amanda raised her voice. 'Don't be ridiculous,' she snapped at Longmore, loud enough for Marion to hear, then marched across the chamber towards her. 'Marion, I don't have much time, but I need . . . ' She dug around in her bag, then handed Marion a registration card – a document employees were expected to carry on their person at all times that detailed warrants for restricted gadgets and identification papers. 'I need you to sign this for me.'

Marion looked at the registration card and the blank space next to a request for a Tranquilliser Pin. The gadget – a needle filled with a dose of diazepam that was concealed in a tie pin or piece of jewellery, and occasionally attached to a timer that would eject the needle into a target when desired – was only ever used by senior Inquirers in the field. Neither Professor Bal nor any member of the High Council would even consider signing the application and the only way Marion could is if she forged one of their signatures, which she obviously wasn't going to do.

She looked up at Amanda, perplexed. 'You can't possibly think *I* could sign this for you? I'm an *assistant* at Gadgetry.'

She waited. Amanda's eyes flickered to the left, to Proctor this time. Marion's skin crawled.

'Why on earth do you want one, anyway?'

Amanda's blunt features changed, turning into something more fearful than angry. Perhaps she realised that if she was asking Marion for an impossible favour, she might as well try to be nice about it. When she spoke next, it was in a hurried whisper.

'*Please*, Marion. Figure out a way. I don't have any other options, or anyone else to go to. *Please*, just . . . think of something.' She wiped a line of sweat from her brow, nodded and slipped from the chamber.

Seconds later, Delia Spragg shuffled to the front of the room, tapped a knife to her glass.

Her clinking echoed off the bare stone walls. Everyone fell silent.

'Good evening, members,' Spragg boomed, touching the arrow pinned to her cardigan, her eyes sweeping the room. 'Shall we begin?'

The drums started up again, their beat rapid now. Spragg cleared her throat, commanded the room to rise, then, in a voice that wasn't quite her own, began to chant:

To reform, to improve, to remain
To reform, to improve, to remain
To reform, to improve, to remain

The rest of the chamber joined in, barring Marion, their voices low, almost cathartic.

To reform, to improve, to remain
To reform, to improve, to remain

Eventually, the chanting stopped. Everyone settled back in their seats.

Spragg shuffled some papers around in her hand. The room buzzed, as though the chanting voices still held in the air.

'Thank you all for coming,' she started. 'As ever, tonight we will discuss an important Truth, one that has been concealed for far too long.'

On cue, the members drew out their booklets, *The Truths*, opened them somewhere in the middle.

Marion's fingertips prickled as she ran them over her own copy. She split it open, paged through.

'The Truth, twenty-eight,' Spragg announced, looking up from her booklet, catching Marion's eye. 'Professor Uday Bal's appointment.'

Marion turned to the appropriate page, glanced down. A photograph of what appeared to be Professor Bal's Miss Brickett's application form, dated January 1952. Alongside the form was a series of short handwritten letters. Marion's eyes swept quickly over the letters, a correspondence between Nancy and the professor, discussing his application to work at the agency, the fact that this was his only chance to avoid deportation. She closed the booklet, looked up.

Spragg was staring directly at her. 'It's not to say we don't appreciate him,' she began, as though appealing to Marion exclusively. 'The professor has done so much to bring the Factory and the Workshop to where it is now. However, I believe the details of his employment perfectly illustrate the extent to which he's been favoured. And I think you'll all agree that his work has been underwhelming of late, stagnant and disorganised.'

Marion pressed her fingernails into the soft flesh of her thighs, digging them deeper and harder until the pain was great enough to distract her. She knew this was Spragg's final test. If Marion resisted or protested, then it would be obvious she could never be a trusted member of the ERPS.

'Therefore, as you may already know, we've put forth a request to the High Council to have our dear professor removed from the position of head of the Department of Gadgetry and transferred to the more suitable post of chief engineer. I'm now happy to say this request was granted and I, Delia Spragg, am now your new head of Gadgetry.'

Marion kept a straight face, only because she knew that Spragg was watching her, expecting a protest. Instead, she clapped along with the group.

It was nearing midnight when the ERPS members finally began to filter from the chamber. The buffet table began to clear and Marion believed it safe to leave. She was barely over the threshold, when a voice called from behind.

'I'm sure you must have forgotten,' Spragg said, holding out a piece of paper, 'but no matter. Here we are.'

Marion edged closer, glancing down at the paper.

'Just your signature here and here. The first is for membership, the second is your approval of the agenda and forthcoming referendum for Professor Bal's demotion.'

Something thick and hot rose in Marion's throat. Even so, she pressed pen to paper against the wall and without hesitation, signed her name.

15

Head of Gadgetry and Gloom

Ambrosia Quinn in tow, Marion arrived at the cafeteria the following Thursday morning to find a large group of employees, including all the second-year apprentices, crowded around the wall near the entrance.

As she got closer, she heard the murmurs, the hushed sniggering. Marion realised the group was staring at a row of newly planted ERPS propaganda posters. She pushed her way to the front – Quinn struggling to keep up – drew a sharp breath as her eyes travelled over the unflattering caricature of Jessica, Maud, Preston and Bill standing in a circle, each holding a pistol pointed at the person opposite. Outside the circle was a slightly more favourable cartoon of Marion, a crown on her head, grinning like a madwoman. The tagline read: 'Deadly betrayal as team DimWit NitWit implodes.'

'So it's true, then,' Maud snarled, stepping up to her side and eyeing the addition to Marion's uniform – the delicate blue arrow pin she wore under her apprentice badge.

'You've joined?' Jessica asked, incredulous, as her eyes travelled from Marion to the poster and back again.

'They're the ones responsible for Professor Bal's *demotion*,' Preston added, striding up to join the mutiny.

'She has . . . she *must* have a reason,' Jessica said hopefully. 'Don't you, Mari?'

Quinn looked left and right over her shoulder, then leaned into Marion before she could answer. 'Don't speak to them. We're not allowed to. And they're watching.'

Sure enough, Marion spotted several ERPS members glowering at her from within the crowd, waiting for her to make a mistake, break her allegiance. She sighed. Was there any feeling in the world worse than being chastised for something you couldn't defend? She turned around, searched the growing crowd. Bill was lingering on the outskirts, his expression indifferent. She tried to catch his eye, consumed by an urge to rush over and embrace him, rest her head against his chest. But he turned, vanished, swallowed by the mob.

This was the part she'd been dreading most – the pretence and lies. Joining the ERPS had given her a sense of guilt and regret, as if she were betraying not only herself, but also her friends, her colleagues and, as Preston had kindly pointed out, Professor Bal. She wondered if the professor knew of her recent tethering to the organisation and what he'd make of it. What would he think if he found out she'd signed the ERPS's referendum requesting his demotion? It made her sick even to consider.

'Are you at least going to warn us before they pass any other referendums?' Maud asked. 'Is it true they're going to ask the High Council to send us all for performance assessments at the end of the month?'

'I don't know anything about that,' Marion snapped, ignoring Quinn's concerned looks and the prickling at the base of her neck, warning her of the eyes watching.

'You'd be fine, of course,' Maud went on, unrelenting. 'You and Amanda would pass easily. Not sure about the rest of us.'

Marion opened her mouth to argue but stopped as she spotted Frank and Nancy seated at a table tucked away from the crowd at the far end of the cafeteria, lounging in their seats, unaffected by the mayhem unravelling around them. She closed her eyes briefly, her throat tight, an unwelcome memory triggered.

Once, when she was fourteen, her mother had disappeared for an entire weekend. Marion spent the days sick with dread. The worst was happening, her nightmares were coming true. But Alice returned on Sunday afternoon, bedraggled though apathetic. She'd smoothed her thinning hair against her scalp and explained with a sheepish smile that she'd been to see a 'specialist', someone who'd promised to help with the depression and sleepless nights. But the truth, Marion later discovered, was that she'd spent the weekend (and a large portion of her wages) at a bedsit across the road pouring vodka and barbiturates down her throat. The deception stung, not so much because of where Alice had been or what she'd been doing there, but because of the indifference and detachment that came with it. And she felt it again now, that same ache of betrayal, easy lies. Frank and Nancy nonchalant, leaving Marion to suffer alone.

She shuffled through the knot of employees and straggling ERPS members, still whispering to each other as they stared up at the posters, distracted.

'Miss Lane?' Nancy hissed urgently, straightening in her seat as Marion approached. 'What are you doing? We can't meet here.' Her eyes scanned the cafeteria. 'They'll see you.'

Frank got up in a fluster, angled himself in front of Marion, preventing anyone from seeing her.

'I thought we agreed only to meet in the Games Room. Is something the matter?'

'Yes,' she said, drawing back as Frank came closer. She took a breath, trying to calm the mix of rage and betrayal bubbling inside her. She'd hardly slept since her first ERPS meeting, her mind racing with doubt, wild dreams. She'd been ousted from her circle of friends, lambasted for a false betrayal and forced to keep quiet about it all. And here, Frank and Nancy were casually enjoying their breakfast as if everything was just fine. 'What happened to Michelle White's body?' she blurted.

Frank glanced around nervously, though only Quinn hovered nearby. 'Please, Marion, keep your voice down.'

'You threw her into the Thames,' Marion persisted, not lowering her voice. 'Spragg told me. She's in control of the ERPS, by the way. And Simpkins and Nicholas have joined, too. I suppose you know they've passed a referendum to have Professor Bal demoted.'

Frank turned to look at Nancy, his grey eyes wide, flickering. 'Marion, you must understand—'

'Is it *true*?' she demanded. 'Did you throw White's body into the Thames?'

'Yes,' Nancy answered coldly, touching the bridge of her spectacles. 'We had to get rid of it.'

'It? *Her*. You mean, you had to get rid of *her*.'

Nancy pressed her lips together. 'What exactly would you have suggested we do instead?'

'Anything, *anything* else.' She turned to Frank, crossed her arms to conceal the tremor in her hands.

'I'm sorry,' he said, reaching for her hand. 'But we must separate now, before we draw attention to ourselves.' He glanced at the thinning crowd behind, some of whom were craning their necks to see who Frank and Nancy were speaking to.

'Right, of course,' she said, suddenly exhausted. 'I'll see you next Monday, then.'

'Good morning, Miss Lane,' Delia Spragg, dressed in a knee-length brown dress and white silk headscarf, greeted Marion at the entrance to the Workshop shortly afterwards.

Marion nodded absently as Spragg guided her across the Workshop, spitting out a list of tasks to be completed that day. 'Where's the professor?' Marion asked as they reached the line of workbenches.

'Off today,' Spragg answered shortly.

'Why?'

'I have no idea, dear. Does it matter?'

Marion decided it best not to answer.

'As you'll see,' Spragg explained, 'we've made a few changes to the department. Just some small procedural things to keep everything running smoothly.'

'Such as?' Marion asked, trying to keep her voice flat and unruffled.

'For starters, you'll find that I've listed everyone's tasks for the day in here . . . ' She patted a large leather-bound book sitting on Marion's workbench. 'Just to make things a bit easier. Then, once your shift is over, I'll need a summary of every task you worked on, how long it took, any problems encountered, who you worked with and so on.'

Marion couldn't help herself this time. 'That doesn't sound like it's going to make things easier.'

Spragg looked very much like Dolores Hacksworth, Marion's estranged grandmother, as she pursed her lips and scowled.

'Well, even so. You're to fill it in. Things have got to be more ordered around here. The professor's mishaps and oversights have already caused the agency terrible trouble in the finance department. We're several weeks behind with our

Factory orders and if we don't streamline things in Gadgetry, we're going to have to . . . ' She paused.

Marion crossed her arms. 'Have to what?'

'The High Council is going to be forced to let some people go, dear. It's as simple as that. We can't afford all the wages if things carry on like this.'

Marion scanned the shift book dutifully, ignoring Spragg's threat. She couldn't let herself get riled again. She didn't have the energy and besides, what good would it do?

'Additional Liar Glass feature to be fitted,' she said, reading out loud the only task listed for her that day.

'Quite right. The professor was against the idea,' Spragg said with a note of menace, 'but of course he's not the one making the decisions now, is he?'

Marion steeled herself. 'What additional feature?'

Spragg didn't answer, so Marion examined the deconstructed pieces of metal, glass and wiring lying on the line of benches — an array of Liar's Eyeglasses. Something indeed had been added — two cords that ran from the magnifying glass handle. She picked one up and threaded it through her fingers, frowning. At the end of the cord was a metal clip with rubber handles. She thought for a moment, deciphering what she was looking at. Then it hit her.

'These are—'

'Electric wires. The High Council loved the addition.' Spragg smiled stupidly as she spoke. 'Though it was actually my idea.' She took the cord from Marion. 'All that's left to do now is to fit the battery into the back of the magnifying glass and adjust the wiring.'

Marion rubbed the back of her neck. 'I don't understand. The eyeglass runs on the battery. Why do we have these cords?'

Spragg seemed perplexed by the question. 'Come now, dear. I know you have a brilliant mind for mechanics, surely you can figure it out.'

'They attach to the finger of the person undergoing the polygraph,' Marion said, voicing her theory.

Spragg nodded encouragingly.

'Which means the person undergoing the polygraph will receive an electric shock?'

'Quite right. But only if the magnifying glass detects a lie is being told.' She sighed theatrically. 'Miss Quinn should be here in a minute to assist. Once you're done, please set all the glasses in here for shipment.' She pointed to a cardboard box. 'You have five days. The shipment *must* leave the Workshop by Tuesday evening. Oh! and just keep one aside, will you?'

'What for?'

'Just in case.'

Spragg's eyes flashed, a glimmer of unease touching her features. She stalled and in the interim, the door to the Workshop sprung open. Quinn entered. Spragg took the interruption as an escape.

'Well, there we are. Now, the two of you can get going.'

A couple of days after finally completing the Liar's Eyeglass order, Marion felt an ounce of relief as she arrived at the Gadgetry Department, for a regular shift. Amid everything that had gone wrong since the start of the year, it was a small wonder that she'd managed to finalise the order and get it shipped to Hanslope Park in time.

But now, as she checked a batch of microdot cameras for faults, her mind began to wander. Why had Spragg insisted that a singular Liar's Eyeglass remain at the agency? Why were all of Spragg's efforts focused on the Gadgetry Department, on defaming and finally removing Professor Bal, on taking over management?

She looked up to see Quinn lingering in the entrance, a detached, worn expression on her face.

'You're not on duty today, are you?' Marion asked.

'No, but I . . . ' She wiped her hands on her skirt, started again. 'I was wondering if you needed any help. All this talk of letting staff go, I want to look busy at least.'

Marion gestured to Spragg's shift book. 'Right, well, I have a few things left to do. Have a look.' She watched as Quinn paged through diligently and was reminded of something. 'I heard your things were destroyed?' she inquired. 'Notebook included?'

'It was just an accident,' Quinn answered quickly, without looking up.

'Right,' Marion said, an eyebrow raised. 'Anyway, I've been meaning to ask what you meant when you told Professor Bal there was a discrepancy with the inventory lists earlier this year.'

Quinn seemed to battle with herself for a moment, as she'd done the past few days, making Marion wonder if the punishment she'd suffered for trying to leave the ERPS was worse than just a bout of vandalism.

'I don't want to cause trouble,' she croaked.

'Your notebook *was* destroyed, wasn't it?'

No reply.

'Do you really think that was because you tried to leave the ERPS, or because someone believed you'd recorded something they'd hoped to get rid of?'

'Both,' she said at last. 'But it was too late, anyway. I'd already explained what I knew to the professor. I noticed the number of batteries listed in the inventory and the number I personally counted in the storage cabinet were different. I didn't immediately think it meant anything – perhaps it was just an oversight by the professor – but I had noticed and I had to understand how it had happened. It's just the way I am,' she added in reply to Marion's look of disbelief. 'Anyway, I flipped back through the past months' inventory lists to see if there was anything off about them. And there was. Up until January, I noticed that Professor Bal counted and signed off on all the lists around the same time every Friday – five in the afternoon. And with the same pen—'

'How could you possibly know it was the same pen?' Marion asked, sceptical.

'I told you. I record *everything*. But you can ask the professor yourself if you don't believe me. He's always used a traditional fountain pen with black water-based ink that bleeds slightly through the paper. I even asked him about it one day, just to be sure. He got the pen from India or wherever he was born—'

'Pakistan,' Marion corrected with a snap.

Quinn crossed her arms. 'Anyway, I noticed that from early February, the inventory list was signed off with a different pen, a ballpoint most likely, but certainly not one that uses water-based ink. You can tell because there's no bleeding through and the lines are less distinct and narrower. The contrast is obvious if you pay attention, and I think the professor noticed it, too.'

Marion's heart beat a little faster as she put together what Quinn was implying. 'So, the lists from February onwards were false copies? Signed off by someone other than the professor?'

'Most definitely. I'm sure you guessed this already, but I believe Mrs Spragg was the one doing it. You see, it was just a matter of timing that I noticed the discrepancy. I'd been cleaning the shelves after the professor had counted and signed off on the inventory, just before Spragg had managed to replace the list with her own false one.

'She was there at the storage cabinet when I arrived. She looked disturbed and irritated and told me to come back later, but I insisted I had to get all of my duties done by six or I'd miss the tube home. Eventually, she wandered off and left me to it, but I'm sure that after I'd finished, she came back and changed the list.'

Marion chewed this over, annoyed with herself that she hadn't noticed the error as Quinn had done and horrified by what it suggested.

'Do you think that means Spragg has been removing gadgets from the cabinet every week after Bal had counted the inventory?'

'It's the only logical explanation.'

'Dammit,' Marion said, pacing now. 'This is how we've been losing money. Spragg's been stealing stock and no one's realised. Have you told anyone this?'

'I only pointed out the issue with the pens to Professor Bal. I'm just a new recruit. I didn't want to get anyone in trouble, and I didn't investigate the issue for any reason other than to satisfy my fixation with inaccuracies and oddities.' She looked down at her hands. 'I like things to be perfect.'

Marion stared across the hall, distracted by the storm of questions and answers this latest revelation conjured. Eventually, she stirred, realising Quinn hadn't moved the whole time.

'Thank you for . . . ' She faltered. Part of her was grateful to Quinn for identifying the issue, part of her was furious she hadn't told anyone until now. But of course, the revelation would likely have been ignored by the High Council (considering Spragg's sway over them now), or worse, got Quinn fired. She touched her on the shoulder. 'Thank you for trusting me with this.'

Quinn shrugged, flipped through Spragg's shift book, then picked up a screwdriver and hammer and got to her feet.

'What are you doing?' Marion asked.

'Replacing the filter on the ventilation duct. It's marked *urgent* in the shift book.' Quinn craned her neck to examine the ceiling above. 'But, eh, it's rather high, isn't it?' she noted under her breath.

Absentmindedly, Marion snatched the screwdriver and hammer from Quinn and ushered her over to a tall wooden ladder leaning against the department's western-facing wall.

'I'll do it. Just hold this steady.'

The top rung was at least twenty feet from the floor and led to a narrow portion of scaffolding from which one could access the ventilation duct. She loaded a small satchel with a collection of tools and a new filter, and started climbing.

'That's not really the point,' Quinn mumbled as Marion began her ascent. 'I was actually wondering . . .'

Marion risked a quick downwards glance as she continued to climb. Quinn was gripping the ladder base with both hands and staring fixedly at the workbench that stood directly below the platform.

'What? Wondering what?' she asked as she reached the top rung.

'It's just something about . . . why are all these tools . . .'

Marion had reached the platform. The ladder trembled slightly as Quinn, distracted, loosed her grip. Marion seized the edge of the scaffolding with one hand and began to haul herself upwards.

'Stop! *Stop!*' Quinn screamed shrilly from below.

Marion teetered, her right foot on the platform, the left still on the top rung of the ladder. She paused and tried to look down, but the shift in her weight caused her right foot to crash through the platform. She tightened her grip on the scaffolding above her, saving herself. She swung backwards, managed to reach the ladder. Quinn was still screaming at her from below, though Marion couldn't make out a word. Her heart was racing, she was drenched in sweat. Eventually, she stabilised herself and edged her way back down the ladder.

'Blast!' she panted. Her right foot throbbed and a trickle of blood leaked from a small cut above her ankle where a shard of wood had pierced the skin.

Quinn was standing at the workbench directly below the platform.

'Thank heavens you're all right!'

Marion hobbled to her side. 'You didn't put these here like this, did you?' She motioned to the carefully arranged assortment of sharp tools: wire cutters, chisels, claw hammers, a bed of nails.

Quinn shook her head. 'I noticed it just in time. But look . . . ' She kneeled down and swept something up with her index finger. 'Sawdust,' she said, presenting the evidence to Marion.

'Someone cut through the platform,' Marion said breathlessly, 'and arranged these tools right beneath, right where I'd have fallen.'

'You'd have been perfectly dead,' Quinn said matter-of-factly.

16

The Inquisition

Marion arrived at the East Eight Chamber for her second ERPS meeting, her arrow-shaped pin fixed perfectly to the breast pocket of her blouse, *The Truths* clutched tightly under her arm.

She raised a hand to knock, then paused. It was less than twenty-four hours since her near-fatal fall in Gadgetry and she was on edge, tense. Someone had set up the platform to break, arranged the tools below. Yes, anyone could have climbed that ladder, fallen to their death, but only Marion was supposed to be on duty that afternoon. She stared bleary-eyed at the chamber entrance. Proctor and Longmore would already be inside and one of them, she was almost certain, would be surprised to see her alive.

Footsteps, quick and strong, coming up behind her.

'Blast!' she hissed, clutching her heart as Kenny appeared at her shoulder, the strap of a duffel bag slung across his chest.

There was a strained moment between them. Marion wondered whether or not he'd forgotten about their last encounter at his room, or whether it mattered to him at all. It was both baffling and frustrating that even now, she cared what he thought of her.

'You've got to stop sneaking around like that. Nearly scared the life out of me.'

He raised an apologetic hand. 'Sorry, just wanted to catch you before you went inside.'

'We can't be seen together. You know how it is.'

'Yeah,' Kenny said, gnawing his bottom lip. 'Frank told me that you're a member now.' He looked with curiosity at the arrow pinned to her blouse, the booklet under her arm, her strung features. 'You look . . . like one of them.'

'Yes, well, that *is* the point.'

He studied her a moment longer. His eyes fell again on the booklet clutched under her arm. Had he heard the rumours circulating the agency, that his caricature, his *Truth*, was coming next? Marion feared the whispers were accurate, for she'd overheard a group of ERPS members muttering: *dead sister, Hugo enrolled in anger management, was he even fit to be a detective?* She shifted the booklet out of sight behind her back.

'Frank also told me about the issue with the inventory lists—'

'Keep your voice down,' she urged, glancing anxiously at the door. 'No one can know about that yet.'

Kenny went on regardless. 'You look shaken. Is everything—'

'Fine, yes.' She averted her gaze.

In her last meeting with Frank, she'd told him only about what Quinn had uncovered concerning the inventory lists. Nothing about the trap in Gadgetry. She was certain if Frank knew she'd been targeted like that, he'd pull her from the investigation immediately. And after everything she'd done to isolate herself from her friends, turning them against her, she'd be dammed if it was all for nothing.

Kenny considered this, then nodded uncertainly. 'Yeah, all right, but still, you need to be careful.' He dug around in his duffel bag and drew out a writing pad. 'You remember the maid who was murdered in Liverpool, the one with the rose branding on her chest?' He didn't wait for a reply. 'She was KGB.'

'The Russian state security police? You're certain?'

'Yeah, pretty much. The case has been taken up by MI5, which means Redding isn't allowed full access to the docket, though he's trying to scratch together what he can for us.'

'Have you told Frank?'

'On my way there now. Look, it's highly unlikely to be a coincidence, which means Eddie Hopper might also have been KGB, or involved with them somehow. And if that's the case, we've probably got a lot more going on here than we realise.' He nodded at the entrance to the East Eight. 'Whatever this is, it's big, Lane.'

Muffled voices came from inside the chamber, Spragg's tenor recognisable among them. Something clanged to the floor, causing Marion to flinch.

'I'd better go,' she said, turning to the door. She was late now. They were waiting.

Kenny grabbed her arm, opened his mouth, sighed, tried again. 'I didn't think you were interested.'

'What?'

'You said, well, you acted as though you weren't interested in me after the stake-out.'

She pulled herself free, looked away.

'You were angry. And I'm sorry, but that's why I . . . Kate and I—'

'Not now, please.'

'Stop brushing me off, Lane. We need to talk about it.'

'Not now, for goodness' sake,' she repeated, a lump rising in her throat. She couldn't let him rattle her moments before she faced Spragg, Proctor and Longmore. She had more than enough to deal with as it was. 'I can't.'

Clearly, Kenny didn't want to let her go, his eyes skirting from Marion to the door behind her. 'Okay. But please, Lane. I mean it. Be careful.'

The second Marion entered the East Eight, she knew something had changed.

Delia Spragg and Rupert Nicholas were standing at the head of the chamber, the rest of the ERPS seated in twenty perfect rows before them. No food or drinks had been set out. No drums sounded. No music. No one was talking. Not even Longmore. At Spragg's side was a table, the spare Liar's Eyeglass laid out on top. Next to it was Amanda, seated in a high-back, her hands strapped to the chair arms.

Marion held a breath as Spragg caught sight of her.

'Where have you been?' she snapped.

Everyone in the chamber flinched. Marion couldn't get her lips to move.

'Never mind. Come. There's no more time to waste.'

Marion forced her legs to carry her forwards while she cast an eye to the back of the chamber. Proctor's blond head was just visible among the line of bodies, all of them as still as if they were cast in stone. Longmore was seated closer to the front, staring fixedly at Amanda, who was trembling wildly, her skin glimmering with sweat.

Spragg stepped forwards as Marion approached. Spragg clasped her hands tightly against her stomach, but even so, a subtle quiver was visible in her fingers. Everyone, it appeared, was terrified.

'Money has been stolen from the Gadgetry Department,' Spragg started abruptly. 'A vast amount. And until I've found out who has taken it, no one will leave this room.'

A chair scraped somewhere near the back. The air crackled with held breath.

'Miss Lane,' Spragg went on, 'since this is your handiwork, you'll be assisting me.' She gestured to the Liar's Eyeglass, its brass rim glittering under the chamber lights.

The room turned their eyes on Marion. Something pressed down on her chest, churned and unfurled inside her stomach. Spragg pushed the gadget into her hand.

'Explain to our members how it works.'

In silence, heat rising up her neck, Marion turned the magnifying glass over in her hand. She straightened the two attached cords, set each of the three dial indicators to their resting positions, then switched on the lithium battery. There was a soft fizz as the glass came to life – the indicators on all three dials jittered, as if awakening from a long slumber. She swallowed against the dryness in her throat, then spoke.

'This is called a Liar's Eyeglass, capable of detecting minuscule deviations in ocular blood flow, pupil size and some other signs of . . . lying.' She touched the thin brass ridge, traced her fingers along the electric cords. She didn't want to imagine what was coming next.

Spragg took her place on Amanda's left-hand side, nodded at Marion. 'Apply it.'

Marion stalled, fiddled with the eyeglass.

'You don't have a choice, Miss Lane,' Spragg said impatiently. 'Either you do it, or I will.'

Marion faltered. She could refuse, but what good would that do? It didn't look as if Spragg was going to relent and at least if Marion applied the polygraph herself, she'd have some control over its features.

She attached one metal clip to Amanda's right thumb, the other to her left. She took Amanda's hand subtly in hers and squeezed it carefully, held the eyeglass over Amanda's eye and turned on the battery. For the first time in her career, she hoped a gadget she'd laboured over would fail to work when put to the test.

Spragg kneeled in front of Amanda. 'Miss Shirley, I'm going to ask you a few questions and it's in your best interests to reply as honestly as you can.' She cleared her throat. 'Is your name Amanda Hannah Shirley?'

Amanda hesitated. Marion watched the dials on the eyeglass quiver. She had no idea which dial represented which physical feature, but all of them seemed to jump at Amanda's silence. Not a good sign.

'*Answer. Quickly!*' Marion whispered in Amanda's ear as she heard the battery fizz and fire up.

'Yes,' Amanda said, barely loud enough for anyone to hear. The dials settled.

'Good,' Spragg breathed. 'And are you an employee of Miss Brickett's Investigations and Inquiries and a member of the ERPS?'

Amanda didn't need prompting this time. She squirmed in her chair. 'Yes. And yes.'

Spragg snarled, twisting her torso like a serpent ready to strike. 'But you've betrayed ERPS, haven't you?'

Amanda shot Marion a look. The polygraph's needles began to quiver once more. 'What?'

'Admit it!' Spragg persisted, drawing out her words.

'No, no. I don't know what you mean.'

The dials shot to the right, then immediately back down.

'You're a thief!' Spragg screeched, trembling almost as much as Amanda now. She paused for emphasis. 'Have you taken anything from Miss Brickett's that doesn't belong to you?'

Amanda's face drained. Her lips twitched as she hesitated. This sent the Liar's Eyeglass dials aflutter, back and forth, flickering like the wings of a trapped moth.

'Answer the question, Miss Shirley,' Spragg demanded.

Amanda stuttered. 'I d–don't know what-y-you m-mean.'

All three dials of the Liar's Eyeglass dashed violently to the right. The battery began to hiss, like water splashed on a hot surface. Electricity pumped through the cords. Marion knew she could remove the glass and Amanda would be spared from answering the question. But if she did so, Spragg would simply take over. Instead, as subtly as she dared, she angled the glass a few degrees off, so that the gauges – the tiny segments of the gadget that picked up changes in ocular blood pressure and pupil size – would be less able to do so.

'Let's try that again,' Spragg persisted, her voice now horribly shrill. 'Have you taken anything, anything at all, from Miss Brickett's premises that doesn't belong to you?'

This time, Amanda didn't hesitate. 'No! No, of course I haven't.'

The dials flickered gently, but the hissing sound from the battery died down.

Marion exhaled, a moment of relief flooding through her. Had her tiny alteration in the positioning of the glass worked? Or had Amanda actually been telling the truth?

'But you have *tried* to steal something from this chamber, haven't you? I saw you looking for it. You remember, don't you?'

'No,' Amanda repeated desperately. 'I told you, *no*. I don't know what . . . ' She stopped short, gasped. All three gauges swung madly back and forth.

'What was that?' Spragg asked, now loud and demanding.

'No!' Amanda spluttered tearfully.

Spragg cocked her head to the side. 'I don't think the Liar's Eyeglass believes you!'

Amanda's head jerked backwards. She made a strange high-pitched sound that set Marion's teeth on edge. Her entire body convulsed, her feet, her hands, her shoulders.

The chamber gasped. Several people got to their feet, perhaps outraged, or more likely intrigued to see what was happening.

Amanda writhed.

Marion removed the glass and fumbled to disconnect the cords. But Spragg shoved her to the side just as another jolt of electricity sizzled down from the battery to the cords and into Amanda. She jerked again, cried out. She was sweating, her mouth agape, horrible wheezing sounds coming from her chest.

'Now, Delia, please,' Nicholas urged nervously, shuffling to Amanda's side. 'I don't think we should continue this. Perhaps there's a better way . . .'

But Spragg was delirious with rage, hissing into Amanda's ear as she pressed the contraption to her eye so firmly, the brass rim left an indentation on her cheek. 'I know it was you!'

'Stop!' Marion pleaded, seizing Spragg by the arm. 'Stop!' The glass slipped, clanged against the floor.

A quick silence. Nicholas gripped Spragg's arm, muttered something to her in an urgent breath. She glowered at him, then turned back to Marion and Amanda.

'Out of my sight,' she said through clenched teeth. 'Both of you. Out of my sight! Now!'

Marion hurried to unhinge Amanda from the chair and disconnect the cords.

Spragg whipped around to face the chamber. 'And the rest of you, go! We'll resume the inquisition as soon as I've gathered more . . . information.'

Marion took Amanda's hands. She was still trembling, her face grey.

'I'm sorry,' she breathed in her ear. 'I'm so sorry.'

Amanda pulled away from her. The look on her face was hard to read – something dark and unexpected.

'Just breathe,' Marion continued. 'Breathe. You'll be all right.'

She waited for the blood to filter back into Amanda's face and for Spragg and Nicholas to move off.

'I'm afraid,' Amanda muttered, barely comprehensible. '*Please*, Marion. They're . . . ' Her eyes darted to the back of the chamber.

Proctor was lingering there, his arms crossed, a scowl on his face.

'Please,' Amanda continued to urge. 'I helped you, now do this for me.'

Marion looked up to make sure no one was listening. 'Helped me? What are you talking about?' She gasped as it dawned on her. The letters. Her informer. She looked over her shoulder. Proctor had disappeared. 'All right, listen,' she whispered as quietly as she could, forcing Amanda to lean in. 'I can't forge a registration warrant for that Tranquilliser Pin. There's no chance that would work.' She nodded to herself, decision made. 'But I'll steal one for you.'

17

Body Count

Fraser Henley crossed the bookshop, made his way down through the trapdoor. It was a Saturday afternoon and although his apprenticeship duties at Miss Brickett's were over for the week, his other duties had just begun.

He stepped out of the lift as it shuddered to a halt, walked eastwards down the Grand Corridor, narrowly dodging Mr Nicholas, who seemed to loiter perpetually outside the library. It wouldn't be a particular trouble if anyone saw him at the agency now, even though he'd told everyone he was going down to Dorset to visit his sister (who didn't exist). But it would seem awry, at least to someone who'd been paying attention to his whereabouts and behaviour the past few months. And awry was the absolute last adjective he wished to be associated with.

Unfortunately, he did bump into someone. The person he'd least hoped to see.

'Amanda,' he said, inclining his head in greeting.

She was already scowling at him, her bare face ragged, drawn, nothing like the woman he'd admired when he first arrived at Miss Brickett's. He'd liked her then. Definitely not love, but something between lust and curiosity. He found her difficult to read, conceited and a bit crazy – exactly how he fancied his women. Things were very different now.

'I thought you'd gone home for the weekend,' said Fraser.

She crossed her arms. Were her hands trembling? He thought so. It had been the same the last few times they'd interacted – a strange mix of anger and fear that she seemed to emit. Obviously, her behaviour towards everyone had soured dramatically since yesterday evening and the Liar's Eyeglass testing spectacle.

'And I thought you went to visit your sister,' said Amanda.

Neither replied to the other's question. Fraser drew the moment out, hoping it would convince Amanda to leave. It didn't work.

'What does she want?' she blurted.

Her voice shook, tears welled. She'd never looked so terrible or desperate.

'Sorry?'

'The inquisitions. Spragg. What's she looking for? Is it really money?'

'How would I know?' Fraser lied, keeping his breath level. 'But whatever it is, she's not going to stop until she finds it, that's obvious.'

Amanda glanced over her shoulder. Someone had opened a door down the corridor. She seemed even more concerned than Fraser that they might be overheard. But still, she didn't move. Fraser looked at his watch. He had to hurry, get her out of the way. He pulled his trump card.

'I overheard you talking to Marion at the ERPS meeting.'

That threw her. She opened her mouth but said nothing.

Fraser continued. 'You asked her to get hold of a Tranquilliser Pin. Don't you think that might get you in trouble?'

Amanda took a while to compose herself. Again, Fraser could see the two sides of her character warring with each other. One was afraid. One was furious. But he knew which would win. She glared at him and left. Finally.

Fraser was mildly disturbed by the interaction. But he had far more pressing matters to concern himself with. He slipped quietly through the ever-winding passageways that broke off from the Grand Corridor until he came to the one that was barricaded but had been partially disassembled. He ducked underneath and continued onwards until he arrived at the East Eight Chamber.

He stepped inside. The floor was scattered with silk banners that had fallen from the wall, a chair and table knocked on their side. The place smelled like stale sweat and fear – Amanda's, mostly.

He retrieved the telephone he'd nicked from storage a few months ago and plugged it into the wall. It wasn't the most suitable method of communication, but it was a hell of a lot better than a rendezvous above ground, especially now.

He picked up the receiver, then put it down quickly. Could the rumour be true, that Nancy and Frank had bugged all the agency telephones? But not this one, surely . . . He'd kept it very well hidden, when not in use, and anyway, he'd scoured the chamber and telephone for bugs every few days. The space was minimally furnished, which meant there was almost nowhere to hide a listening device. But you could never be too careful. He'd even tried to use one of those nifty Wire Catchers to weed out any well-hidden bugs, but despite having observed the second-year's SpyCraft lecture where the contraption was demonstrated, he still hadn't quite got the hang of it.

After scanning the walls and telephone three times over, he breathed a sigh of mild relief, picked up the receiver and dialled.

The line went quiet for a second. Fraser twitched with unease.

'Is it secure?' came a hushed foreign accent.

'Yes.'

'Ah, well then. Good afternoon, Mr Henley. Good of you to call at last.'

Good of you to call? As if he had a choice in the matter.

There was another pause, longer this time. The line crackled.

'Any updates?' the Florist drawled.

Fraser took a moment to reply. There were lots of things he could tell the old man – trivial things such as the quiz night and string of propaganda that followed, which was intended to encourage agency members to join the ERPS but instead had only created vast swathes of chaos and distrust. He wasn't sure the Florist would be happy about this. The ERPS was entirely that idiot Spragg's idea. He suspected it was her way of controlling the High Council and Miss Brickett's, ensuring the various light orbs, skeleton keys and miscellaneous gadgets could be produced and shipped from the Workshop to Moscow, no questions asked. But the fiasco was now very much out of hand, the ERPS an untameable beast set loose. The propaganda and false news, the agency rotting from the inside, Spragg driven mad by her power-hungry agendas. Meanwhile, the most impor-tant shipment of all had disappeared. And Fraser was being punished for it.

He clenched his fist, considering the innumerable ways he'd failed. The whole purpose of his recruitment had been to keep an eye on Spragg, clean up any mess she created and deal with anyone who got in her way. He'd botched his second (and very likely his last) chance and proved himself truly unworthy. He knew what was coming next.

'Mr Henley?' the Florist cooed maliciously. 'Have you fallen asleep? I asked you a question.'

'I don't know where it is,' Fraser spat, unable to hold off the tremor in his voice any longer. 'Spragg is trying to find out what happened, but there's not much I can do. You told me to make sure she doesn't identify me.'

'Yes, I see your dilemma. However, I wasn't asking you where the shipment is.' A pause, a long sigh. 'I'm due a body, aren't I?'

Fraser curled his damp fingers tightly around the receiver. His heart was thumping so fiercely now, he could hardly take a breath. He obviously knew it hadn't worked, the trap he'd set in Gadgetry, the fragile platform and array of tools below. It was a pathetic attempt, but the only one he could think of at the time. 'Yes, I . . . I tried, but—'

'Tried?' the Florist cackled. 'Oh dear, young man. We don't use that word in this business, do we? It's been four days, Mr Henley.'

Fraser held the telephone a few inches from his ear and closed his eyes. He might not be in immediate danger, down here, several miles below the streets. But he was under no false illusions as to what would happen to him if he didn't convince the old man he was worthy of keeping alive. Again.

His mind filled with grisly images – the Florist's branding iron, a rose singed into flesh. It wasn't death he feared, but all that would come before.

'You know the rules,' the old man continued. 'Spragg hands over what's mine, or you hand over a body.' Fraser tried to interrupt, but the Florist spoke over him. 'Now, since neither of you have done as I asked, I'm afraid I must increase the toll.' He waited, only because he knew the pause would turn Fraser's stomach thrice over. 'Two bodies, if I haven't got the shipment by Tuesday. Do we understand each other?'

Fraser saw it then, clear and pristine in his mind. He'd been mulling over an escape plan for weeks, plotting a way he could extricate himself from the horrors the Florist would inflict upon him should things turn sour.

He turned to look at the satchel he'd already packed – there was a bottle of water, a few items of clothing, some money, fake identity papers. He could do it – he was almost sure. He just had to get the timing right.

'Absolutely,' he said in reply, his voice breaking, though not with fear this time. Purpose.

18

Final Warning

Spring loomed in London. The pale sun turned to gold, the skies swelled with humidity and the scent of ripened earth filled the air. But below the streets, winter endured. An icy darkness stretched through the corridors, its fingers suffocating the light, unravelling the shadows.

It was Sunday, two days since the incident in the East Eight with the Liar's Eyeglass. Several employees (mostly non-ERPS) were gathered in Regent's Park for Bill's twenty-fifth birthday. The group settled beneath a large birch tree whose leaves shivered in the breeze as finches and sparrows called from their perches above. Marion settled next to Bill while Jessica, Maud and Preston lounged on a picnic blanket a little further off. Marion's ever-present chaperone, Ambrosia Quinn, hovered a few yards away.

At a glance, everyone seemed perfectly untroubled, but Marion knew they all felt it – the tremor in their foundations. Rumour of Spragg's violent inquisition had been unleashed and a low rumble of unease carried in the air like a threatening storm. Money had been stolen from the Gadgetry Department. There was a thief among Miss Brickett's and Spragg would track them down, one way or another. But the worst of it was that most agency employees, who were now ERPS, actually seemed to *want* the inquisitions to continue. *The thief must be unmasked*, they uttered, nodding to one another, a righteous mob. And although Marion had told Frank what had happened at the East Eight immediately afterwards, he'd been strangely reserved, unsurprised. She'd watched him warm his hands by the Games Room fire, thoughts taking shape in his mind. 'What do we do now?' she'd asked, to which he'd answered in a deadpan voice: 'We wait, just a little longer.'

Now, Marion looked over Bill's shoulder. Amanda was sitting near the lake, alone, her back to everyone. It had been this way since her inquisition. Physically, she'd recovered from what could only be described as her torture session. But emotionally, psychologically, something grim had come over her.

Yes, Marion would do as Frank asked. She'd wait. But to do absolutely nothing in the interim seemed foolish. Spragg's inquisitions would surely resume on Monday and Marion feared Amanda would be put under the Liar's Eyeglass again. And so, without overthinking it, Marion kept her promise, stole a Tranquilliser Pin from the Workshop and handed it to Amanda. During the hushed exchange outside the library late last night, Marion hoped to confirm a theory: 'You're the one who's been sending me those letters, aren't you?'

Amanda's eyes had flashed wildly. She'd snatched the pin from Marion's hand.

'Leave me alone. Just leave!' she'd snarled, then disappeared before Marion could say anything more.

She considered trying again, perhaps today in the park, but guilt and fear and a dreadful sense of foreboding told her this was a bad idea. Spragg was sure to be watching everything Amanda did and any awry behaviour or interactions would put both her and Marion in further danger. Whatever Amanda's purpose in sending the letters had been, she'd have to wait until things cooled to find out.

Marion bit her lip, pushed the memory aside. She handed Bill an ale and plate of snacks: vanilla muffins, several slices of cheese, crackers, some cold hams.

'Happy birthday.'

'Thanks,' he said, trying to smile. 'I thought you weren't allowed to speak to me alone?'

Marion nodded at Quinn, still hovering nearby. 'We're each other's chaperones, I think. Thankfully, she doesn't seem to take her role too seriously. Besides, I hardly think Spragg's going to jump out of the bushes and scold me.' There was an awkward pause. 'I have something for you.' She opened her bag and pulled out a gift, wrapped in white tissue paper.

Bill tore apart the wrapping, revealing a chrome bookmark engraved with his initials and adorned with a teardrop light on one end. He turned it over, a smile playing on his lips.

'It's a normal bookmark – I just added the light. It switches on automatically when it's dark. And the battery is a spare from our expensive collection in Gadgetry, so it should last a long while.'

'Blimey, it's brilliant. Thank you,' he gushed at last, though Marion still sensed a note of reluctance in his voice.

He slumped back against the birch tree, the bookmark in his hands, staring wistfully at the branches above. He'd been so withdrawn since their argument, not just with her but with everyone. She wondered what he thought about in those long moments of solitude and silence, what he hoped for. She believed she knew him better than anyone (at least anyone at Miss Brickett's), and yet there were times when he seemed so caught up in his own world, so absorbed in things he didn't speak of, that she wondered if perhaps there was a side to Bill she knew nothing about.

'Twenty-five, eh?' he said quietly to himself, taking another sip of ale and placing the bookmark in his haversack.

Marion followed his line of sight. Golden light beamed through the boughs above, flooding the leaves as if from within. She watched a finch hop carelessly through the branches and imagined for a moment what it must be like not to think, or have to feel, to be impervious to your memories and mistakes. The human mind was so often a chasm of pain and regret. A gift no doubt, but an inescapable curse, too.

'Do you think you'll move into the agency next year?' she asked, the question sprouting from the notion that having Bill around more often might dull the nagging sense she couldn't shake that an eternal darkness lingered within Miss Brickett's corridors.

'I suppose. Derek's leaving after Christmas and I can't afford the rent on my own,' he said, referring to his cousin with whom he'd shared a flat in the East End for as long as Marion had known him. Unlike many of the apprentices at Miss Brickett's, Bill's parents were both still alive. They lived somewhere in the North of England, though he hardly ever visited or spoke of them. Apparently, they'd cut him from their lives after he left home at eighteen. It was a touchy subject, Marion realised, and she never pressed him for further information. She knew all too well what it was like to have a difficult family and a fractured history.

'It'll be nice to have you there. It takes a bit of getting used to though, living almost permanently underground.' She laughed ironically.

Bill seemed to consider this for a long while. 'Do you miss it ever? Your old life. Before Miss Brickett's, I mean?'

Marion dialled her memory back to that first day, at the beginning of last year, when she was recruited, taken down through the bookshop trapdoor into the Grand Corridor, with its glittering marble floors and vaulted ceiling. She'd stepped into the Gadgetry Department and laid eyes on Professor Bal's vast array of improbable gadgets, aware that this was where she'd spend the rest of her working life, surrounded by things she understood and people who were misfits just like her. Did she miss what her life had been before that? She didn't think so. And yet, the reality of being an apprentice Inquirer had so quickly darkened, as the shadows swooped in like vultures. Perhaps there was a small part of her that yearned for the ignorance of her pre-Miss Brickett's self, perhaps.

Bill looked as if he might say something else on the topic. Instead, he took another sip of ale and changed the subject.

'I feel like I've hardly seen you all week. You know Spragg cancelled all of my shifts in Gadgetry? She said my skills are better used elsewhere.' He snorted and mumbled something under his breath that sounded a lot like *bloody hag*. 'I think she probably doesn't want me to see what you're up to.'

Marion prickled. 'What *I'm* up to? Come on, it's not like that.'

Bill looked at her in a way that suggested he knew she was hiding something from him, though he didn't really want to know what. 'I don't know how you're managing with her.'

'I don't like her, you realise that, I hope?'

'I heard about Amanda's inquisition. Will there be more?'

'I don't know,' she lied. 'Probably not.'

Bill gave her a noncommittal shrug. 'And is it true that she's ordered a batch of spy snakes to patrol the corridors at night?'

Marion cocked her head, another rumour she hadn't heard about.

'Some of the third-years were talking about it,' he elaborated. 'They went for a stroll last night and bumped into one of the snakes.' He stopped, a muscle in his jaw twitched – a sign that he was holding back a wave of irritation almost certainly directed at her. 'You could have told *me* at least. It's not something I'd have liked to find out by accident.'

'I didn't know. And anyway, I thought you didn't want to talk about the ERPS.'

'I do if it's going to get me fired or killed. God knows what the purpose of those snakes are now.'

'I'm sorry, then,' Marion retorted. 'It's hard to keep up with what everyone wants and doesn't want. I have my own problems to deal with.'

Bill grunted. There was an awkward pause as he thought of something else to say. 'How's Bal coping with Spragg?'

The truth was that the professor had hardly emerged from his new office for nearly two weeks. And each time he'd looked pale, thinner and more haggard than ever. It had taken every ounce of Marion's reserve not to break down and admit how much she despised and disagreed with Spragg and the ERPS.

'He's really struggling. I wish I could do something.'

'You're doing more than enough already. And I don't think your infiltration of the ERPS—'

'Please, not this again.' Marion cut him off. 'I know you don't like it. I don't, either – it's been impossibly hard. What happened to Amanda . . . ' She broke off, swallowed back another wave of guilt. 'And on top of all that, I have to deal with you lot as well.' She gestured to Bill, then to Jessica and Maud sitting further off. 'Behaving as though I'm doing this just to spite you. But I trust Frank . . . '

Bill reacted to this with a subtle shake of the head. Marion decided to ignore it.

'Until he tells me to quit the ERPS, I'm going to stay on and make the best of it.'

She looked across the park, to the sea-green fields, the thicket of birch trees and their glittering reflections in the lake. She inhaled deeply through her nose, absorbing the clear spring air, the lightness and warmth of it, so at odds with the dim world she was accustomed to – a world others might find cold and unwelcoming but which she loved as if it were a living thing. She thought back to something Edgar Swindlehurst had said to her last year (just before he tried to kill her) about the way the twisted tunnels of Miss Brickett's can feel so much like home one moment and prison the next. She wondered if this transmutation would ever begin for her, or if it already had.

This memory unravelled another and tears filled her eyes.

'Mari?' Bill shuffled closer, placed an arm over her shoulder, all trace of anger replaced with concern. 'What is it?'

'*Everything*, Bill,' she said, choking up. 'Do you remember what we promised each other last year after we went into the tunnels beyond the Border and you told me everything you'd been keeping from me about David and the map?'

Bill shifted himself so that he was sitting directly opposite her. 'Yeah, of course I do. We said no more secrets.' He smiled a little. 'Even when it's hard. We tell each other everything.'

Marion nodded. 'I suppose I've broken that promise. I don't even know why. Maybe because I didn't think you'd want anything to do with what's been happening. Maybe because I thought you'd point things out I didn't want to be reminded of. But I can't keep it from you any more. It's destroying me. And I really don't know what to do . . . ' She trailed off.

'I know, I mean . . . I don't know what it is you've been hiding, but I've known there was something since, well, a while. It's my fault, too, Mari. You're right. I didn't really *want* to know. That's the truth of it. I could tell you were struggling with the ERPS, and I didn't press you because I was just so tired of the problems and drama. I didn't want to know.' He took a long breath. 'But I do now.'

A storm cloud moved in, the sky transforming to silver-grey. A tree nearby swayed as a brisk wind picked up from the north. Marion waited for the last of the partygoers to gather their things and leave. Even Quinn. Once they were alone, she told Bill everything – about her mysterious informer whom she now believed to be Amanda, about the 'accident' in Gadgetry that had almost got her killed, about *The Truths*.

Bill seemed to struggle with himself for a moment. And then he laughed.

'What on earth could be funny?' she quipped, caught off guard by this unlikely reaction.

Bill shook his head and waved his hands apologetically. 'No, it's just that last part. Ambrosia Quinn saved your life? Bloody hell, that's brilliant.'

Marion couldn't help but grin a little. 'If you say so.'

'I mean, you can't ever have a go at her again for being pedantic. You're only alive because she is!'

'All right. Enough of that!' Marion laughed, her chest swelled. To see Bill carefree again, even for a fleeting moment, to laugh with him – it made all the difference.

'Anyway, about the rest of it . . . ' He ruffled his hair in an agitated manner. 'About *The Truths*...'

'Some of it really *is* true,' Marion blurted. 'I asked Nancy about White's body and she admitted that they dumped it in the Thames.'

She let out a breath, for the first time realising just what a relief it was to voice her concerns. She trusted Frank with her life, she did. And yet she'd been unable to dismiss entirely the suggestion that there were, or had been, happenings at Miss Brickett's that the High Council kept a secret from everyone. It wouldn't be the first time.

'Yeah,' Bill said easily. 'Look, there *are* things the High Council keeps from us. Of course there are. Professor Bal was an illegal immigrant. White's body was dumped in the Thames. The Holding Chambers are real. Who knows what else. But that doesn't mean you should trust the ERPS by default. Spragg is trying to make you afraid, turn you against the people you love. She wants you to think the ERPS is on your side and everyone else is just lying to you, tricking you. That's how these things work. If you want to control and coerce someone, you first have to isolate them, make them believe everything they knew before was a lie, everyone they trusted has or will betray them.'

Marion mulled this over. She *had* almost turned against Frank and Nancy after Spragg showed her the newspaper clipping. And it only took one ERPS meeting. And even now, even though she *knew* she'd been manipulated, a fragment of doubt remained, unbidden, inexorable. She shook her head as though to dispel the thought.

'And what about Amanda? Do you think I'm right in assuming she's my informer?'

Bill paused to think. 'I don't know. Could be, I suppose, but the only problem is, how the hell did she know all that stuff? The answer to the bonus question at the quiz I can understand, though I've no idea why she'd want to tell *you*. But the rest of it? About one of the recruits not being trustworthy. Blimey . . . ' Bill interrupted himself. 'I just remembered something Jessica said a while back.' He looked off into the distance for a second. 'She was convinced Amanda and Proctor had . . . you know, cavorted in the bed linen.'

'Really? Are you sure?'

Bill shrugged. 'I'm not sure. But that's what Jessica suggested. So maybe that's who she got all her information from.' The first drops of rain had started to fall. Bill looked up and sighed. 'Another beautiful day in London, eh?' He stood, pulling Marion to her feet. 'Listen, I've got to stop by my house for a bit. It's the only day of the year Derek wants anything to do with me. I can't miss it.'

Marion laughed. 'Tell him I say hello.'

'Will do. And, Mari . . . ' Creases formed around his eyes, softening his expression. 'I'll be back at the agency tomorrow morning and we'll figure all this out. Together. I promise.'

She planted a kiss on his cheek, waved him off, then made her own way through Clarence Gate. But instead of heading towards the agency, she turned east.

It was pelting by the time she arrived at 16 Willow Street. She removed a set of rusted keys and unlocked the front door.

The hallway was barren and musty. The rug at the bottom of the staircase seemed to have aged a decade. It had been nearly six months since she'd last visited the battered flat she'd once shared with her mother and then her grandmother. It had also been about six months since she'd heard anything from Dolores. According to her latest letter, she was now happily settled in Ohio with Marion's cousins, Reginald and Erin.

But now that Marion was back at Willow Street, she felt that familiar twinge of the past, of frayed memories and the old self she'd left behind the day she joined Miss Brickett's. She wasn't quite sure why she'd wanted to come back today. Maybe because of what Bill had asked, about whether or not she missed the life she'd had before. Perhaps she needed a reminder of what it had been like, cloistered here in Willow Street, alone and desperate. Or perhaps it was because of what she'd recalled Swindlehurst saying – about the hold Miss Brickett's had on everyone who worked there.

She wandered through the hall and up the stairs to her old bedroom. The wardrobe stood with its doors pulled open. The bed was unmade, the sheets crumpled and ruined from the damp that leaked in perpetually through an array of holes in the ceiling. She lay down on the bed. It creaked beneath her weight and a plume of dust lifted. Even so, she fell asleep almost instantly.

When she woke, it was just before 5 a.m. She hadn't intended to spend the night, but it was a relief to wake to sunlight streaming in through the windows rather than an alarm clock.

She reached into her bag for a handkerchief.

Instead, however, her fingers touched something coarser. Her heart rate piqued even before she'd lifted the envelope from her bag.

She ripped open the sleeve and pulled out the letter inside.

Marion,

It's been a while, hasn't it?

Anyway, there's something I think you'd like to know, something I discovered a while back. Forgive me for taking so long to get this message over to you, but I needed time to gather further information.

It appears the Florist is upset and from what I understand, two people are going to die because of it. The first death was supposed to happen on Thursday, something that might have looked like an accident. But for reasons I'm unaware of, this 'accident' was avoided.

Regardless, a death will occur on Monday morning at exactly five minutes past eight. And the second murder? Well, I'll tell you when I see you.

Do come along and we'll have a chat, face to face at last.

This time, however, I'll need something in return.

Bring your leather roll of tools.

19

Illegal in London

Marion was delirious with terror, but she pushed it aside. There wasn't time.

She'd made it to the bookshop, through the trapdoor, into the Grand Corridor. The journey had taken her less than an hour and had been a blur. She couldn't yet formulate theories or connect the dots of everything she knew. But one thing was clear enough: someone was going to die that morning.

'Steady on, darling!' Jessica said as Marion collided with her at the end of the Grand Corridor. Jessica righted herself and looked up. It took her less than a second to realise there was something wrong. 'What's going on?'

'Has Amanda arrived yet?' Marion asked abruptly, ignoring Jessica's question.

'I'm not sure. What's the matter?' Jessica repeated. 'You look a fright.'

Marion pulled her hair from her face, shook her head in frustration. She had a strong suspicion that everything was going to unravel within the next twenty-four hours. The ERPS's hold over Miss Brickett's had reached a tipping point and either there was going to be an uprising from the rest of the agency, or something worse would push the situation over the edge.

A murder, quite possibly.

'I'm afraid, too, Mari,' Jessica admitted after a moment's silence, glancing left and right over her shoulder. 'People are saying things. Spragg has taken over. Everyone seems to think Nancy and Frank have stolen the money. What if they're fired or forced to leave?' She didn't wait for an answer. A clink of metal echoed through the corridor. 'We really shouldn't linger here. You're not supposed to talk to me and . . . the snakes . . . ' She trailed off. 'I'm going to the common room. Will you come? At least we won't be alone.'

Marion didn't know what to say. Someone was going to die and she was certain it would happen here, at Miss Brickett's. She needed to speak to Frank. She needed to speak to Amanda. But traipsing around the agency now *did* seem like a bad idea. And could she leave Jessica alone? Would she be the victim? What about Bill? Kenny? Maud? Preston? She wished she could gather everyone she loved together and watch over them. But there just wasn't time.

'Listen,' she said, coming to a rushed conclusion, 'something horrible is going to happen here at five minutes past eight.' Jessica went deathly pale, but Marion didn't comfort her. She went on hurriedly. 'Make sure you're not alone at that time or doing anything . . . dangerous. Okay?'

'I don't understand.'

Marion was breathless now. 'Just promise me, Jess! Stay in the common room with the others.'

Jessica faltered, then nodded slowly as Marion took her hand. 'Okay, okay. I promise. But wait, where are you going?'

'To fix this.'

She kissed her on the cheek. Her lovely, beautiful Jess. She wouldn't allow herself to imagine what it would be like to lose her. She wasn't going to let that happen.

'Marion?' Frank appeared weary-eyed at the door to his night room.

Marion had never visited him here before but was eager to get inside, or at least away from the winding corridors. There was nothing but shadows ahead and yet she was certain she could hear it, the distinctive schlink-schlink that sent a shiver of recognition through her. Without visual confirmation, she was certain – the spy-snake patrol was nearby.

Frank's gaze travelled to the stack of letters and torn envelopes in her hand. He seemed instantly on edge, but Marion wondered if it were solely because of her early morning visit, or the strange shuffling, slinking sound driving down from the western tunnel.

'What's going on?' he asked, perhaps to both.

Gooseflesh rose on Marion's arms. A draft whipped up from somewhere behind her, as if something had swept past. 'Can we speak in your office?'

Frank looked over his shoulder at the clock on his bedside table, then briefly past Marion and down the corridor. 'Give me half an hour and—'

'No. It has to be now!' Her tone was shrill and urgent, close to tears or delirium or both.

Frank relented, pulled a robe over his nightclothes and they began a painfully slow walk to his office on the other side of several convoluted corridors. Marion was numb – her limbs, her body. Only her mind seemed alert. At one point, Frank placed an arm across her chest, bringing her to a halt. He tilted his head to the side, listening. Marion could hear it too, the methodical clink-schlink of scales. They stood there for at least five minutes, still as statues, waiting for something to slither past. But when nothing did, they continued their journey in peace.

'Marion, there's a lot going on at the moment,' Frank said as they entered the office. 'I think we have to . . . ' He stopped, eyed the letters again, which she'd placed in the centre of the desk between them. 'What are those?'

Marion began to explain, as thoroughly and speedily as she could, making sure she included everything – the letters, even the near fatal 'accident' in the Gadgetry Department.

When she'd finished, Frank dropped his head into his hands for a moment. Thankfully, he didn't ask her the most obviously pressing question: why was she only telling him this now? He reached forwards and read each of the letters in turn.

'And you're certain it's Amanda who's been sending you these?'

This was the part Marion had been struggling with since she'd left Willow Street.

'No. I suppose I'm not. Not any more. It doesn't make sense if it is her, but it doesn't really make sense if it's not, either.' She inhaled quickly. Her chest was struggling to expand. She knew she wasn't making sense. 'I was convinced it was Amanda after what happened in the East Eight with the Liar's Eyeglass. She said she'd *helped me*. I assumed that meant she'd been sending me the letters for my own good. Problem is, it doesn't make complete sense. For starters, how did Amanda know all the things she told me? Some of the information had nothing to do with the ERPS and most of it was quite random. Also, this one . . . ' She picked up the last letter and read a part of it out loud: '. . . *do come along and we can have a chat, face to face at last*. What does that mean, face to face at last? I see Amanda in person nearly every day.'

Frank eyed the letter. 'Do you believe it's a warning? Or a threat?'

'I don't know. It could be either. It depends if it's from Amanda or not.' Frank didn't look terrified enough, so Marion elaborated. 'I know it seems ludicrous, someone dying at exactly five minutes past eight, but after what happened in the Gadgetry Department—'

'This one,' Frank said, pointing to the letter Marion had received before the Miss Brickett's quiz night. He frowned. '*The answer is string.* What does that mean?'

'It was an answer to the bonus question at the ERPS quiz night.'

'The correct answer?' Frank asked tentatively.

It seemed he was the only member of Miss Brickett's who hadn't heard of Marion's illustrious – and bizarre – win against Team ERPS.

'Yes.'

'So that was a play to get you to believe whatever they claimed next,' he said, nodding to himself.

'Well, it worked. Which is why I'm here. We have to do something, Frank.' She looked at her watch. It was already seven o'clock. 'Before it's too late.'

Frank got up and began to pace, muttering inaudibly to himself. Marion picked her nails as she waited for him to come up with a solution. She wondered what he'd been doing all this time, since Friday evening, since she'd told him about the inquisition in the East Eight. He'd promised her everything was under control, and yet things were so much worse now. She decided she had to ask.

'People are saying Spragg has control. Over everything. Is it true? What are you doing about it? Why aren't you stopping her?'

'We're trying, Marion. You must understand, our power is dwindling, especially now that Spragg has convinced everyone a large sum of money has been stolen from them. By me or

Nancy.' He averted his gaze, muttered something Marion only caught half of: '. . . mistake, it seems.'

Marion twisted in her seat, trying to clear her head. 'But on Friday, you said you had a plan.'

'We did. We do. Nancy and I were hoping we'd be able to draw out Spragg's conspirators this weekend. I just didn't think it would lead to this.'

He turned to her as if he had just realised something, then moved over to the filing cabinet. He retrieved a file and placed it on the desk.

Marion could hardly bear the anticipation. The minutes seemed to be ticking by furiously and all the while, if the letter was to be trusted, someone at Miss Brickett's was about to take their final breath.

Frank looked at his watch, his expression registering panic. 'Did Hugo tell you what Redding uncovered about the case in Liverpool?'

'What? I mean, yes but . . . ' She blew out a frustrated breath. 'What are we going to do about the letter, Frank? We don't have time for anything else!'

He made a placatory gesture. 'Please, just listen. It's important you understand why I did it.'

He opened the file, ran a finger down a list of handwritten notes. Marion didn't have the breath to ask what he meant by *why I did it.*

'As Hugo mentioned, the woman who was found dead in a hotel in Liverpool was KGB, working undercover in England. The murder was handled by MI5, but Redding finally managed to glean some details on the case, which he passed on to me a few days ago. It appears the rose branding is associated with a division of the Russian state security police known as Directorate S, the department responsible for training Illegals.

He said he couldn't squeeze anything further from MI5, but it was enough to put me on the right track.'

Marion's brain was spinning, too much clutter, too many words. 'Illegals?'

'KGB spies posted to foreign countries without diplomatic cover. Generally civilians, trained to blend into society, gather intelligence and so forth. Once I knew this information, I sent a letter to a colleague of ours who has contacts within the Soviet Union. I asked if he knew anything about the rose branding. What it might mean. He wrote back immediately.

'Apparently, the head of one particular division of Directorate S was a man named Leonid Oblonsky. He was specifically responsible for running the section that trained Illegals posted to Britain. Oblonsky's history with the KGB has always carried a mark of supreme violence and control, notably his habit of branding KGB traitors with an English rose, specifically agents in his division who'd double-crossed him, and the Soviet Union, by turning to our side. It's believed the Florist marks these traitorous spies with a rose before death, thus they take their final allegiance to the grave.'

'You're saying the Florist is Leonid Oblonsky?' She didn't wait for an answer. 'Which means Eddie Hopper was a Soviet spy, too, who double-crossed the KGB.'

'Indeed. Eddie and his partner, who is one of our recruits. According to Redding, two British nationals have been on MI5's radar since August last year. Both were apparently recruited by the Florist, Oblonsky, several years back. He trained them in Moscow, then sent them on a series of missions throughout Europe. Their most prestigious operation began last year when they were posted to Milton Keynes, Buckinghamshire to pose as junior technicians in the communication centre.'

Marion felt a chill creep down her spine as the pieces fell slowly into place.

'Again, we don't have the full picture. My Russian contact was extremely helpful but also very aware that he was putting his life at risk with every word. He wanted to say as little as possible to lessen the blow of a double-cross if one came. Thus, the information I have is patchy and incomplete. However, putting together everything we've learned, I believe it only makes sense that these two Illegals – Eddie Hopper and our very own recruit – were sent to Hanslope Park in Milton Keynes, under the Florist's instruction, to collect intelligence on what surveillance equipment was being produced at the centre for MI5 and MI6.

'There's a rumour Hopper had second thoughts once he arrived at Hanslope. Perhaps he considered turning himself over to MI5 in exchange for clemency. The Florist must have caught wind of this, thus the rose marking and his painful death. The other spy, however, was forced to continue his mission.'

'Which would have led him here,' Marion concluded. 'You're saying you think that's what this is all about?'

Frank was hesitant to answer, maybe because he didn't understand the scope of what he'd discovered, or because he didn't want to accept it.

'Well,' he said at last, 'it makes sense, doesn't it? You see, the Soviets have always tried to procure scientific and technical information from Britain. It's a major part of their Cold War effort against us. You can't defeat your enemy if you don't understand the nature of their campaigns, the tools and methods they use to gather intelligence. But I'm afraid I think it's even more complex than that.

'The KGB don't just want to know what gadgets we produce for Hanslope Park, they want to arm their own spies with the same contraptions.' His gaze drifted to the bookshelf and the old clock facade wedged there. 'We've been supplying the British and American secret services with superior surveillance devices for more than a decade. It's not entirely unfair to say we make the best in the world. If Russia wanted an upper hand in intelligence gathering, shipping our gadgets to the KGB in Moscow would be the perfect solution.'

'Are you certain you're right?' It seemed pointless to be incredulous now, after all Frank had said. But the notion that she'd been interacting with a Russian spy all these months, helping them to navigate the tunnels, showing them Miss Brickett's every secret . . . She pressed her fingernails into her temples.

'It's as unbelievable to me as it is to you. But yes, I'm afraid Spragg's inquisition on Friday proved the theory.'

'I don't understand.'

'It's just a cover, Marion. Spragg has convinced the agency she's trying to find out who has stolen money from the Gadgetry Department. But it isn't money that's gone missing.'

'Oh . . . '

The Florist was KGB. One of the new recruits, too. Together, they were using Spragg to ship Miss Brickett's gadgets to Moscow. Chaos had been unleashed just days after the largest shipment had left the Workshop. The batch of Liar's Eyeglasses. Her throat dried up as it dawned on her, Frank's previous words reverberating in her head. *It's important you understand why I did it.*

'You have the shipment, don't you?'

'It all fell into place once you told me what Quinn had uncovered about the inventory lists and I learned what Redding had uncovered about the rose branding. But I had to be sure. I suspected the Liar's Eyeglass shipment wasn't going to Hanslope Park, after all, and I wanted to see what Spragg would do if the shipment vanished. The test worked and backfired at the same time. Spragg has turned the entire agency against Nancy and me, cultivating the seeds of doubt she'd sowed right from the beginning.'

'So where is it now? The shipment.'

His lips twitched, words held back. 'I'm afraid to tell you. If Spragg finds out you've spoken to me, she'll interrogate you.' He inclined his head slightly as though to indicate that what he was about to say next was worth taking note of. 'It's just a bit too close to home at the moment.'

Marion nodded dumbly. Was this code for something? She was too anxious to think it out just now. She looked at her watch. It was seven thirty – thirty-five minutes until someone died.

'Anyway, we can deal with Spragg and all that later. I have to speak to Amanda before it's too late.'

Frank reached for the letters on the table. 'Let me, please. This mess is all my fault.'

'She won't tell you anything,' Marion said impatiently, drawing the letters towards her. 'For whatever reason, she chose to send the letters to me. I'm certain I'm the only one she'll speak to.'

'Then at least take Hugo with you.'

She got to her feet and started for the door. Her legs felt like rubber. 'Yes, all right.'

'I'll call him and explain the situation to save time. He should be in Intelligence at the moment. By the time you get there, he'll be up to date. Amanda usually arrives for work around seven forty-five – you should catch her in the Grand Corridor. Find out what she knows and meet me back here. We'll take it from there.'

20

The Courier and The Informant

Marion slipped from Frank's office after he'd checked the corridor and given her the all-clear. She dashed silently down to the Intelligence Department, where Kenny was waiting.

'Frank's filled you in?' she asked breathlessly, ignoring the ache in her chest.

Kenny nodded, his eyes darting back and forth down the corridor, looking for eavesdroppers. 'I wish you'd told me about the letters, Lane. This is such a darn mess now.'

Marion pursed her lips. This being a rare opportunity for her to get a jab in when Kenny had no time to retaliate, she went for it. 'I might have done if you hadn't always been so preoccupied with your love life. Besides, I *did* tell you. My "secret admirer", remember?'

Bullseye, she thought, as he shook his head and grumbled. 'Anyway, you ready? Let's beat feet.'

Moments later, they were waiting furtively at the end of the Grand Corridor. No one else was around, though Marion couldn't shake the sense that they were being watched. She checked the time: seven forty-nine.

'Where is she?'

As she said it, the lift at the other end of the corridor shuddered and creaked and the doors split open. Amanda stepped out, catching sight of them immediately. She froze, stared for a moment, bewildered, then dashed back into the lift and pounded the control panel, urging the doors to shut.

'Stop her!' Marion screamed at Kenny.

He bolted down the corridor and dived through the lift doors just as they started to close. Amanda yelped as Kenny dragged her out and into a broom closet nearby. By the time Marion had caught up, Kenny had Amanda pinned against the wall.

'We know!' he spat, angrier than Marion had ever seen him. 'You've been sending Marion letters, manipulating her.'

This wasn't really true. Marion still wasn't sure the letters were from Amanda, but Kenny had insisted that the best way to get her to tell them the truth was to pretend they already knew most of it.

Amanda spluttered and hissed like a caged animal. 'Let me go! Let me go, you idiot!' She gasped for breath. Fury distorting her features, the pent-up emotions she'd been holding back ever since the demonstration with the Liar's Eyeglass now spilled forth all at once. She glared at Marion. 'Haven't you done enough already? Torturing me in the East Eight wasn't sufficient?'

Marion let the accusation hit her square on. It was out of context, but it was true. 'I'm sorry. I really am. The Liar's Eyeglass wasn't my idea. I didn't ever think they were going to use them on employees.'

Amanda snapped her teeth together, almost growling with rage. She wriggled some more, but her narrow build was no match for Kenny's bulky frame. He switched his grip to around her neck.

'Kenny! You're choking her. Let go!' Marion pleaded.

Kenny lessened his grip and fired off a rapid series of questions. 'Tell us what you were trying to achieve by sending Marion those letters. Tell us who's going to die. Tell us who you've been working with.' Amanda didn't reply, so Kenny went on: 'It's one of the new apprentices, isn't it? Which one?'

'You said you'd helped me,' Marion tried, taking over the questioning. 'At the end of Spragg's inquisition, remember?'

Amanda looked even more wretched now. She thrashed about with all of her strength, though she barely moved an inch. Eventually, she relented, nodding hastily.

'Fine, dammit!' she muttered. 'I'll tell you. I'll tell you. Just-let-me-go!'

Kenny released his hold at last. Amanda dropped to her knees, clutching her throat, gasping for breath.

She hauled herself upright, glared at Marion and Kenny. 'I sent the letters to Marion. Yes.' She touched the bracelet on her arm. 'But that's all. The letters weren't *from* me. I was told when and where to deposit them and to make sure I wasn't seen doing so, but nothing else.' She took a long breath. 'I don't know what you mean about someone dying, really, I have no idea.'

'Who told you to send them to me, then?' Marion asked, exasperated. 'Who are they from?'

Amanda didn't answer. She looked at Marion's watch and a strange expression crossed her face. Was it fear? Anger?

'Please, Amanda. We don't have time for this. We know Spragg is communicating with an agent from the KGB. They're after our gadgets and heaven knows what else. One of the new recruits is involved, too. Someone is going to die this morning. I don't know why. I don't know who. Help us understand. Before it's too late, *please*.'

Amanda looked up. 'The KGB? Soviets?' She wheezed, then laughed like a lunatic – high-pitched and hysterical.

Kenny squared his jaw, his arms twitching with rage. 'Don't play games with us, Shirley! If you sent Marion those letters, you must have known who they were from and what was written inside.'

She held up her hands in a plea of defence. 'I didn't! I swear.' She turned to Marion instead, perhaps sensing she had no chance of convincing Kenny of anything. 'You have to believe me. I'd never have been involved if I thought the ERPS was going to destroy Miss Brickett's. I thought they were helping, improving things. It was only much later, when I was already too deeply rooted to get out, that I realised they weren't all they appeared to be.

'I was offered a small pay rise to assist them with internal politics and logistics, but that was all. I never . . . ' She swallowed. 'I didn't know anything about Soviet involvement. The KGB? Come on, Marion, of course I didn't know that! And the letters . . . ' She hesitated. 'I had no idea they had anything to do with the ERPS.'

There were too many things Marion needed to understand to complete the puzzle. She closed her eyes briefly, picking out which were most urgent.

'A few days ago, I was working in Gadgetry with Quinn. Spragg had written in the shift book that the filter on the ventilation duct needed replacing. The task almost got me killed. Someone had sawed through the platform on the scaffolding and laid out a row of sharp tools on the workbench below.'

'What?' Kenny said, sounding both disturbed and reproachful. 'You didn't tell me that.'

Marion ignored him. 'I, or someone else, was supposed to be killed that afternoon. Do you have any idea why?'

'No. I mean . . . unless it was for me.'

Kenny cursed and started to pace.

Amanda eyed him warily, then continued. 'It's just . . . I have a feeling I'm in the way of a few people and things would be easier for everyone if I wasn't around any more. I suppose it started when I called things off with Jerome—'

'Longmore?' Marion said, slightly confused as she thought back to what Bill had told her about Amanda and Proctor's failed romance.

'Yes. I broke things off with him and started seeing Proctor for a bit. They didn't like each other anyway, but this created a bigger rift between them. Longmore wanted to cause trouble for Proctor, make him think we were still together. And it worked. Proctor was furious and I think that's why he . . . he showed me the caricature Spragg had drawn of me.'

Marion gritted her teeth. 'So the caricatures were her doing?'

'They were Spragg's handiwork, but they weren't solely her idea. The one of me, for example, I'm convinced it was Proctor's design.'

'I thought caricatures were only for non-ERPS members?' Kenny asked, still glaring and impatient.

'In the beginning, yes. But really, they were the ERPS's way of blackmailing anyone who didn't do as they were told. As I said, mine was truly awful, I can't . . . ' She steadied her voice. 'I-it showed me in a grotesque pose with Longmore, Proctor standing behind us with a sword plunged right through the both of us, skewering us together. Proctor showed it to me as a threat, I think, and told me to "watch my back". That was when I asked you for the Tranquilliser Pin, in case either Proctor or Longmore tried anything.'

'Right,' Marion said hurriedly. 'And what about the inquisition? Spragg asked if you'd stolen something. Why did she think you had?'

'That was your fault. I begged you for the Tranquilliser Pin at your first ERPS meeting. That was just hours after Proctor showed me the caricature. I was terrified and you were the only one I could think of asking. I thought you could forge Bal's signature, or at least steal a pin from storage.'

'I did, dammit. And it wasn't easy, let me assure you.'

Amanda went on as though she hadn't heard. '. . . but when you didn't right away, I decided to take matters into my own hands. A couple of days after that meeting, I went to the East Eight alone. I have a key, of course, so it was easy. I searched the place high and low until I found a collection of documents Spragg had signed. Being a High Council member, I knew her signature would be accepted on the registration warrant and I thought it would be easy enough forging it once I'd had a good look, but . . . she caught me.

'She'd left something behind and she came back to fetch it, right when I was in the middle of sifting through her things. I've never seen someone so furious. And scared, actually. I don't think she knew what I was actually looking for, but later on, after whatever it was that went missing, she became convinced I was the culprit.

'That's why the Liar's Eyeglass shocked me, I think. When Spragg asked if I'd stolen something, I said no. But it wasn't exactly true. I *had* tried to steal something, just not the thing she assumed.' Amanda faltered, rubbed her wrist, twisting an old bracelet she wore. She lowered her voice to a whisper. 'I lost it, you know. For five hours yesterday. I wonder . . . '

'What?' Marion leaned in, but Kenny cut her off.

'You still haven't answered our question. Who told you to send Marion all those letters?'

Amanda's eyes darted around the dark, cramped closet, as if she expected someone to pop up from behind the line of brooms. 'I was just the courier.'

Kenny gripped her by the blouse collar. 'Answer the darn question!'

'Harry. It was Harry.'

Marion and Kenny looked at one another.

'What?' Marion said. 'Harry, the barman?'

'Yes, yes,' Amanda answered hurriedly. 'I collected letters from him when he told me to and sent them on as instructed.'

Marion rubbed her temples. Harry – that old, quiet, nondescript long-time Miss Brickett's employee, who, as far as she knew, couldn't even spell? It couldn't be true.

'Harry asked you to hand the letters over to me?'

Amanda nodded dully.

'In exchange for what?'

Amanda shifted her footing, crossed her arms. 'Three months ago, just after the formation of the ERPS, I asked Harry for a supply of expensive alcohol from the library bar: Scotch, bourbon, vintage champagne. I thought the collection would secure my chances of joining the ERPS. I had every intention of paying Harry for the alcohol, but he offered to waive the cost in exchange for a favour. When he explained that all I'd have to do was slip some letters into your bag now and again and make sure you didn't see me, well, of course I agreed.'

Marion still wasn't convinced. She could believe Amanda would do something like that to bribe her way into the ERPS. What she couldn't wrap her mind around was the idea that Harry was the kingpin – Marion's secret, all-knowing informer.

' . . . so, you'll have to ask him,' Amanda concluded. 'I have no idea what the letters are for, or what they mean.'

'That's actually a great idea,' Kenny said immediately and with an edge of menace. 'I'll go and fetch Harry right now.'

Amanda's posture stiffened. 'Well . . . maybe we should—'

'No,' Kenny said easily but certainly. 'You aren't going anywhere and we're not delaying this.' He looked at Marion. 'Wait here with her. I won't be long.'

Kenny was gone before Marion or Amanda could get a word in edgeways. They stood together, so close that if either moved even an inch, they'd bump into one another. Amanda avoided eye contact, preferring to stare fixedly at her feet. Marion felt her breath catch in her chest as footsteps echoed in the Grand Corridor, closer, closer. The door to the broom closet swung open and Kenny stepped inside, pushing Harry before him.

'Right, old man,' Kenny said. 'Tell Lane what you just told me.'

Harry looked up at Amanda. She bit her lip and turned away. He then set his gaze on Marion and she realised it was the first time she'd ever really *looked* at him – his sunken black eyes, his crooked teeth and leathery skin. She waited for him to speak.

'I'm not the one who's been writing those letters,' he said in a raspy, cutting tone.

'Amanda said it was you!' Marion snapped.

'Aye,' Harry said, looking unperturbed by the accusation, 'it was me she got the letters from. But it wasn't me who wrote them.'

She waited for him to continue. She was tired of asking the obvious.

'Swindlehurst.'

'What?' Kenny looked at Marion.

'Why?' Marion asked, her voice unsteady.

'I don't know,' Harry said simply.

'How did he know all the things he told me?'

Harry shrugged and picked his dirty nails. 'It's complicated.'

'How is he getting the letters to you?' Kenny asked.

'That's also complicated.'

'Just tell us!' Marion snapped.

Harry took a step backwards. Kenny elbowed him in the ribs. Harry gasped, cursed and doubled over but recovered remarkably quickly when Kenny threatened to pummel him a second time.

He wheezed a little, then spoke. 'I oversee meals to the inmates at the Holding Chambers. There's a pulley system fitted into the kitchens — a little box that I use to lower plates, food, water and whatnot directly through the kitchen floor and' — he stamped the ground with his boot — 'down. That's how Swindlehurst and I have been communicating. He writes the letters and passes them up to me along with his dirty dishes. I reply with whatever he asks for.'

Marion decided not to bother asking how Swindlehurst had got hold of a pen and several sheets of paper or anything further about this odd pulley system she was hearing about for the first time. 'And what *does* he ask for?'

Harry rubbed his hands together anxiously. 'Information.'

He must have recognised the fury in Marion's eyes, because he raised his hand in a mollifying gesture and began to dig around in his trouser pocket. Eventually, he produced a small black box and handed it to her.

'What is that?' Kenny asked, craning his neck.

'A voice recorder,' Marion answered, turning the object over in her hand as she contemplated its significance. 'Of course. Hidden in the East Eight, I presume.'

'In a room behind it,' Harry said while casting his eyes around the space they were standing in. 'A tool room, a bit like this one. I'm the only person who uses it and definitely the only one who knows there's a broken water pipe that connects the two. I put the recorder in the pipe, nice and easy.'

'And then?' Marion urged.

'And then, after a week, I send the recorder down to Swindlehurst. After he's listened to it, he sends it back up and we start again. Sometimes, he sends a letter up with the recorder, which I hand to Amanda. That's it.'

'Right,' Marion said, taking a quick breath. There was an endless list of questions she needed answered – such as how all this had started in the first place – but they were running out of time. 'Why are you doing this for him?'

'Because he's my friend and I don't think it's right what happened to him.'

'Fine,' Marion said curtly. 'We can chat about morals and the facets of justice another time. The last letter you gave Amanda to send to me. It said someone is going to die. Who is it?'

Harry squirmed under her gaze. 'I-I don't—'

'You have to *think*. Who is it? Who's going to die?'

'I told you,' he shrieked, backing even further away. 'I put the recorder in the pipe and I leave. I don't eavesdrop, myself. I don't listen to the tapes and I don't read the letters Swindlehurst sends up for you.'

Amanda was crying now. Tears poured down her face. She began to sob violently.

Kenny turned to Marion. 'What now?' he whispered, leaving Amanda to whimper behind them.

'I don't know.' She checked her watch – six minutes to eight. She could feel how close it was, the grim abyss of dread and hopelessness and fear.

Kenny was about to say something but was interrupted by a strange gurgling sound. He cocked his head to the side. 'What is—'

The sound had transformed. It was no longer gurgling, but rather a horrid choking.

Marion and Kenny dived to the floor. Amanda was doubled over. Her lips already blue. Rivulets of foamy spittle leaked from the side of her mouth. Her eyes lolled back in her head. In the panic, Harry dashed from the closet, gone.

'Help! Someone, please!' Marion screamed.

Kenny ran after Harry.

Marion lifted Amanda to her knees. She didn't know what was happening. Was she choking? Was she having some sort of seizure?

'Amanda, please. Come on. *Come on! Breathe!*'

Amanda's face was purple. Her mouth stretched open in a hopeless attempt to draw air into her lungs.

'Oh, God!' Marion said as Amanda's last ounce of energy faded, leaving her limp and immobile.

She collapsed to the floor with a hideous, lifeless tumble.

It seemed liked an age before Kenny returned with the agency doctor and a small crowd of horrified, whispering onlookers. Marion didn't look up. She didn't move as the doctor and someone else crouched down, checked Amanda's limp body for signs of life.

There was no need for any confirmation, though. Amanda Shirley was very clearly dead.

21

Death Pin

Marion lay on her bed, staring at the cracked grey ceiling, watching the shadows from her gas lamp flicker and drift. A deadened ache had settled in her chest, her thoughts jumbled.

Amanda's body had been removed from the broom closet and taken somewhere to be disposed of, forgotten, disgraced. She hoped not dumped in the Thames. Her family would be told she hadn't turned up for work today and nothing more. But like most of those who'd been recruited to Miss Brickett's, Amanda's family was sparse and distant and their questions, if any came, would be a minor inconvenience.

Without instruction, everyone had returned to their rooms, offices or the common spaces. No one was sure what would happen next. Earlier, the corridor outside had been filled with voices, sobs, a shuffle of limbs as someone – Marion was too weary to discern who – was apprehended, taken away. For questioning? Counselling?

But now, a sickening lull hung in the air, the shrill quiet of a churchyard.

Marion breathed deep and slow, but it did little to keep the demons at bay, now snapping and slavering at her heels. If she closed her eyes, she was plagued with flashes of Amanda's face, her dead, staring eyes, tear-stained cheeks. She didn't know how it had happened, or what exactly had killed Amanda. She didn't want to think about it, or the fact that she'd failed. And worse still, she knew Amanda wouldn't be the last.

Eventually, she pulled herself from under the covers, swaying with fatigue. She would have liked to fall into a dreamless sleep, but her mind was growing restless, congested with what-ifs and maybes. She needed something useful to do. She ripped off the white cotton blouse and grey skirt she'd been wearing since the day before, both rank with sweat, the blouse blotched with yellow stains near the collar where she'd held Amanda as she'd choked. Even her silver apprentice badge was smudged with something red and sticky. She wiped it clean, pulled on a pair of trousers, a clean blouse, picked up the black box from her bedside table – the voice recorder Harry had given her – and dismantled the backing. As she'd expected, however, the tape inside had already been removed. Swindlehurst.

She cursed, stumbled over to the basin, washed her face and neck, scrubbed her nails until they were raw. Her reflection was miserable, pathetic. Pallid and drawn like a wax figurine. She opened the door and stepped into the corridor outside. It was quiet, though it was already the middle of the day. She lumbered across to the common room, not for any particular reason. She just needed to be elsewhere. And not alone.

It was the most crowded she'd ever seen the place. In fact, short of counting, Marion was certain that nearly every Miss Brickett's apprentice was present. But not Kenny. She scanned the room twice over as she entered. A low rumble of voices rose. Some of her colleagues stared blatantly, some even scowled. Others squirmed awkwardly in their chairs, turning away as if merely looking her in the eye was bad luck. Quite probably true, all things considered.

Bill, Jessica, Preston and Maud were seated in their usual spot near the fireplace and, after a moment of hesitation, Marion joined them.

Jessica was staring blankly at the grate, her face paper white, streaked with mascara. Preston was comforting her while Maud and Bill watched Marion settle. No one said a thing.

Marion wanted everything to be over, though she knew it had only just begun. She looked again across the common room, avoiding the sea of biting glances as best she could. 'Where's Kenny?'

'He's being kept—' Bill stopped short, realising something. 'Mari,' he added with an awful whimper, as if he were about to tell her more bad news, which was surely impossible. 'There's something I'm supposed to give you . . . ' He looked at his hands, which Marion now realised held a crumpled letter.

With trembling fingers, he handed it over.

A wave of dizziness flooded through her, reading the letter, everyone watching.

High Council Order A34I. Miss M. Lane for Tribunal.
Date: 15 April 1959.
Time: 8 p.m.
Transgression: Suspected murder.
Signed: Delia Spragg

Marion stared blankly at the paper, her thoughts whirling, heart rapping.

'Kenny and Harry are being kept away from you,' Bill explained at last, 'until your tribunal tomorrow evening. As witnesses, you know.'

Marion couldn't process this, nor the letter in her hand. She read it again: *Suspected murder. Tribunal.*

Maud groaned impatiently. 'Amanda died from a dose of shellfish poison, Marion.' Her tone was brash and accusatory.

Marion opened her mouth. Everything was a mess. Nothing made sense. All she could think to say was: '*How?*'

'Why don't you tell us?' Maud snapped.

'Excuse me?'

Bill gripped Marion's hand. 'Nicholas found an unregistered Tranquilliser Pin concealed in a bracelet Amanda was wearing when she died. He said there was no way she should have been able to get hold of one. And, eh, the pin wasn't loaded with a tranquilliser like it should have been. The injection needle was filled with shellfish poison – a dose large enough to kill five adults.' He paused, looked cautiously at Maud, then back at Marion.

He obviously knew Marion was the one who'd given Amanda the pin – she'd told him as much on his birthday. But surely he didn't think she'd given her one loaded with poison?

He started to stutter, surrender to his nervous tic – finger to thumb, finger to thumb, tap-tap-tap. 'I'm *so* sorry. I was . . . I told Maud and Jessica that you gave Amanda the pin. I didn't mean it as an accusation, I was just thinking out loud, trying to understand how this could have happened.' He paused, mouthed something, tried again. 'Someone must have overheard me and now Nicholas and the council—'

'Think I *murdered* her?' Marion provided, barely able to believe her own words. Her gut turned in on itself. A burning wave of nausea rose in her throat and she thought for a moment she was going to be sick. She looked at Bill, greasy black hair matted to his scalp, a flicker behind his dark eyes – regret, confusion, betrayal. She didn't know. 'How could you, Bill? How could you even *think*—'

'I don't. It's just, the pin was set to eject at exactly five minutes past eight this morning. It did, obviously. It shot right into Amanda's wrist vein.' He looked at the crumpled order in her hand, nearly torn in two by frustration. 'And since you know how to set the timers . . . it just doesn't look good for you, Mari.'

'You can't be serious?' she retorted, looking aghast at each of her friends in turn. 'You *actually* think I killed her? All of you?'

'No,' Bill said immediately, awkwardly. 'Of course not. *I* don't. We just want to understand what happened.'

Maud wasn't so kind. 'Tell us what you were doing in that broom closet. You, Amanda and Kenny.'

'It's a long story,' Marion snapped.

'As usual,' Maud said, leaning back in her chair. 'There always seems to be something you can't tell us. How can you expect us to think any differently? You gave her the pin. And since Amanda definitely didn't load the thing with poison and set the timer herself, what are we supposed to believe?'

Marion remembered something. She didn't bother addressing Maud, who was clearly not interested in hearing anything other than a confession. 'Amanda told me just before she died that she'd lost the bracelet for five hours. Yesterday evening, I think. So, someone must have set the timer and loaded the pin with poison then.'

'But why did she have the pin in the first place?' Maud asked, crossing her arms and facing Marion square on.

Bill intervened. 'Marion gave it to her because she begged for it. Right, Mari?'

Maud sneered at this. 'She begged you for a Tranquilliser Pin?'

'Yes, Maud. She asked me to help her get a registration warrant signed, but I told her that was impossible. I couldn't sign one myself and no one on the High Council would give a second-year apprentice a Schedule 3 gadget for personal use. But then I-I realised she was terrified of something, so I stole one for her. I thought I was helping. I thought I was protecting her. I never imagined this would happen.'

No one (other than Bill and maybe Jessica) looked satisfied by this story, so Marion took another long breath and elaborated.

'I was in Gadgetry last week, completing a task that nearly got me killed, because someone had set the entire thing up as a death trap.' She went on to explain, for the second time that morning, exactly how the platform on the scaffolding had been partially cut to break when stepped on and a collection of sharp tools laid out on the workbench below. 'Someone has been trying to kill off employees. The trap in Gadgetry was their first attempt. The second was in the broom closet,' she croaked, 'with the pin . . . Amanda.'

Jessica blinked, the first re-emergence of her familiar character – comprehension and compassion – etched across her face. 'Who is the killer? Do you know?'

'Proctor or Longmore. I'm absolutely certain.'

'Oh, I believe that,' Preston said immediately. 'Don't trust either of them. Never have.'

'Don't be an idiot – this isn't a joke.' Maud glowered then turned to Marion. 'We're talking about calculated murder here. What makes you think either of those two are capable of something like that?'

Marion ignored the question only because she'd just noticed something. She was wrong. Not all of the apprentices were in the common room.

'Where are they? Proctor and Longmore?'

Everyone glanced around the room. No one knew.

Their absence made Marion's skin crawl. Amanda's killer had to be one of them, maybe even both. And if they'd disappeared, did that mean they were planning something else? Another murder? She was certain it did.

'We have to find them!' she said, panicked, getting to her feet.

Bill pulled her back down. 'We can't, Mari. *You* can't, especially. Nicholas is guarding the corridor here and the snakes are everywhere. You're a murder suspect now, remember?'

They were all staring at her again, the rest of the common room, too. It looked very much as if they weren't yet convinced she had nothing to do with Amanda's death. Because of this, she decided there was no longer any option other than to tell her friends the whole story, right from the beginning.

She composed herself and turned to Maud, Preston and Jessica. They were shaken, yes. They were angry and confused, partly with her, no doubt. But there were unmistakeable traces of compassion in their faces, too. Camaraderie. Fellowship. And she realised then what a fool she'd been. Maud was right – how could she have expected them to believe her, with all the inconsistencies and omissions? Of course they'd understand, of course they'd help her. They were misfits and outcasts and nobodies just like her – the flotsam and jetsam of London – and they'd stick together because they were all each other had.

She began, carefully, slowly, and in incredible detail to explain – about the letters, about the ERPS and the propaganda Spragg had used to break apart the High Council, about the Florist and his KGB illegals from Moscow and their plan to use Miss Brickett's gadgets to gain an upper hand in the Cold War. When she'd finished, it felt as though the smallest spark of hope had ignited inside her.

The group shifted uncomfortably in their seats. They seemed to contemplate her, perhaps still somewhat unconvinced.

Eventually, Jessica stirred, squeezed Marion's hand. 'Oh, darling. I'm sorry you got caught up in all this.'

'Yeah, we're sorry,' Maud agreed blandly. 'But still. You should have told us. We could have helped.'

'She's right, of course,' Jessica said. 'But never mind.' She looked each apprentice in the eye, as though analysing something. 'We're all in this together now.'

Bill nodded, drew his chair closer. 'Right on, Jess.'

'Mari,' Jessica added with a spark of determination, 'you said Longmore or Proctor is a Russian spy working with the Florist, correct?'

'Not exactly a spy, but working with the Florist, yes. And definitely after our gadgets. That's what Frank believes, anyway.'

'That last letter . . . ' Maud said. 'It claimed there would be two deaths. Do you think that means . . . ' She trailed off, turning to the fireplace, then to the crowded common room. 'Is one of us next?'

'I don't know,' Marion admitted, 'but yes, I think there will be another death if we don't figure out who the killer is.'

'Then where do we start?' Jessica asked, frustration cutting through her smooth Mayfair vowels.

She was, without question, the most intuitive of the group, which is perhaps why she now sounded so on edge. She knew Marion was feeling it, too, the desperation and hopelessness.

'We could just go straight to Spragg,' Maud suggested. 'Give her a taste of her own medicine and interrogate her until she tells us everything. She must know if the spy is Longmore or Proctor. I, for one, wouldn't mind giving the old hag a few in the ivories.'

'No,' said Marion immediately. 'We can't risk it. We don't know the rules of this game. If we act openly, it could mean a swifter death for the second victim, or more than one. Especially since we don't know where Proctor or Longmore are.'

'Yeah,' Bill reasoned. 'It would be a balls-up *and* a waste of time. If Spragg knows who the killer is and is willing to tell us, she wouldn't have given Marion a tribunal order. Either she's covering for Proctor or Longmore, or she really hasn't a clue.'

'What about going to Frank or Nancy?' Jessica asked, gnawing at her nails. 'Maybe they know something.'

'They know just as little as I do,' Marion said despondently.

'And, eh . . . ' Bill added, again looking as though he'd rather not say whatever was on the tip of his tongue. 'Both of them are being watched. Spragg's convinced herself and everyone else on the ERPS that they've stolen this alleged sum of money. As far as I've heard, members have been asked to report untoward activities of non-members. That means, they're watching you and they're watching Frank and Nancy. Every second of the day and night.' He nodded to the left, where the rest of the common room had gathered in a closely packed circle.

Every one of them was a member of the ERPS and all were staring at Marion, Bill, Jessica, Maud and Preston with a look that screamed fury and betrayal. Clearly, they now knew Marion had turned against them.

Bill added in a whisper, 'Think about it. If you were one of them, entrapped and manipulated by Spragg, you'd believe Frank and Nancy *had* stolen the money and in the ensuing chaos, their favourite apprentice had, maybe accidentally, killed Amanda.'

'So we're on our own, then?' Preston concluded with a sigh.

Marion addressed the group at large, emboldened by their concern, the fight in their voices. 'I think Bill's right. Even if Spragg knows who's going to die next and how, she won't tell us anything. She has all the power. For now.'

Bill gave her a look that suggested he knew where the conversation was leading. He fell back into his nervous tick – *tap, tap, tap,* finger to thumb – more wildly than ever.

'There's only one way I can solve this, and it has to be done before my tribunal tomorrow.' Her eyes swept over Bill, Jessica, Maud and Preston. 'But in the meantime, I need you to stay together. I don't know how or when the second murder will, *might,* happen, but it'll certainly be easier for the killer if one of you is wandering around alone.'

Jessica shuffled to the edge of her seat. 'We'll stick together, of course. But what about *you*? If Spragg won't tell us anything, then who . . . ' She watched Marion, tilted her head, pupils dilating. '*Oh* . . . '

Maud looked from Jessica to Marion, confused. 'Oh? Oh what?'

Jessica took a swift breath. 'Swindlehurst.'

Marion confirmed this with a nod. 'Harry said he never listened to the recordings he collected from the East Eight, or read the letters he gave Amanda to send to me. He could be lying, but I don't think so. Which means Swindlehurst is the only person who knows who the killer is and how we can stop the next murder. I have to speak with him.'

'But he's locked up,' Maud ventured. 'Swindlehurst is in the Holding Chambers. No one even knows where they are.'

Marion glanced at Bill. He shrugged.

'Finding them isn't the problem,' she answered vaguely. 'But I can't go traipsing around the agency with an order for tribunal hanging over my head.' She paused to think. 'I need to get past Nicholas. And soon. Any ideas?'

'I could bribe him,' Preston suggested as he drew a rucksack onto his lap, scratched around, pulled out a polished cedar box. He flipped it open to reveal a line of cigars covered in brown-gold foil. 'Harvesters. Very expensive, from America. I know he has a taste for the good stuff.' He shrugged. 'It might work.'

'It won't,' Jessica insisted. 'Nicholas is steadfast. Trust me. He wouldn't help us even if he wanted to. He's too afraid of being on the wrong side of things. So long as Spragg has everyone convinced of her authority, he'll trail her like a puppy dog.'

Maud rolled her wrists, wet her lips. 'I'd offer to pummel him, but I don't suppose that lot' – she motioned to the group of ERPS on the other side of the room – 'would be too happy about it.'

'Something more subtle, then,' Jessica proposed, turning to Marion. 'Halothane, from Gadgetry? That'll put him out for a few minutes.'

'Come on, be a little more imaginative than that,' said David Eston, sauntering over, hands in his pockets.

Everyone tensed as he made himself comfortable within their circle. Marion was certain he'd been sitting with the ERPS, far away on the other side of the common room, out of earshot. Clearly not.

He leaned back, stretched his arms behind his head and grinned. 'Ah, the looks on your faces. Priceless.'

'Piss off, Eston,' Maud said, her posture wound tight as a spring. 'What are you doing here?'

'Steady on,' David drawled. 'I'm here to help.' He sighed, rubbed the sparse stubble on his chin. 'I mean it. I know you don't consider me part of your little NitWit gang, but maybe you could give me a chance for once.'

'We've given you lots of chances. But you've proved your-self a prize shit and now we don't trust you,' Maud said matter-of-factly.

Jessica put a pacifying hand on Maud's thigh, then turned to David, lips pressed together. 'You're ERPS, David. You must understand that we can't just—'

'So is she,' he interrupted, pointing a finger at Marion. 'Just hear me out, okay?' He threw a glance over his shoulder, but the group of ERPS, with whom he'd been sitting, had now dispersed. 'Nicholas is guarding the common-room door with specific instructions not to let Marion go anywhere other than her quarters—'

'We know that already, Sherlock,' Maud said, unimpressed. 'And we'll figure out a way to get Marion past him without your help, thanks very much.'

'Nah, you won't. You're clueless, the lot of you.' He turned to Marion. 'Nick's no mug—'

Bill scoffed. 'You sure about that?'

'You can't bribe him,' David continued, heedless of Bill. 'And he's not just standing guard. He's supposed to check on you every hour, then scamper back to Spragg to tell her you're not up to anything . . . *suspicious.* You can't knock his lights out, or he'll miss his cue and Spragg will raise the alarm.' He clasped his hands together and leaned forwards conspiratorially. 'But, lucky for you, I just heard Nicholas complaining that he can't stand guard all night and all morning. He'll need a kip, yeah? He'll need a shift change.'

'And you've offered?' Marion guessed, mildly hopeful as she passed the others a sidelong glance.

David raised an eyebrow, his small black eyes filled with intent. 'I'm on duty from three a.m. onwards.'

'That's six hours away. Far too long—'

David threw his hands open. 'We've not got a choice. And before you ask, the reason you can trust me is because . . . I want revenge. Amanda and I were friends. She understood me, somehow. And if it wasn't for Spragg and the ERPS, she'd still be alive.' He swallowed, masking a break in his voice. 'I want to bring those bastards down.'

'Just so you know,' Maud said after a short spate of silence, 'if you turn on us, I swear on my parents' grave, I'll hunt you down and cut off your—'

'Okay, I'm sure he gets the point,' Jessica added quickly, patting Maud on the thigh. She gave David a thorough once-over, her eyes tight with concentration, scrutinising him as though she could see something no one else could. She turned to Marion, nodded. 'I believe him.'

Marion got to her feet. Even with Jessica's assurances, she wasn't entirely convinced David's change of heart could be relied on, but since he already knew exactly what she was planning to do, she had no choice but to trust him. 'I'm going to my quarters,' she said to the group. 'There are a few things I need to plan. David, I'll see you at three. The rest of you' – she gave them each a pleading look – 'stick together, okay?'

Bill rose, came to her side, where he always was, always would be. He placed a hand on her shoulder and, despite the circumstances, despite the horrible churning of dread in her stomach, she felt a brief interlude of strength and comfort.

Marion and Bill crossed the corridor and returned to Marion's room under the watchful eye of Rupert Nicholas.

'We're really going there, eh?' Bill said once inside the room, the door locked behind them. He slumped down on the bed looking flustered.

'We?'

Bill shrugged. 'Of course. What did you expect?'

She shook her head, kissed him on the cheek. 'Then, yes, I'm afraid so. I wish there was another way, but Swindlehurst wants something from me in exchange for the information we need. It's our only option.'

Bill might not have heard, for he spoke again in a swift, dutiful tone that suggested he hadn't yet fully considered just what they were about to do, or how dangerous it would be. 'Thing is, even if David keeps his word and you're able to leave this room, we still have to get all the way to the Border without anyone seeing us.'

Marion let Bill ramble while she pulled out the small brass box from under her bed. She flipped back the clasp. It sprung open. Bill inhaled sharply, catching sight of the three items inside: a brass monocle, a frayed piece of rolled parchment and a small crystal vial wrapped in purple velvet.

'First off, we need directions to get to the Holding Chambers,' she said, lifting the parchment from the box and smoothing it out on her side table. The frail paper crackled as it unfurled and under the flicker of the gas lamp's flame, a web of silvery furrows appeared.

Muscles tightened in Marion's chest. The sight of the old map had woken sleeping memories, most of which she'd hoped never to think of again. She wavered for a while, considering. She'd promised herself she'd forget. She promised herself she'd keep a distance from the shadows that haunted Miss Brickett's. Was opening the map now not going against all that?

She drew out the monocle – the only gadget with which one could read the invisible ink map – attaching it to her right eye. Hundreds of once invisible lines appeared on the parchment, intersecting each other, diverging and disappearing. Marion scoured the page, tracing corridor and chamber, passage and hall until she found it: the Holding Chambers.

'It's not going to be easy, but if we follow this route, we'll be okay.' She removed the monocle and handed it to Bill.

The Holding Chambers appeared to be miles away from the corridors and tunnels that splintered out across Miss Brickett's proper. Worst of all, it appeared that the only way to get there was by traversing the dark and confounding labyrinth across the Border. A searing fear rose inside her, resurrecting past mistakes. She knew that crossing the Border and attempting to find one's way through its never-ending passages was a suicide mission. But, as she'd explained to her circle in the common room, Edgar Swindlehurst was almost certainly a large part of what was going on at Miss Brickett's and if they were going to uncover the truth, he was their only hope.

Bill removed the monocle from his eye, nodded despondently. 'I suppose we don't have a choice. But, Mari, you haven't answered my question. How the bloody hell are we going to get all the way down to the Border without raising the alarm? The snake patrol is everywhere and it's not just Nicholas roaming around at night. The entire ERPS is watching you.'

Marion flashed him a quick smile, picked up the only other item remaining in the brass box. A crystal vial wrapped in purple velvet. 'This is how.'

22

The Red Gutter

The common room was empty by the time Marion returned. Scatterings of cigarette butts and dregs of beer left in tankards suggested it wasn't long since the last apprentices set off for bed.

Marion wondered who among them would survive the night.

It was 3.30 a.m. A grandfather clock chimed sharply in the shadowy recess behind the fireplace.

Marion's nerves twitched and jumped as a pair of footsteps echoed through the corridor outside. It was several hours since Bill had left for the Gadgetry Department to collect whatever tools and contraptions he could pilfer, and then the library for a book he insisted they'd do well to have with them on the journey. In that time, just as David had warned, Nicholas checked in on Marion once every hour until the end of his shift.

But now, as Marion waited alone, the room still and dark, a part of her mind was screaming – *the second victim might be you.*

She held her breath as the door swung open and Bill stepped inside.

She exhaled, relief flooding through her. Bill looked flustered. One shirtsleeve rolled up to the crook of his arm, the other pulled down over his wrist, the cufflink undone.

'Everything fine?' she asked, worried now. 'Did someone see you?'

'Just David and . . . ' He muttered something inaudible.

'What?' Marion pressed.

'Spragg and the gang have moved things down to Gadgetry.' His fingers fluttered, another nervous tic. 'The interrogations, I mean. I was down there, obviously, trying to get some supplies, but . . . Kenny was hooked up to the Liar's Eyeglass. The High Council was there, everyone except Nancy and Frank. They were asking him about the murder. About you. Why you were questioning Amanda, why you'd joined the ERPS in the first place. What you had planned.' He stopped, looked at his hands. 'He was lying, but they wouldn't stop asking. I don't know how long it had been going on for, but he looked nearly . . . unconscious. They've stopped now, but . . . it was horrible. I'm sorry . . . '

Marion turned around, swallowed back the lump in her throat.

'I'm sorry,' Bill repeated. 'You were right about Kenny. And I was a git. He's got your back.' He smiled as Marion turned back to face him. 'And, like me, he'll do anything for you. Which is all that counts.'

Marion nodded, gave him a quick hug. Knowing she couldn't continue the conversation without breaking down in heaving sobs, she changed the subject. 'Did you manage to get anything from Gadgetry, then?'

'A few things.' He placed a leather haversack on the couch and unzipped it, pulled out two light orbs, a Skeleton Key, two coils of Twister Rope. 'Don't suppose you care that those are Schedule three and we're not authorised to use them?' he asked, pointing at the Twister Rope.

'Not one wit.'

Bill nodded. 'Thought so. Did you bring the map?'

'Of course.'

'Good. Good . . . okay.' He fiddled with the bag, drew out a worn paperback. 'I, er, found that book I told you about: *The History of Miss Brickett's: Legends, Facts and Falsehoods.*'

Marion gave him an impatient look. 'We don't have time for legends and falsehoods.'

He ignored her, flipping the book open to somewhere near the middle, his expression harried. 'Apparently, there's a trap that guards the Holding Chambers, the Red Gutter.' He ran a finger down the page, muttering under his breath. 'The Red Gutter exists to deter potential trespassers on their way to the Holding Chambers. Though no one on record has encountered the trap, rumour suggests the ground shifts, throwing travellers off balance and into a gutter lined with stakes and—'

Marion whipped the book from Bill's hands, slammed it shut. 'Enough, please. I don't need another thing to worry about. Besides,' she added, more to herself and as a comfort, 'if there really is a trap guarding the chambers, it wouldn't be listed in any book you're able to find in the library. Nancy probably made it up to convince everyone that looking for the chambers is a bad idea. Which it is, in case you forgot, trap or no trap.'

Bill flung his hands into the air in an 'I give up gesture'. Marion handed him a coil of Twister Rope and a light orb. She slipped the map into the haversack, along with the remaining supplies Bill had pilfered from the Gadgetry Department.

'Now, let's just get this over with.' She retrieved a small crystal vial from her pocket, held it up to the dim light, watched the flecks of grey and silver dance within. 'There isn't much, but it'll be enough to get us to the Border at least.'

She and Bill wrapped their nose and mouth with a damp cloth, then dabbed the last remaining drops of the curious translucent mist onto their wrists and clothing: the Grey Eagle – the same alchemic substance that Swindlehurst had used last year during Michelle White's murder.

Bill rubbed his arms, gooseflesh rising on his skin. 'You really think this will fool the snakes?' he asked, his voice muffled beneath the cloth. 'And everyone else?'

Marion swung the haversack over her shoulder and gestured to the door. 'Time to find out.'

They stepped into the corridor outside, passing David, who was lounging on a chair, a pint of ale and a folded newspaper on his lap. He frowned at the door creaking open (apparently of its own accord). 'Marion, Bill? That you?'

But before he could comprehend what he was seeing, the mist had taken effect – disorientating him, causing his vision to blur, his thoughts to tangle and lag. He rubbed his eyes and stared stupidly at the door as it clicked closed again and two cloudy figures pushed past him.

Marion and Bill arrived at the base of the long stone staircase a while later, just as the alchemic mist began to wear off.

Marion pulled the map and monocle from her bag. It was the second time in just over a year that she'd traversed the tunnels that lay across Border, and this time was no less terrifying than the last.

'Just remember, we have to stay together. If either of us gets lost down there, we won't be able to find each other again easily.' *If at all*, she thought to herself.

Bill nodded and they moved on, over the Border, into the dark.

The first part of the journey – where a singular tunnel ran perfectly straight – they walked in utter silence, each lost in their own thoughts and fears. The way was easy, the ground smooth and the tunnel roof high enough to dispel claustrophobia. But Marion knew from experience this wouldn't last and soon they'd be in the very bowels of the earth, so far from sunlight and fresh air that it would seem suicidal not to turn back. She knew the tunnel walls would close in, the darkness grow so thick it was almost tangible. She knew it wouldn't be long before even breathing seemed an insurmountable task.

Bill, despite the discontent he'd emanated at the start of their journey, seemed to become more light-spirited as they walked. Marion knew this wasn't because he was enjoying himself or feeling any better about things, but rather because he'd realised Marion was feeling worse.

'Apparently, White used to keep a cat down here,' he said. 'Siamese, I think. She called it Ghost and fed it only biscuit crumbs, poor sod.'

They'd arrived at Michelle White's old office. A painted wooden sign, bearing the words 'Border Guard', hung above the door, creaking as it swung in a soft breeze that came from somewhere deep within the tunnels ahead.

'You read that in your little paperback, too?' Marion asked with a grin.

'Hah, no. This is true. I even saw the cat once, up in the Filing Department. Nasty, vicious thing. Nearly scratched my eyes out.'

'Probably because it was starving.'

They paused outside the deserted office, peered in. It had been cleared out long ago, all of Michelle's possessions removed, leaving only an old desk and two chairs. Cobwebs stretched across the lintel, the floor was covered in a carpet of dust and rat droppings. It still troubled Marion that Nancy had actually thought this was suitable living quarters for anyone – feline or human.

'What happened to it, anyway? The cat?' Marion asked, taking the lead as they passed the office and turned left into the first of many low-roofed passageways that stretched out before them.

They jumped over the thin underground stream that fed off from somewhere along the River Fleet. But the further on they went, the more unfamiliar and sinister the tunnels became. And, as Marion had anticipated, the roof sunk in, the lights dimmed and the smooth stone floors transformed to sharp rock and wet gravel.

Bill shrugged. 'Got lost down here and never came back. Poor Ghost – ironic end, isn't it?'

Marion scowled. 'Delightful story, thanks.'

Moments later, Bill stopped. 'Which way now?'

Marion studied the four-way split in the tunnels before them. 'Light, please.'

Bill held up his glowing orb as she placed the monocle over her eye and looked down at the map. She attempted to trace her finger along the path they'd come down, the passage that led off from the base of the long stone staircase, past White's office and left into the low-roofed tunnel. But the silvery line was no longer there.

'Blast.'

She turned the map around, angling it to orientate herself. Beside her, Bill was muttering something – a prayer, it sounded like.

'And?' Bill said impatiently after a long silence.

'I don't know. I can't see where we are. Look . . . ' She handed Bill the map and monocle. 'There was a line here representing the tunnel that runs past White's office, but it's disappeared.'

'Does that mean the tunnel has—'

As if in reply, a loud scrape came from the corridor behind them. They turned around, Bill whipping the monocle from his eye.

Another sound – as though a large stone was being dragged across the gravel floor.

An echoing thud, silence and utter darkness.

Marion took a few steps backwards and walked right into a wall. 'I think . . . ' She felt around the stone facade; it was cool and smooth and solid. 'Great.'

'Is there another way out?'

'We'd better bloody hope so.'

She pulled her coat tighter about her shoulders and the pair continued onwards, following the stream as it flowed through the tunnel gutter, deeper and further underground.

'I have a question,' Bill said as they took a sharp right. 'Who took Swindlehurst to the Holding Chambers in the first place and how did they get there? Because they definitely didn't come this way.'

'There's probably a safer route only Nancy knows about.'

After all, the agency's prison cells were a closely guarded secret – where they were, what they were, how they operated, even that they existed – and if Nancy found out Marion and Bill were attempting to reach them, it might have been the last thing they did at Miss Brickett's. Especially now that Marion was embroiled in yet another agency murder, this time as the prime suspect.

'Mari,' Bill said, drawing her from her thoughts. 'Did you see that?'

They were standing in a relatively wide corridor, the underground stream trickling at their feet. Just ahead, the corridor forked, then merged back into one.

'What?' she said, casting her eyes to the ground two or so yards ahead of them, where Bill was pointing.

He took a step back, bumped into her. 'Something moved over there.'

'A rat,' Marion said without thinking or bothering to investigate. She couldn't see whatever Bill was pointing at, but there was at least a 90 per cent chance that if it was moving, it was a rat.

'No, it . . . ' He faltered, raised his orb. 'There! Look!'

It took only a fraction of a second for Marion to realise what was happening. The stones that had once formed a solid surface beneath their feet were starting to rearrange themselves, shifting left and right, overlapping each other or falling away entirely to reveal gaping black holes.

'The Red Gutter?' Bill gasped, leaping over a newly formed hole just in time.

'Don't drop the map or monocle, please,' Marion said, panicked as she and Bill were separated by a foot-long gouge.

Bill shot her an irate look.

'And don't fall in, of course,' she added to pacify him.

The stone she'd been standing on started to move. She looked around at her feet. She was on an island now, surrounded by open trapdoors. Bill had his back to her, shaking as he tried to keep his balance. Marion swayed, lost her footing. She could see a solid piece of ground to her right, not too far to attempt a jump.

Everything went black.

'Bill!' she shrieked. 'Your orb?'

His voice was distant, strained. 'Dropped it. Sorry. Yours?'

She didn't answer. Her orb was in the haversack, which was hanging over her shoulder. There was no way she could fumble around and get it now, in the dark, balancing on a moving rock.

'Luckily,' Bill stammered in between a string of shallow breaths, 'I . . .   did r-read the rest of that p-passage about the Red Gutter. Watch out for—'

A shrill whistle cut him off, followed by a series of synchronised clicks.

'Darts!' Bill said, his voice even further off. 'Duck!'

At that moment, a dart whipped past Marion's cheek, followed a split second later by another that would have caught her in the arm had she not shifted left.

But the move cost her.

She knew she was going to fall before she did – that split second that precedes a cataclysm, when time stops. She teetered, called out as the ground gave way. Cold air rushed past her. She landed hard and awkwardly on her feet.

Utter blackness.

'Mari!'

'Here,' she groaned. 'Down here.'

'Are you hurt?'

She had no idea. She waited a minute, attempted to lift her arms, move her legs. A stab of pain caught her in the neck, the shoulder. She was bleeding, the warm liquid leaking from a wound near her spine, halfway up her back. 'I don't think so, not badly at least.'

'Okay. Okay, good.' His voice was strained, breathless. 'Well, your fall has closed most of the trapdoors up here. And,' he panted, groaned, 'I can't keep this last one open much longer.' Clang, clip, something moved. Bill moaned as though in pain. 'The bag? Do you have it with you?'

Marion patted the ground around her. Her haversack was still there. She lifted it in front of her and scratched around for the orb, finally managing to switch it on. She glanced upwards. Bill had wedged himself into the last remaining trapdoor, his feet pressed up against one side of the rim, his arms stretched out behind him, pushing backwards into the other. But despite his efforts, both rims were moving towards each other.

'*Hurry*,' he breathed. 'I can't hold them for much longer.'

'Blast!' Marion said, the light of her orb reflecting off something long and silvery, which had just sprouted up from the ground several feet away.

No sooner had it appeared than it sank back into the ground, replaced by another, a foot closer.

'Stakes!' She turned her eyes skywards again. Her neck and shoulders throbbed. 'Twister Rope,' she said, calling up to Bill. 'Do you still have yours?'

'Yeah, but if I let go . . . ' He wheezed, spluttered.

Marion stole a glance over her shoulder, just as a stake strung up within touching distance. 'You have to try, please!'

She pulled out her coil while Bill readjusted himself in the swiftly sealing trapdoor, pushing his neck and shoulders against the edge where his arms had been.

'Okay, got mine,' he gasped.

'Right. On the count of three. Ready?'

Bill winced, the trapdoor aperture crushing his shoulders and feet. 'Just do it. Now!'

Marion crouched slightly, holding her coil at her side. The stake behind her had disappeared into the ground. A few seconds later, it would reappear, more than likely right where she was standing.

'One, two, *three*.'

She launched her Twister Rope upwards at the exact moment Bill let his down. The ends of the two coils touched, immediately magnetising each other, twisting themselves into a tight knot. Marion didn't have time to test the connection. She placed her foot on the lowest overhang and began to haul herself upwards.

As she reached the lip of the gutter, Bill shimmied out of the way, allowing her a split second to crawl to safety before the trapdoor shut with a violent clang.

She fell backwards, gasping, aching. The ground around her was solid, unmoving. She breathed a sigh of relief.

'The Red Gutter, eh?' Bill said, stretching his neck. 'Told you it was real.'

★

Several hours and countless wrong turns later (though with no further incidents), they finally arrived at a rusted steel gate. There was no signage, no obvious indication that these were the Holding Chambers, but something about the sinister atmosphere told Marion they were at the right place.

'No lock,' she said, pushing the gate open.

Bill raised his eyebrows as they stepped through. A short path led off from the gate, terminating in an antechamber, encircled by towering stone pillars that stretched several feet upwards to a domed ceiling. The space was bare, featureless, save a gargantuan block and pulley contraption built against the far wall.

She approached the contraption, studied it, her eyes tracing three gears and axles, the taut belts to which they were attached and the strange pits beneath them. She kneeled, touched one, a shallow depression in the dusty floor. There were twenty at least, all criss-crossed by chains and attached to a belt, which was in turn connected to its own cumbersome gear. Most of the pits were open, their iron doors lying off to the side. Three were sealed shut.

'These are them, I think,' she said at last, her tone low and careful. 'These are the chambers.' She shuddered, imagining what lay beneath – a dark, deep, suffocating well that extended to unknown depths, a tomb from which there was no escape. Panicked thoughts raged through her: *this could have been Frank's fate — this might be mine.* She rose to her feet, unsteadied by another wave of terror.

Bill had crept up beside her. 'You all right?'

She touched her neck, her arteries thumping fast beneath her fingers. 'I just . . . I can't believe we're here. I can't believe this is where—'

'I know, I know,' Bill soothed. After a moment, he added, 'The book said they're impossible to open once they've been closed.' He pointed at the open chambers, cells, whatever they were. 'Once you seal the door, they can't be opened again. Not from the inside. Not from the outside.'

'I doubt that. Nothing's impossible, in a mechanical sense,' she said, echoing Professor Bal's favourite motto.

She slipped a hand into her haversack, touching her leather roll of tools. In some sense, she already knew what was coming next.

She walked over to one of the open wells, seized the cord of her light orb and, careful to hold the end tightly, lowered the glowing bulb into the hole.

'There's no ladder, no stairs,' she said, thinking out loud, 'so either you're dropped' — she shuddered at the thought — 'or . . . ' She turned back to the iron door, its attached belt and accompanying chains, her eyes tracing upwards to the contraption lodged against the antechamber wall. 'Lowered,' she whispered to herself, pulling the light orb up again and wrapping the cord around her wrist.

She turned to Bill. There was a clanking scrape. A small box appeared on a chain from somewhere near the ceiling of the antechamber and began a slow and staggered journey down towards the floor. It then slipped through a small aperture in the circular chamber door and disappeared.

Moments later, Marion thought she heard a voice drift from the depths beneath her feet. The scraping, clanking sound started again and in seconds, the box reappeared through the aperture.

She looked at her watch. 'Harry,' she whispered.

Bill nodded. 'Breakfast time. But he's only sending food down into one chamber. Suppose that means—'

'The other two don't need it,' Marion provided, stepping up to the aperture, peering down through the blackness.

'Mari,' Bill said, pulling her back again. 'You're sure you want to do this?'

'We came all this way.'

'I know, but . . . it's not too late to change our minds.'

Marion didn't reply. She crouched down, bringing her face right up to the aperture, the one through which Harry had just lowered a box of food. A faint light flickered from below, scarcely visible. A draft wafted upwards, sickly and rotten. She coughed, pulled the collar of her blouse over her mouth and nose.

Bill turned away as he smelled it, too – the rot of human waste.

Marion took a shallow breath and spoke down into the hole. 'Hello, Edgar. I believe you're expecting me.'

23

Swindlehurst's Bargain

'Edgar, can you hear me?' Marion faltered, repeating herself. This was the most bizarre, awkward conversation of her life. It was also one of the most important.

There was no reply. But Marion could hear Swindlehurst breathing, seething. She was suddenly grateful for the vast depth between them.

'I know it's you who's been sending me the letters,' she said into the dimness. 'I know you gave them to Harry and Harry gave them to Amanda.'

She waited for a reply, but again all that came was deep breathing, as if he – if it really was Swindlehurst she was talking to – were pulling air in through a pair of barely functioning lungs.

'I also know you asked Harry to plant a voice recorder in the East Eight.'

She waited. Nothing.

'Amanda is dead. But you already know that.'

She let the statement settle in the air, wishing she could see Swindlehurst's reaction. He couldn't have been surprised, but was he upset? Regretful? Proud?

'How did you know that was going to happen? Who orchestrated her death?'

She turned to Bill. His face was twisted into something that resembled a frown, his eyes darting nervously from Marion to the metal gate behind them. Had it just clicked shut?

'Mari, we can't be here for long,' he whispered, mirroring her thoughts. 'I don't like it. Maybe we shouldn't have come at all . . . ' He trailed off, muttering something about the dark and cold and shadows that moved.

Marion was sure something had shifted just beyond the gate, something low and close to the ground. She hoped it was only the dance of a shadow from her light orb. She turned back to the ground, the sealed entrance to Swindlehurst's Holding Chamber.

'Please, Edgar. You sent me all those letters, all that information. You asked me to come here. What for? Why me?'

There was a horrible scratching sound, as though a fingernail were being dragged against glass.

'I wanted you to come, yes,' came a low hiss from beneath.

The voice wasn't recognisable as Swindlehurst's – it was thinner, softer, more strained than what she remembered. But she knew it was him. She could almost taste the malice in his words.

'I chose you because I knew you were the only one who *could* come, and the only one who *would*. The others are dead, did you know that? One died of some infection. I had to listen to him scream at his hallucinations for five days before the fever took him. The other was even weaker. I heard the soft thump of his head against the wall for hours before the silence came. But it was the smell of their rotting corpses that nearly drove me mad. Can you imagine what that's like?'

Marion rubbed the stump on her left hand – why was it throbbing now? She knew who Swindlehurst was talking about – his accomplices, the two men who'd been with him at

Turnchapel Mews in Clapham last year when he'd attempted to bribe Nancy for his freedom. One of them had killed a woman in front of Marion's eyes, the other had assisted Swindlehurst in pouring an alchemic acid over her finger, disfiguring her for life. She hadn't given their fates – to perish here alone, terrified – a second thought. She didn't even know their names. But if she didn't feel any trace of pity or sympathy for what had become of them, why did she feel that ache in her chest now?

Swindlehurst heaved several long breaths. 'You put me in here to rot alongside them, but I can forgive you. I realised a long while ago that holding on to hate won't get me anywhere.' He coughed and spluttered. 'I don't want revenge. I just want a second chance at another life.'

Marion straightened, began to pace. Bill watched her anxiously, touching her occasionally on the shoulder, as if to remind her he was here, watching over her.

'I presume you have that old map of Ned's,' Swindlehurst continued.

Marion caught Bill's eye. He raised an eyebrow. As far as they knew, Swindlehurst had never actually seen the map. They knew he'd known about it – his friend and fellow apprentice, Ned Ashbry, had once owned the thing – but how did he know it belonged to Marion now?

'Yes,' Swindlehurst said, answering this thought. 'I figured it out. I've had a lot of time to think down here, as you can imagine. I wondered how it were possible that you found the laboratory last year when it was concealed so brilliantly from everyone else. Well, you must have stolen the map from our dear Michelle White, I presume?' He cleared his throat again, a thick, phlegmy sound.

Marion wasn't going to waste her time answering Swindlehurst's questions. It was supposed to be the other way around. 'Why did you tell Harry to plant the voice recorder in the East Eight in the first place? Are you involved with the Florist, too?'

This earned a condescending laugh from Swindlehurst. 'Of course not. I'm merely an observer. You see, Miss Lane, I knew the moment I arrived in this godforsaken pit that I'd find a way out. But I didn't know how. I thought of every-thing, but escaping seemed impossible, even in the early days when I still had hope. And strength. I realised then that the only way I was getting out of here was the same way I got in – bribery, using the agency's secrets against them. But in order to do that, I needed outside help.'

'And you chose Harry,' Marion interjected, still somewhat baffled by the fact.

'He was my *only* choice, the only person I could contact. Fortunately, I had a feeling he'd be interested in working with me. He knew how I was suffering. He knew that the others had died such awful deaths and I don't think he believed I deserved the same fate. And so, sometime around autumn last year, I asked Harry for some paper and a pen.

'This in itself was a monumental task. I had to scratch a message to him on a stone with a butter knife he'd sent down to me for breakfast. But I had time enough for anything. And I suppose having something to do in this eternal hell gave me hope, even if I wasn't convinced it would be worth much.

'With the first reel of paper Harry sent down, I wrote him a letter. I thanked him for his trust in me, mentioned how much I valued his company – even though I couldn't see or hear him, just the thought of another human being to interact with was a priceless comfort. And I suppose in some respects, he felt the same way. No one had ever really paid him much attention at Miss Brickett's. No one even knows his second name.'

Again, Marion caught Bill's eye. He looked contrite. She was certain they were thinking the same thing: Swindlehurst was a brilliant manipulator – and to be so, he often picked up on things others dismissed. Harry *had* always been ignored, taken for granted. Marion could see now how easy it would have been for Swindlehurst to coerce him into anything, provided he pandered to this void.

'None of it was a lie,' Swindlehurst elaborated, 'but my flattery towards Harry did serve another purpose, of course. After a few more frivolous letters, simple communications about how his day had been, how work was going, what he was doing for the weekend, I decided it was time. I started asking more interesting questions: what was going on with Nancy and the High Council, how was Frank and Nancy's relationship, how was the selection of new recruits going. I told him I simply wanted something to keep my mind occupied and he seemed to understand this perfectly.

'Over the weeks and months that followed, Harry sent me scraps of gossip he'd picked up, mostly during his shifts in the library bar. The majority of it was uninteresting and useless and as the months slipped away, I started to worry that I'd never learn anything worthy of corruption.' He cackled again; the sound echoed throughout the antechamber. 'But then it came, more secrets, lies and deception than I could ever have dreamed of.

'Early in the year, Harry sent me a letter saying that Spragg and several other employees had been gathering in the library bar on several occasions, usually following a High Council meeting. He didn't know what they were chatting about, but he sensed it was something no one else was supposed to hear. He tried to eavesdrop, but they were careful not to be overheard, which of course raised our suspicions even further.

'I told Harry to go and buy a simple voice recorder. Nothing fancy like we make here, just something plain and easy to use. I asked him to plant it behind the bar counter and turn it on whenever Spragg was around, then leave. I thought this would work, assuming that Spragg would feel free to talk in Harry's absence. But the bar was too big and the recorder too weak. The only thing we were able to discover was that Spragg was looking for a place to hold a series of "private rendezvous". All she needed was an isolated room that wasn't being used for anything else, preferably with a telephone line already installed.'

Marion nodded to herself, realising she already knew this part of the tale. 'So, Harry recommended the East Eight Chamber.'

'Exactly. He knew it would appeal to Spragg because it was so isolated. But, more importantly, there was a smaller room behind it that only he knew existed – the perfect spot to conceal a voice recorder.

'Indeed, things fell perfectly into place after Spragg and her cronies moved into the East Eight. Harry sent me the recordings once a week and I wrote down everything I heard. I started to realise the society was planning something I could capitalise on. I had information, delicate and fragile and so easily corrupted. All I needed was someone who would value it.

'Of course, I chose you, Miss Lane – not only because I knew you'd be too curious to push aside the letters, but also because, ultimately, you were the only one who had something to offer me in return. You were the only one who could find me, with that map of yours, and you were the only one who could set me free.'

Marion pressed her fingers to her temples. In some way, she'd foreseen this moment, played it over and over in her head, trying to imagine what she'd do if Swindlehurst – in exchange for providing her with the information she needed – asked her to help him escape the Holding Chambers.

'I can't, Edgar. The doors are impossible to open once they've been closed,' she said, echoing Bill's statement, though without really believing it.

'There's no key, certainly,' he agreed. 'But there *is* a way.'

Marion crouched, ignoring Bill's cautious glare. She placed her hand on the cold metal disc at her feet, ran her fingers over its surface, feeling for bolts, divots, latches, keyholes. She felt a line of ridges, tiny elevations that reminded her of something she'd encountered twice before in her time at Miss Brickett's.

'It's a—'

'Trick Lock, yes,' Swindlehurst rasped, a smile clear in his tone. 'A padlock that can only be opened by pressing a series of symbols in the correct order, the sequence gleaned from a riddle.'

'But I don't know the riddle,' she said, then shook her head. Why was she trying to figure out how to open it? Why was she even considering doing such a thing?

Bill pulled her upright. 'Mari, don't. Please. Let's just leave. He isn't going to tell you anything else and you can't . . . ' He looked at chamber door, his expression twisting with angst. 'Nothing he says is worth it.'

There was a change in the atmosphere, a heavy, raw quiet. Bill was saying something more, but she couldn't hear. Or chose not to. She opened her haversack and pulled out the leather roll of tools Swindlehurst had asked her to bring. How convenient.

'You've disarmed a Trick Lock without the riddle before, haven't you?' Swindlehurst asked expectantly. 'If you do it again, I'll tell you who is going to die next. I'll tell you how to stop it, too.'

Marion blinked into the darkness, heaved for breath. Yes, she'd opened a Trick Lock once before, bypassing the riddle and sequence of symbols on the day of her recruitment test last year, the day her new life had begun. She unfolded her roll of tools, laid each out on the dusty floor, a chill slithering down her spine.

'I'll get us going, then,' Swindlehurst went on, warming to his theme. 'The Florist is angry. He knows the shipment of Liar's Eyeglasses has been stolen from the Workshop. In case this hasn't dawned on you yet, the shipment wasn't ever meant for Hanslope Park. It's destined for Moscow and if it doesn't get there, well, I think you get the picture already. The Florist called Spragg the day after the shipment was supposed to arrive and told her to find out what had happened. Then he spoke to his accomplice, the recruit I warned you about, instructed him to take a life as punishment for the mishap.

'There was a problem with that, as well . . . '

Marion nodded. The trap in Gadgetry, her failed assassination.

'. . . now, two people have to die. Both Spragg and the recruit are in a panic. Spragg knows that if she doesn't locate the shipment soon, the Florist will send an anonymous letter revealing what she's been doing to a list of contacts, including Scotland Yard. The Florist's accomplice is in even more trouble if the shipment isn't located. Either he hands himself over, or he hands over another body.'

Marion didn't have time to let this settle or contemplate the fact that she'd played such a pivotal role in the entire thing – designing the Liar's Eyeglass, working tirelessly to ensure the commission was completed in time, all the while believing it was a Hanslope Park order. She turned around. Bill was no longer at her side but rather a few yards off near the gate, crouched on the floor looking at something.

'Who's going to die next? And how?' she asked Swindlehurst breathlessly.

'Ah, yes. The most vital question. Longmore and Proctor have disappeared, haven't they? I must admit that until a few hours ago, I still didn't know which of the two was Fraser Henley, Eddie Hopper's partner and killer. But I've figured it out now. I will tell you, Miss Lane. But you know what I want in return.'

Sounds drifted up from the depths, scuffling, scraping, breathing. Marion peered again through the aperture, though all she saw was the same faint, flickering light. She wondered whether or not Swindlehurst was plotting something grand down there, or simply waiting for her to relent. And in the darkness and silence, her thoughts began to reform, to shape into something she despised but couldn't ignore: guilt, regret, pity.

She'd feared as much when she'd made the decision to locate the Holding Chambers, feared how she'd feel about the part she'd played in Swindlehurst's fate. And now, something was working itself out in her subconscious – that guilt and regret mixing with her desperation to seize what Swindlehurst was offering. She watched the desire build in her mind's eye. She let it happen.

She turned again towards Bill. He'd stop her if he knew what she was going to do, and in some way, she wished he would. But he was nowhere to be seen. She placed her fingers on the metal disc, then traced them along her roll of tools. Swindlehurst was right – she knew exactly how to disarm the Trick Lock by unhinging the pentagon-head bolts on its underside. It would take her less than five minutes.

'Where will you go?' she asked, drawing a screwdriver and penlight from her leather roll.

'Very far away.'

There was a note of hopefulness in his voice now, which only made Marion's hands shake more.

'As I told Nancy last year, I have no desire to cause trouble here. All I want is to start my life again.'

In the back of Marion's mind, she knew she was being manipulated, and yet she inhaled his words like oxygen. 'And how will you get out of here, the agency, without being seen?'

'I've had a very long time to plan it all. You needn't concern yourself with any of it. Unlock the door and release the lever. The door will lower itself down. I'll step onto it. I'll tell you everything you wish to know as soon as the pulley is in motion. And all of this will be over. For both of us.'

Without further thought, she held the penlight in her mouth and set about dismantling the Trick Lock.

Click.

The backing of the lock sprung open, even easier than the first time.

She straightened her spine and, hands shaking, pulled the lever downwards.

Immediately, the iron door shifted and clanked as the belt, and pulley connected to it, began to move. She watched the disc — part door, part lift — sink into the darkness below.

She waited for the thump as it landed on the floor, then leaned over the gaping hole and peered down. A shadow moved in the depths — a shrunken, withered form. The chains that surrounded the platform clunked as the belt pulled taut and Swindlehurst stepped onto the platform.

'Up,' he said.

Marion pulled the lever again and stepped back. Bill was lingering somewhere out of sight. She knew Swindlehurst might be armed. Who knew what else Harry might have passed down to him? She had to be ready for anything. She planted her feet firmly on the ground, squared her shoulders, clenched her fists, felt her muscles quiver.

Amid the clunking of the pulley and squeal of rusted metal, Marion heard Swindlehurst's voice.

'Proctor and Longmore are meeting the Florist at Chestwells scrapyard in South London. One of them is Fraser Henley. The other is the second victim.'

'I already know it's Proctor or Longmore!' Marion snapped, her heart rapping wildly. 'You said you knew which one was Fraser. Tell me!'

The chains continued to clank as the belt moved around the pulley, rattling, grinding.

'I'm sorry, Miss Lane. Fraser never referred to himself by his alias.'

'You lied!' Marion was shouting now, frantic, desperate, aware that she'd made a horrible mistake.

Swindlehurst seemed unperturbed and continued to speak in a level tone. 'The only way to stop the second murder is to take the shipment of stolen gadgets and deliver them to the scrapyard. That's what the Florist wants. If he doesn't have it, Fraser will have to kill another and another. It'll never end.'

Marion stepped forwards, peered into the hole, her light orb held above her head. Swindlehurst came into view, inches from her now, crouching on the platform, gripping the chains at his side desperately – his once tall, broad frame had withered to nothing more than a skeleton. His eyes were sunken, his skin a blueish-grey. Wisps of greasy, dishevelled hair stuck to his face. A wild beard grew on his chin. He turned away to shield his eyes from what must have been the first bright light he'd seen in more than a year. Despite everything Swindlehurst had done and said and ruined, she couldn't stop the aching pity gnawing at her insides.

A long moment passed, seconds dragging, as though time had expanded, slowed. Marion's thoughts ticked furiously, her senses struggling to take in what was unfolding in front of her.

Swindlehurst straightened, drew a kitchen knife from somewhere on the platform. He leaned forwards, one leg on the platform, one on solid ground.

Bill's voice echoed from somewhere behind. *Move. Run. Duck.*

Swindlehurst thrust the knife forwards. Then back. His posture changed, folded. Marion felt something hit her in the stomach as Bill pushed her out of the way. An object whipped through the air, a large rock or some type of tool, and collided with the pulley system on the wall opposite.

There was a loud crack, a sharp scratch of metal. The system jammed. The chains clanked. The belt became slack, slipping through the gears so fast it blurred.

Swindlehurst's eyes widened, horrible pools of desperation, pleading, hatred. He screamed. Then, in the fractured second before he fell, he said: 'I won't be the last.'

A bone-crunching thud.

Silence.

Marion couldn't move. She held her breath until Bill took her hand.

'You okay?' he asked, his voice indefinite, faint. 'I'm sorry . . . I-I didn't know what else to do.'

They stepped forwards together. Marion lowered the light orb halfway into the chamber. They could just make out Swindlehurst's unmoving form below, a glint of something white among a knot of matted hair, framed by a pool of red. Bone, blood. All wrong.

'I'm sorry,' Bill repeated, though not to Marion this time.

24

Battle Yard

Marion stood immobile, watching Bill as he turned it over in his mind. He'd killed someone. If he hadn't, Marion might have a kitchen knife protruding from her chest. She might be dead. But still, he'd *killed* someone. She took him by the hand, felt the pulse in his wrist thump erratically beneath her fingers.

'Bill,' she urged, pulling him away from the gaping pit at their feet. 'I'm sorry, but we have to go.'

He was silent as he turned to follow her, back through the antechamber, out through the gate, swift down the splintered corridors towards the Border. Using the map and intuition, Marion managed to guide them safely through a Red Gutter bypass, right, right, left until they reached the underground stream on the gutter's other side. She knew they didn't have time to be careful, to calculate their next move or ponder the fact that they'd just committed a murder. Proctor and Longmore were certainly already at the scrapyard (if Swindlehurst had actually been telling the truth about that), and if Marion didn't find the shipment and deliver it in time, another life would be snuffed out for nothing. But still, if Bill was going to make it through the next few hours, she needed to give him the chance to process what he'd done.

'Look,' she said, coming to an abrupt halt a few yards from the stream. 'I know you're in shock – I am, too. Swindlehurst is dead because of us and—'

'Me, because of *me*,' Bill corrected, finally emerging from his reticence. He wiped his brow with the cuff of his sleeve. 'It happened so quickly. I wasn't *thinking*. I saw the knife, imagined . . . ' He pressed a hand to his chest, breathed. 'I just wanted to push him away from you. I didn't think—'

'I know,' Marion interrupted. 'I *know*. I feel the same about Amanda. It's awful. I shouldn't have got twisted up in all this. I shouldn't have involved you. I wish I could go back, change things. But we're here now and if we give in, someone else is going to die. You understand that?'

He cast an eye around him, at the dank tunnel walls, as though he wasn't sure how they'd got here. Eventually, he nodded solemnly, coming back to himself. 'Swindlehurst said we have to find the missing shipment. How?'

'Blast!'

'What?'

Marion rummaged through her haversack, hands shaking. 'I left my tools at the chambers.'

Bill seemed momentarily perplexed by her level of angst. Then he realised, thinking out loud. 'Evidence.'

'Nancy knows those tools are mine,' Marion said, her courage wavering. She turned around to look at the dark thread of tunnel behind them – the Red Gutter. Did they have time to go back?

Bill took her light orb, held it aloft as if to take command of the situation. 'You said it yourself, Mari. We can't go back. We'll worry about the toolkit later.' He sighed, nodded to himself. 'Now, how are we going find the shipment?'

Marion swallowed back the fear, pushed it aside. He was

right. She was right. They couldn't go back. 'I know where it is,' she answered, earning a bewildered look from Bill. She took the map and monocle from her bag and tried to orientate herself while explaining what she'd recently come to understand. 'Frank wanted to tell me where it was at our last meeting, but he said he couldn't in case I was interrogated by Spragg.' *Like Kenny*, she thought but didn't say. She recalled what Frank had said: *It's just a bit too close to home at the moment*. 'It's at Willow Street. He hid the shipment at my old house.'

Bill contemplated this, shook his head. 'Okay, great. But there's a bigger problem. We don't know who it is yet. Longmore or Proctor. One of them is the killer and if we get to the scrapyard without knowing which, well, we won't know who to protect.'

Marion had turned this problem over in her mind already, not coming up with any solutions. Fraser could just as easily be Jerome Longmore or Thomas Proctor. She looked at her watch. Less than twenty-four hours until she was due at her tribunal.

'We'll just have to rely on our instincts. Anyway, at this rate, one of them might be dead by the time we get there.' She ran her finger along a silvery line on the map – the tunnel they were in – that would steer them directly back to the Border, provided no walls rolled into their path, forcing a detour. She detached the monocle from her eye and pointed ahead. 'This way.'

Chestwells Scrapyard overlooked the eastern bank of Deptford Creek in South London. Beyond its gates, which stood ajar, lay a collection of broken car parts, piles of jumbled metal threaded with weeds and mud and litter. The tide had retreated in the creek below, revealing a muddy path that twisted north to reach the Thames.

It was several hours since Marion and Bill had found their way back across the Border and into Miss Brickett's proper. It was either sheer luck or something to do with Spragg's takeover of the agency that they hadn't bumped into a single employee on their way out through the bookshop and off to Willow Street. The shipment *was* there – in the kitchen, in the pantry, wrapped in an old bed sheet. The sight of it sent relief and guilt surging through Marion in equal measure. The box was nondescript, about thirteen square inches, filled to the brim with ninety-nine carefully stacked Liar's Eyeglasses – the cause of so much suffering. Would things have turned out differently for Amanda if Frank had told Marion where he'd hidden the box in the first place?

'Well, this is the correct address,' Bill said now as they approached the scrapyard gates. He shielded his eyes from the sun beating down hot and clear. 'You think the Florist and his friend are actually here, though?'

Marion wasn't sure. Swindlehurst could certainly have lied. In fact, she had no idea why he'd have told her the truth about where Fraser Henley and the Florist were meeting. She had to admit, however – the scrapyard *did* look like the perfect setting for a murder, or a rendezvous, or whatever it was they were about to interrupt. Off the beaten track, isolated from public view and the throngs of Central London.

Bill placed the box of gadgets on the ground, stepped up to the gate. He ran his hands along the mesh, paused.

'What is it?' Marion asked.

He pressed his fingers into her hand. She felt the residue of something sticky.

'Blood. And it's fresh. They must have come through here,' Bill said.

Marion wiped her hands on her trousers and rolled up her sleeves. She didn't want Bill to know it, but she was terrified. Was this a foolish move, seeking out the Florist – a known KGB official and killer – alone in a scrapyard with nothing but some fanciful gadgets as protection?

'I know,' Bill said, sighing slightly and appearing to have read her mind. 'But we're here now and we've been through worse.'

She handed Bill his coil of Twister Rope from earlier. 'It's better if you have it on you, just in case.' It slithered up his shoulder as she spoke. 'Keep it magnetised and be ready.' *For anything*, she added in her mind. 'If anyone has a gun, try to get it off them using the rope.'

Bill winced as the coil twisted and writhed around his forearm. 'And is this a bluff, or are we *actually* going to hand them over?' he asked, motioning to the box of gadgets he'd repositioned on his shoulder.

Marion chewed her lip, mulling this over. If everything she'd uncovered about the Florist's infiltration of Miss Brickett's was accurate, Spragg had already seen to it that the KGB was in possession of a number of agency gadgets: lock picks, orb lights, transmitters, bugs. Admittedly, those were relatively innocuous contraptions, unlike the Liar's Eyeglass, but still, as she said now, thinking out loud: 'If handing over the shipment is going to save a life, then yes.'

The scrapyard was desolate and quiet, save for the seagulls that screeched overheard. Towers of ripped tyres and rusted hubcaps lined a path that ran directly to the banks of the creek. Here, there was a small tool shed, surrounded by a wall of broken chassis and mismatched engine parts.

As they came around the back of the shed, a voice called, cracking the silence like a whip: 'Looks like you have something for me.'

They froze. Something tickled the nape of Marion's neck. She flinched, wiped a drip of sweat away.

'Well?' the voice rang through the scrapyard, sound waves bouncing off the scattered car parts, making it impossible to know which direction it was coming from.

But Marion recognised the accent instantly. Russian. The Florist.

'Where are you?' she answered, ignoring Bill as he mouthed something to her.

'Down here, near the water.'

Bill tried to stop her but again, she ignored him and marched quickly to the creek's edge. She looked down, squinted against the sun's glare – mud, reeds, flies, nothing.

'Look,' Bill whispered, crouched at her side. He touched the wet earth, a shoe imprint. 'It's going that way.' He pointed back towards the tool shed.

A break in the silence. The flies in the creek below buzzed wildly, as though disturbed, followed by a clang of metal. Marion turned to the noise. Something blinded her – not the sun, something human, man-made.

'Get down!' Bill screamed, pulling her to the ground as a bullet zipped above their heads. 'This way, follow me.' He belly-crawled to a dismantled chassis a little way off, teetering on the verge of the creek.

Marion followed, reaching shelter just as another bullet cracked through the air. Her skin was clammy, cold. She turned to Bill. He was trying not to shake, trying to breathe.

Several minutes slipped past in near silence. Marion watched her chest rise and fall in rapid intervals.

A guttural scream. Marion's body jerked involuntarily at the sound, coming from the other side of the shed. She peered around the chassis, then dived back just as a bullet cracked through the air. She looked at Bill, mostly to check he hadn't been hit. He shook his head as a drawn-out groan followed another scream.

'It's happening,' Marion breathed urgently. 'The second murder. We have to stop it!' She craned her neck around the car shell, scanned the yard. Nothing.

'Get back!' Bill gasped as yet another bullet hit the chassis, followed by three more in quick succession, one of which ricocheted onto the ground at his feet. 'We've got to move!' he urged, pushing Marion to the left.

The Florist cackled, began to sing:

'Two little mice, all caught in a trap, two little mice nowhere to go.'

Click. The pistol reloaded.

'We have the shipment,' Marion called, realising a bargain was now their only hope.

Silence.

She looked at Bill, at the Twister Rope still curled around his arm. 'Hide it,' she whispered, disentangling her own from between her fingers and around her wrist. She demagnetised it, tied it around her waist, under her blouse.

'Either I kick them over the edge of this creek,' she went on, 'and they break, or you put your gun away and let us bring them to you.'

There was a shuffling sound. Walking? Something being dragged?

'Yes, yes, all right,' the Florist answered, a fraction less controlled. 'Come round to the front of the shed.'

'What's the plan here?' Bill whispered as he shoved the Twister Rope under his shirt, hauled himself upright. 'He's got a gun. There might be others.'

'We can't run and we can't stay cowering behind the chassis.'

They'd started to move, across the open space towards the shed, too close now to have a long conversation, or change their minds.

'Just wait for the perfect moment, okay?' Marion said.

They reached the front of the shed. Looked around. Something flashed behind a honeycomb stack of tyres, catching the sun. Carefully, and with Bill in tow, Marion followed the light, edging closer to the wall of tyres until the light was just a foot away. The light: a dagger, glittering in the sun.

'Leave him!' she gasped, lurching forwards.

Jerome Longmore was lying flat on his back, pinned to the ground by Thomas Proctor, who held the dagger to his throat.

'Mari, no! Wait!' Bill yelled, catching her by the arm.

'Let him go!' she commanded. 'Let him go!'

Proctor faltered for a second, looking up. Longmore took the opportunity to cough, take a breath.

Click. A pistol was cocked. Marion turned to the sound, just to her left.

The Florist's face twisted into a grin as he aimed the gun at Bill. 'Ah, there you are, little mice.'

Bill dropped the box of gadgets at his feet. Held up his hands.

'Names?' the Florist asked.

'We work at Miss Brickett's,' Marion answered quickly. 'That's all you need to know.'

'And we're here for an exchange,' Bill added, tapping the box of gadgets with the toe of his boot.

The Florist's wiry eyebrows arched in surprise. 'Exchange?'

Marion looked at Proctor, his posture stiff, a long cut across his forehead, faint streaks of blood through his white-blond hair. Then at Longmore, drawn and trembling. Her mind ticked, analysing. Killer, victim, killer, victim. But even before reaching the scrapyard, she'd assumed that Proctor was the killer. He'd troubled her since they'd met, with his sinister mannerisms and habit of threatening employees with foul ERPS caricatures, his inexplicable night-time wanderings. He even had a motive, other than self-preservation, to kill Amanda. Jealousy over her relationship with Longmore.

'Longmore in exchange for the shipment,' she said, meeting the Florist's eye.

'No!' Proctor begged, holding the dagger steady against Longmore's throat. 'No, you idiots! Longmore is . . . I am . . . *Please!*'

There was a momentary silence. Even the seagulls above stopped screeching. The flies in the creek stopped buzzing. The Florist frowned, then smiled as something dawned on him. Longmore opened his mouth, glowered at Proctor, then gargled, wheezed, muttered through his teeth: '. . . going to kill me.'

'He made me!' Proctor tried again, looking at the Florist. 'He said it was my life or his. I didn't have a choice.'

'True,' the Florist chimed in after a short interval. 'That *is* what I said.' He laughed softly, causing the pistol to quiver in his hand. 'And I *am* a man of my word.' He gave Proctor a quick nod. 'Do it. Kill him now or I'll shoot you all.' He glanced at Bill. 'Starting with little mouse number one.'

Longmore squirmed, breathing hard. Proctor steadied the blade against his throat.

Marion's eyes were darting, calculating. The Florist had his gun aimed at Bill. He was at close range. He wouldn't miss. And if she moved, tried anything, the Florist would shoot. Bill was dead. If she didn't, Longmore was dead.

'Tick-tock,' the Florist cooed. 'Slit his throat, nice and quick.'

Proctor closed his eyes, then changed his grip on the blade, pressed down. Longmore heaved, screamed out. A trickle of blood swept down his neck, onto his shirt collar.

Marion slipped her hand subtly under her blouse, up to her waist, to the Twister Rope. She looked at Bill and mouthed, 'Two . . . '

He nodded.

In order to do anything useful with it, she'd have to untie and magnetise the rope before anyone stopped her. And before Proctor sliced through Longmore's jugular.

'Three . . . '

The tips of her fingers tingled as she began to untie the knot. She locked her focus on the Florist and called, 'Hey, over here.'

The Florist's eyes flickered, fell on her, unable to resist.

It was the shortest pause, but Marion knew it was their only shot. She ripped the Twister Rope from under her blouse as she lurched forwards. Bill dashed left, cast his rope at Proctor. The Florist re-aimed, this time at Marion. But she was already at his side.

She kicked him in the shin. The blow unsteadied the old man long enough to allow her to throw the rope at his hands. The coil tightened around his wrists instantly, binding them. The pistol slipped from his grip. Marion picked it up and aimed it at him while Bill pinned Proctor to the ground, Twister Rope binding his arms to his chest. He prised the dagger from Proctor's grip, threw it to Longmore.

'Move and I'll shoot,' Marion warned, addressing the Florist. Without turning, or losing her focus, she addressed Proctor. 'And you, Thomas, don't struggle. The rope will tighten every time you do.'

'Damn fools!' Proctor protested, his dark eyes flashing with hatred.

He paused to take a breath, just enough time for Bill to stuff a handkerchief into his mouth, silencing him.

Longmore collapsed several yards away, trembling so much Marion thought he might be having a seizure.

Marion held the pistol steady in her grip, aimed at the Florist's temple. She'd never shot a gun before and she wasn't planning to now. But no one had to know that. At Bill's side, Proctor tried to back away, but before he'd managed to move even an inch, the Twister Rope writhed. He cried out, then coughed as the rope tightened, squeezing the breath from his lungs.

For a split second, Marion was relieved. Proctor and the Florist were disarmed and unable to move. The box of gadgets was still in her possession and no one was dead. But then she remembered where they were – a scrapyard in South London with two Russian spies bound in silvery rope. There was no chance she and Bill could haul the Florist and Proctor back to the agency in Fulham without raising suspicion or being seen.

'Longmore,' she said, looking over. 'I need you to go back to the bookshop and fetch help. Frank or Nancy.'

Longmore, who was trembling less than before though still obviously harried, passed a fleeting glance at the Florist, as though he expected him to leap up at any moment. But the old man was utterly still, observing the scene with unwavering focus.

'You're still in favour with Spragg and the ERPS,' Marion went on in reply to Longmore's silence. 'At least if you encounter either, you'll be able to talk your way out of trouble.'

Longmore pressed a hand to his neck, winced. 'Yes, all right. I should manage. And you'll stay here?'

Marion looked down at the Florist, who'd still not moved an inch. Then over at Proctor, who was no longer fighting his bonds but still groaning, wheezing through his gag. Bill was crouched beside him, sweating but seemingly in control.

'Yes,' she said. Then, looking at Longmore's chest, 'Your apprentice badge, where is it?'

He patted his breast pocket nervously, then cast a searching gaze around the ground. 'I . . . don't know. Must have lost it when Proctor dragged me here.'

She bit her lip in frustration. 'Well, you can't get into the agency without it. I'll have to come with you.'

'Just give me yours,' he suggested hastily.

'I can't. Badges only work if the person they're registered to uses them.' She faltered for a moment, trying to dismiss the vague misgiving rising inside her. She didn't like the idea of leaving Bill alone with Proctor and the Florist, even if he was armed.

'Don't worry; I'll be fine,' Bill said in a whisper, reading her concerned expression. 'Just hurry.'

Marion and Longmore arrived at the bookshop forty minutes later. The sun had started to fall and a sheet of deep grey cloud obscured the last rays of light, casting the Georgian shop in a grim, eerie shadow. Marion allowed Longmore to take the lead, trailing behind him as he unlocked the door, pulled down the lamp post disguised as a lever and weaved his way through the cramped shelves of the bookshop. The journey from Chestwells had passed in a silent blur, though now Longmore appeared more hurried, agitated.

'You're going to have to go and find Spragg on your own,' she said as they reached the butler's desk. 'I'll use my badge to open the lift, but I'll have to wait here. I'm still supposed to be in my quarters. And there's an outstanding High Council order in my name. If you bump into Spragg, insist on speaking with Nancy or Frank. Make up any excuse, just don't tell her the truth. If Frank's able to call Constable Redding and he arrests the Florist, it should be enough to start untangling the mess Spragg's got us all wound up in.'

Longmore clutched his chin, wiped his forehead with the back of his hand. The thin cut on his neck had stopped bleeding, but his shirt collar was now soaked in red. 'Fine, okay.' He turned to face her. He looked past her, to the bookshop door, still open, then bent down and retrieved a duffel bag wedged between two bookshelves.

'What's that?' Marion cocked her head. Her skin prickled. 'We can't leave Bill with the others at the scrapyard forever. What's the matter?'

'Actually, I think you should go down there instead. I'll wait here.'

'What? I just told you, I have an outstanding order against my name. I can't go traipsing around the agency and Spragg will never let me speak to Frank.'

Longmore pushed one hand into his pocket, the other still clutching the strap of the duffel bag. 'I can't,' he said simply, starting for the door.

'What are you doing?' Marion asked, her voice rising.

'I'm leaving. Just . . . let me, okay?'

'What on earth? Leaving for where?' She blocked his path, wedging herself between the butler's desk and the wall, pressed her hands onto his chest, forcing him to a halt.

'I forgot something at the scrapyard.'

'Have you lost your mind? We've got to . . . '

Longmore's expression darkened. Something had changed. He spoke again, this time rushed, breathless. 'I have to run, get away. I've failed them. They'll never stop hunting me. You *have* to let me go.'

She gasped, her head reeling, understanding. She didn't move, though every muscle in Longmore's body was jumping to get past her, tensed, ready to bolt. 'Fraser Henley,' she muttered, barely able to get the words out.

He shifted on his feet. His right eye fluttered.

A pause. Longmore, Fraser – whoever he was – shook his head. He launched forwards, drawing out a dagger – the one Bill had thrown to him in the scrapyard – and swiping it through the air like a man possessed. It missed her neck by half an inch the first time, less the second and third. She ducked and weaved and danced around him. Then, thinking on her feet, she grabbed a book from the shelf next to her and lobbed it right at him. He ducked, giving her a second's grace. She reached for the dagger but tripped, lost her composure.

He caught her by the shoulders. She struggled – but like a coil of Twister Rope, this only made him tighten his grip. He brought the dagger to her face.

'I told you to let me go!'

He pressed the blade into her cheek. It pierced the skin. Blood trickled into her mouth. She spluttered, inhaling the liquid with what felt like her final breath.

'I don't want to kill you. I didn't want to kill Amanda. Or Eddie. I just want to *disappear*.'

'Okay, okay! Go. Leave. I won't stop you, I promise.'

He took a breath, lessening the pressure of the blade against her cheek, then staggered backwards into the short passage behind the butler's desk that led to the trapdoor.

Marion edged sideways, pressed a finger to the cut on her face, stemming the blood. She watched Fraser analyse her, the threat she posed. She might let him leave, but she knew who he was now. His cover was blown.

He lowered the blade. Took a step forwards.

Then everything paused.

Fraser froze. Marion held her breath. Someone was coming up the stairs towards the trapdoor.

The latch on the other side clanged as it slid loose.

Fraser was standing to the left of the butler's desk – he would get the first look at whoever it was.

'Jerome? What's going on? What . . . get away from me.'

'No!' Marion screamed. She couldn't see around the corner, she couldn't see who'd come through the trapdoor and called out Fraser's alias, but she knew exactly who it was. 'Jess! No! Get back. Run!'

Fraser blinked, turned to face Jessica instead and twirled the dagger in his hand. He reached for the light switch and everything went black.

Marion stretched her hands out in front of her, searching for the light.

There was a scuffle – Fraser and Jessica – which went on for several seconds. Marion couldn't see a thing but heard the swish of the dagger as it cut through the air. Over and over, back and forth. Jessica cried out. Something thumped, hit the floor.

Marion staggered forwards, finally found the light switch. She could already smell the thick metallic scent of blood as it filled the cramped space.

There were only two people left alive in the bookshop now.

She flicked on the light.

25

Atonement

A couple of weeks later, Marion found a seat in the auditorium alongside Bill, Preston, Kenny and Maud. Nancy was standing in her usual spot at the head and looked every bit as serious and impatient as ever. Next to her was Frank, Professor Gillroth and Mr Nicholas (with Harry cowering at his side). Everyone was wearing a memorial band – a strip of black silk, either tied around their arms or folded and tucked into their coat pockets.

Marion wove her own strip through her fingers, feeling the silk glide over the callouses on her palm, remembering – the bookshop floorboards soaked with blood, the body. Everything that had occurred after her encounter with Fraser had happened in such a blur of chaos and confusion that, looking back, it seemed surreal. Following the pandemonium, however, she'd come to her senses, bolted down through the trapdoor, to the common room. Thankfully, David was still there, on watch.

Following Marion's instructions, he'd located Nicholas, convinced him there had been an *incident* in the bookshop. After a hurried explanation from Marion and presentation of Fraser Henley's fake identity papers – retrieved from his duffel bag – Nicholas had allowed Frank to inform Constable Redding that the Florist was tied up in Chestwells scrapyard alongside the body of his latest victim. Leonid Oblonsky was arrested and – to simplify things and prevent unanswerable questions from being raised – charged with two counts of murder.

It was partial justice at best, but it was all that could be expected under the circumstances. And, as Marion had assumed, Spragg was quick to back down once she'd learned of the Florist's fate. Even so, Marion and Frank had used all the information gathered from Swindlehurst and Quinn – the exact method Spragg had used to defraud the Workshop by altering inventory lists and shipping documents – to convince the majority of the ERPS that Spragg wasn't entirely who she claimed to be. They then delivered their own version of *The Truths* – evidence (albeit circumstantial) – that Spragg had been accepting money from Leonid Oblonsky, a KGB official, who'd used Spragg's influence at Miss Brickett's to ship agency gadgets to Moscow. Indeed, nearly everyone on the EPRS had agreed that Spragg deserved a turn under the Liar's Eyeglass herself.

Now, Marion glanced at her fellow apprentices scattered throughout the auditorium. Some looked pensive, others apprehensive, tense. Though all ERPS propaganda had been removed and destroyed and no meetings had taken place since Amanda's death, the society lingered, albeit deconstructed, fragile and ineffectual.

Even after Spragg's hasty confession, the ERPS, as a unit, didn't implode completely. While they vehemently agreed that Spragg had been in the wrong defrauding the Gadgetry Department and conspiring with Oblonsky, they seemed reluctant to accept that this meant everything the ERPS stood for was, by default, wrong. After all, the establishing principles of the society held firm: truth, reformation, security. In fact, Marion wasn't sure if cohesion would ever return to Miss

Brickett's, especially after the trauma everyone had suffered, Amanda's death and then . . .

Kenny turned to Marion, flicked this thumb across her cheek. 'All right, Lane?'

She looked at his fingers, the blue-grey marks still etched across them, a reminder of his time under the Liar's Eyeglass. She'd still not asked him exactly what had happened with Spragg and the High Council in the Gadgetry Department, but she knew he'd lied, over and over for hours, to stall things, to protect her.

'I don't know. Are you?'

Kenny nodded and kissed her hand. He'd been different towards her since the bookshop incident – gentler, warmer. He'd hardly left her side all week, even when Kate had tempted him with her most amorous smile and seductive expressions.

'Yeah, think so,' he said, studying her anxiously. 'You'll get there, promise.'

How could he be so sure? She looked again at her colleagues scattered throughout the auditorium – Spragg, Harry, the remaining members of the ERPS. How could anything go back to normal when Miss Brickett's was infested with liars and con artists?

'Oh, and look who it is,' Maud pronounced, breaking the tension, catching Marion mid-thought. 'And as bright and polished as ever. How *does* she do it?'

'I shower occasionally and sometimes I even bother to brush my hair, quite the family secret,' Jessica laughed softly as she sat down. She reached across Kenny's lap and took Marion's hand, squeezed it firmly – a signal of solidarity and understanding.

Jessica, like Marion, hadn't been the same since the ordeal in the bookshop the week before. It wasn't murder, Marion kept reminding her. Fraser had tripped, fallen on his dagger.

But that didn't take away from the fact that Jessica had witnessed a colleague bleed to death in front of her eyes. It didn't matter that he was a Russian spy, a murderer, a liar. In that moment, he'd been a colleague, a fellow recruit and a human being.

Marion turned in her seat. Professor Bal caught her eye, beckoned her over. She climbed over Maud and Jessica, shimmied through the row of seats to the back. The professor removed his beret and pulled her into an embrace.

'You look rested,' she said with a small laugh. 'Or are my eyes deceiving me?'

The professor, whose skin was certainly brighter and his clothes less tattered, confirmed this with a brisk nod.

'Your eyes *are* deceiving you, most definitely,' he said with a wink. 'I haven't slept all week.' He shook out his beret, put it back on. 'But even so, I *am* feeling better. Miss Quinn has been a delight in the department.' He lowered his voice conspiratorially. 'Actually, she's a little infuriating at times, but very helpful.' He chuckled. 'That notebook habit of hers, I've never seen anything like it.'

'She's a special one,' Marion agreed wholeheartedly, recalling Quinn's shock and excitement when she learned that it was Marion who'd made the High Council aware of her incomparable skills, resulting in a new role – Gadgetry design assistant – which Quinn accepted with gusto. 'She deserves it.'

The professor gleamed, as did Marion, warmed at the spark of joy flickering across his face. He'd been reinstated as head of the Gadgetry Department just days after Spragg's confession, slipping back into the role as though he'd never left. And if he held even a trace of disappointment for the part Marion had played in his demotion, he never showed it.

She pressed her hands together and looked him in the eye. 'I wanted to say thank you.'

The professor cocked his head to the side, causing his beret to slip an inch to the left. 'For what?'

'For never doubting my intentions. Even after you found out about, well, everything. I never had to explain to you why I joined the ERPS. Or why I signed your demotion referendum. But I hope you know, everything I did was done to bring down Spragg and the society. Signing the referendum, especially.' She took a long breath. 'I hated it all and I'm so sorry you suffered because of it.'

He waved this off, turned to look at the head of the auditorium. Nancy was standing at the podium, her hands resting on either side of the microphone. The professor tapped Marion's hand, nodded at the ceiling, from which a swathe of twinkling white clockwork stars appeared, just as the main light was extinguished.

'You and I make a wonderful team. We always will,' the professor said as the stars released a rain of miniature origami.

Along with the crowd, Marion caught one, unfolded it and read the note she and the professor had written inside: *In loving memory of Amanda Hannah Shirley. Friend, colleague, detective.* She looked up. Thomas Proctor was standing a little way off, clutching an origami, his eyes wet. He noticed her staring, and for once his expression wasn't searching or unpleasant but rather warm, trusting and yes, sad.

Following the incident at Chestwells, guilt and regret from both Marion and Proctor had brought a certain level of understanding to their interactions. Marion had apologised for misjudging him, while Proctor provided an explanation for his odd behaviour. He'd suspected Longmore of foul play at the agency since their recruitment, which was why she'd seen him stalking around at night in the staff quarters. Yes, he'd tried to undermine Longmore, but only because he believed he was after Amanda — first romantically, then nefariously. He also explained that he'd only shown Marion and Amanda their respective caricatures (both of which were Spragg's creations) to warn them of what was to come, not to intimidate or threaten them.

'But I know,' he'd concluded, eyes cast to the floor, 'I don't come across as I mean to sometimes. And I'm sorry for that. I wish I could tell *her* that, too.'

The main light flickered back on after a moment's silence. Proctor raised a hand to Marion, then vanished into a throng of employees.

'Thank you for coming,' Nancy announced from the podium, mannered and constrained, banishing the chatter.

Marion returned to her seat alongside Jessica, Maud and Bill. She clutched her black silk band even tighter. Kenny placed a hand on her thigh.

'Tonight we are here for two reasons: to honour the life and work of our dearest colleague, Amanda Shirley, and to fix what has been broken. I realise that the past few months have been exceedingly challenging for us all. We've lost a great deal here at Miss Brickett's. Not only life, but also trust, respect, solidarity. It may seem impossible for us to come together again, to seal the rift that exists between those who were a part of the ERPS and those who were not, but I do believe it's possible.'

To Nancy's left, Nicholas shifted on his feet. Just behind him stood Delia Spragg, dressed in a grey-and-white skirt and stained blue blouse, her lips cracked, her skin taut and discoloured.

'We have been torn apart by lies and distrust,' Nancy continued, 'and it is my firm conviction that the only thing that will bring us back together is the opposite — honesty and empathy. I expect each one of you to take responsibility for your part in what happened here over the past months, admit your failures and learn from your mistakes. And, of course, I think it is only fair that I do the same.' She seemed to lose herself for a moment, composure draining from her expression bit by bit.

Marion had always found Nancy's cold, controlled character both unsettling and admirable. But now it seemed that the smallest fracture had formed and through it, a tendril of vulnerability was evident.

The auditorium looked at one another, unsure what to expect and hesitant to believe that anything Nancy said could undo the catastrophe that had swept through their ranks, tearing down their foundations and disrupting their sense of order.

Nancy steeled herself, perhaps sensing the monumental task before her. 'I deeply regret allowing the ERPS to seed and spread at Miss Brickett's when I had the opportunity to put an end to it. I am not completely sure how it happened so quickly, or why I didn't see it for what it was right from the beginning. All I can say in my defence is that I was preoccupied with other problems at the time.'

Marion and Kenny glanced at one another knowingly. By 'other problems', they were certain she meant the Harrogate murder case.

'I was naive and inattentive, and I take full responsibility for the damage my inaction caused. I promise you that this will not happen again.' She broke off, turned to Frank.

For the first time in memory, it seemed as though Nancy was expecting some degree of approval from him to continue. He gave it with a subtle nod.

'One thing I hope we can all learn from this ordeal is to be aware of the power of persuasion. So often in life we are blinded by promises from corrupt individuals and organisations, assurances of community and safety and togetherness, a better life, perhaps even happiness. We are presented with something that pledges to fill the void inside us, for we all have one to fill. Instead we find ourselves manipulated and ensnared. For as long as human beings have been on this Earth, cults and sects and societies have taken advantage of the weak and vulnerable, flourishing in troubled times, for that is when their apparent solutions become so much more desirable. We cannot expect to stop the barrage of con artists and conspirators in this world – they will always exist and they will always try their luck. Therefore, I leave you with this simple advice: think for yourself. The truth is very often just an opinion. Be sure to form your own.'

She stopped and for a while the auditorium was still. The members of the ERPS shifted in their seats.

'Delia,' Nancy said minutes later, 'will you get us started?'

Spragg looked as if she were considering refusing Nancy's request, then swiftly changed her mind.

'Hello, everyone,' she began, wringing her hands against her chest and speaking in a detached monotone, as though she'd practised the speech several times. 'I should start by explaining how I met the Florist.' She swallowed. 'I oversaw the Factory order forms at the time and one day I received a commission inquiry for a batch of polygraphs. I knew I shouldn't respond – the inquiry had come from a private source, not Hanslope Park or the CIA. But the request had promised a small fee in exchange for it being signed off and, well, I wanted the money.

'In the beginning, that's all it ever was for me. I didn't know the man who'd requested the commission was Russian, or working for the KGB. I never even met him. I didn't know he'd orchestrated the recruitment of Mr Henley and, although I realise this is hard to believe, I knew nothing about Mr Henley's role in the whole ordeal. Nothing at all . . . I . . . ' She cleared her throat and cast her eyes to the floor, as though embarrassed by the statement. 'I didn't know it then, but that first letter was a test. A way that the Florist could judge whether or not I'd be a worthy partner in his business venture. I suppose you could say that I passed.

'Following this, every week he sent me a list of gadgets he wished to acquire and a sum of cash. I had no idea where the gadgets were going.'

Nancy interrupted with a small cough.

Spragg took a long breath. 'I-I know it was wrong of me to keep the money for myself. I know it was wrong to take the orders without permission and to fix the inventory list. I was greedy and . . . it all just got away from me.

'I realised I might get caught out, so I created the ERPS to distract everyone from what was going on in Gadgetry. I distributed the propaganda to gather members and create mistrust. As time went on, it became less about the money and more about the power. I liked being at the top. I liked being in control. I know you won't believe this,' she added with a slight stammer, 'but I regret it all. I really do. I hope you can forgive me . . . eventually.' She lowered her voice and muttered something more that only Nancy could hear.

'Thank you, Delia,' Nancy said, gesturing for Spragg to step aside. 'Even though we may not fully understand your motivations, I'm sure we can agree that you have demonstrated courage tonight. As we have seen, not only with Delia and the members of the ERPS, but also with Mr Henley,' she went on, addressing the auditorium at large (while Spragg's expression grew more shameful and pitiful), 'weakness and desperation are easily moulded. None of us are immune to this. Let us keep that in mind, always.'

There was a long moment of contemplation.

'Now, before we move on to Miss Shirley's memorial service, I think it is imperative that I address several rumours that have been circulating since last week. To start, as I'm sure you already realise, the Employee Rights and Protection Society are no longer permitted to exist in any formal capacity, to hold meetings, to sign referendums or to distribute propaganda of any sort and in any format. I would also like to make it clear that the High Council and myself are once again in full control of Miss Brickett's.' She glanced to her left, to Spragg, Mr Nicholas.

They looked away.

'However, there have been some necessary adjustments to the board. As such Mr Stone, Professor Gillroth, Miss Simpkins and myself remain on the council, while Delia Spragg and Rupert Nicholas have been removed. I would also like to state, for the record, that Professor Bal is once again head of the Gadgetry Department. As for Mrs Spragg, despite the pivotal role she played in establishing the ERPS, I would ask that you all respect my decision to keep her on as a Miss Brickett's employee. I have discussed this at length with the High Council and we have decided that she will remain here as my general assistant, under our close and constant watch.'

'*What?* Is she having us on?' Maud growled, followed by a similar rumble of discontent from the crowd.

'She doesn't have a choice,' Bill pointed out amid the chatter. 'Think about it. If she fires her, she'll likely turn on us, expose us, who knows what. This way, she has her chained. She says she's keeping Spragg as an employee' – he sniggered, raised an eyebrow – 'sounds more like a prisoner on parole to me.'

'He's right,' Jessica said assuredly. 'Nancy isn't being kind, she's being Nancy. Protecting the agency at all costs.'

Marion watched Spragg cower under Nancy's glare, all trace of her former poise and righteousness wiped away. Perhaps Jessica and Bill were right, perhaps this was a punishment worse than any other Nancy could have given.

'Miss Lane, one minute, please.' Nancy ushered Marion to the side directly following Amanda's service.

'Yes?' She shuffled closer.

Nancy's blank expression gave absolutely nothing away. 'Two things: I didn't want to announce this to the auditorium, for obvious reasons, but I thought you'd like to know that Harry has also been reprimanded for his little espionage operation.'

Marion chewed the inside of her cheek. Ridiculous as it was, she'd hoped Frank would have found a way to explain to Nancy everything that had unfolded without having to tell her about Marion's secret informer. Obviously, he hadn't.

'However, I don't think we will have any further problems from him now that his accomplice is out of the picture.'

Marion wound the strip of black silk through her fingers, distracting herself. She was rather certain she knew who his 'accomplice' was.

Nancy waited for a moment, perhaps expecting Marion to ask what she meant. Eventually, she gave up.

'Mr Swindlehurst is dead, Miss Lane. It appears he fell from a considerable height, broke his neck, shattered his skull.'

Marion braced herself, prepared for the worst. 'I'm sorry to hear that.'

Nancy stared her down for one long and intolerable minute, then turned to the briefcase lying on the table behind her. She drew out a tattered leather roll of tools, handed it over.

'Never again, do you understand?'

Epilogue

Eight months later

In the weeks that led up to Christmas Eve, 1959, Miss Brickett's Investigations and Inquiries transformed into a wonderland of colour and extravagance. The marble floor of the Grand Corridor glimmered with the reflection of stringed crystal lights. Red and gold streamers encircled the lamp statues and the faint chime of Christmas carols echoed from the ballroom. Here, an enormous frost-tipped pine reached to the ceiling, decorated in hundreds of glittering, dancing embellishments. Some of these were ordinary Christmas trimmings, most were rather more bizarre: silver clocks that hopped from branch to branch of their own accord, white gold pine cones that sprouted wings every hour and soared across the room, expelling a rain of prismatic glitter.

The library bar was permanently stocked with food and drink brought in from across Europe: iced scones, French pastries, gingerbread twirls, specially blended whiskies from the Scottish Highlands. The corridors closer to the kitchens were invariably thick with the scent of spiced wine, nutmeg and honey, while the common room was adorned with Christmas-themed board games, sprigs of holly, red stockings and the general cheer of the holiday season. It was the most dazzling, brilliant Christmas in Miss Brickett's history and yet Marion had chosen to spend the eve of the twenty-fourth at 16 Willow Street.

Now, standing at her old bedroom window, she watched a sweep of grey water flow through Willow Street and into the storm drain, gushing down into the sewer. She imagined the grimy stream disappearing into the tunnels below the city streets, flowing east towards the River Fleet. But not all of it would make it there, some destined to seep through London's oldest foundations, down, down, down until it reached the gloom of another world. A place that, for all its dazzling decorations and brilliant disguises, held a darkness Marion now realised could never be completely excised.

'Ghastly out there, isn't it,' Frank said, coming up beside her. He was dressed for travel in a hooded coat and scarf, boots, a folded umbrella at his side.

'You sure you won't stay?' Marion asked, turning to face him.

Dressed for a night of fizz and celebration, she was wearing a sheath dress in port red, her favourite colour, which brought out the streaks of bronze in her otherwise monochrome hair.

'Thank you, but I shouldn't. I promised my sister I'd spend the evening with her and since we hardly see each other these days . . . ' He trailed off, his gaze flickering. 'Besides, Christmas is always such a busy time for me.'

Sheets of rain were now falling faster than ever, drumming against the window, the roof. Marion knew what he meant by *busy*. Christmas was traditionally when Frank compiled his shortlist of new recruits and prepared their tests and interviews. She couldn't help but wonder if he'd do things differently this year.

'One more year,' he muttered, stirring from a thought, 'and you'll be an Inquirer.' He shook his head wistfully. 'I always believed bringing you to Miss Brickett's was a way to protect and watch over you. But it's been very much the other way round, hasn't it?' He placed a hand on her shoulder. 'Thank you again, my dear. For everything. I'm so grateful and . . . proud.'

Marion smiled, nodded subtly. Something transformed inside her. Frank was and always would be her greatest source of comfort. But over the course of the year, her desperate urge for his approval and validation had tempered, if only by a fraction. Failure and loss had finally washed her clean and, in their wake, something stronger bloomed – trust in her own decisions and capabilities. As Bill had rightly pointed out, she *did* deserve to be an Inquirer, just as much as anyone else. She had nothing left to prove, not to Frank, not even to herself.

She looked again out of the window where a knot of cloaked figures was bumbling ungracefully down Willow Street, one umbrella between them. They paused outside number 16.

'I believe that's my cue to leave,' Frank said as the doorbell rang.

Marion pulled him into a hug. 'I'll see you next year, then.'

'Indeed. I'm looking forward to it,' he pronounced with a certain degree of effort. 'Have a wonderful Christmas, my dear.'

Bill, Preston, Maud, Jessica and David had settled in a circle on tattered cushions and threadbare woollen blankets arranged around a blazing gas heater in the centre of Marion's old bedroom. Between them was a game of Miss Brickett's Cluedo and, of course, several bottles of assorted liquor. Kenny was there too, lying on his side, propped up on his elbows, bantering with Bill whenever the opportunity presented.

The bedroom had been decorated mostly by Jessica hours earlier. Nothing like the frill and indulgence of the Grand Corridor or ballroom, but still good enough to recognise it was Christmas. Red, gold and green tinsel adorned the wooden rafters and a small pine sapling that Preston had bought from the local Christmas tree farm stood near the window. Arranged around the base of the tree were seven presents roughly wrapped in glossy festive paper – six of which Marion had bought with her share of the prize money from the ERPS quiz.

'How do you turn these sodding things off?' Maud snapped. She pointed at the ceiling where one of the only gadget decorations Jessica had managed to 'borrow' from Miss Brickett's was fluttering between the roof beams unchecked. It was a specially designed bronze Distracter programmed to emit Christmas carols every couple of minutes. Maud scowled at Jessica. 'Out of all the things you could have stolen, you chose a singing bird?'

Jessica continued handing out the Cluedo tokens unperturbed – small wooden figurines of past employees. 'I see you're in the Christmas spirit already, fabulous. And for your information, I didn't steal the Distracter. I'd never take a gadget from the agency without permission—'

Maud rolled her eyes. 'Oh! Spare us the righteousness for one night, please.'

Jessica continued to ignore her. 'I found it in my bag when I arrived here. Must have flown in.' She fluttered her eyelids at Marion.

Marion smiled and swiftly confirmed: 'Sounds like something a Distracter would do. Anyway' – she jumped up – 'I'll get it.' She climbed onto Preston's shoulders, he being the tallest of the group, and snatched up the Distracter mid 'Silent Night', adjusted the dial she knew so well and turned it off. Permanently.

'Would have much rather you'd brought us one of those bottomless mulled-wine tanks Bal set up in the library bar,' Maud mused, pulling her tokens and cards towards her. She turned to Marion, a mischievous glimmer in her eye. 'How did you two make that thing, anyway? It's brilliant!'

'Simpler than it looks, actually,' Marion said, though this wasn't quite true.

She, Bal and Quinn had spent the best part of a month designing the liquid level sensor, the automatic switch, the pump machine. It had been a wondrous distraction to spend the long months that followed the Florist's arrest with Bal and Quinn in the Workshop, doing what they loved best. And although it seemed like a waste of time and money to some – designing gadgets for no other purpose than festive pleasure – Marion sensed it was well worth it in the end. Things had certainly changed for the better since that poignant general meeting in the auditorium. No one had mentioned the ERPS in months, its remaining members having abandoned their arrow pin badges and air of superiority, while Delia Spragg spent her days under Nancy's close watch, haggard and nearly forgotten.

Marion beamed now at the sight of her friends, snug around the heater. Like her, somehow they'd all felt that, despite the wonder of the holiday party Nancy and Gillroth had organised beneath the streets, this was an evening the second-year apprentices (and Kenny) should spend with each other, for once away from all that had brought them together.

It was Christmas Eve, but it would also have been Amanda Shirley's twenty-ninth birthday.

Jessica completed the handout of tokens and cards while Maud poured everyone a tankard of golden ale.

Then, as if they'd rehearsed it several times, the group raised their tankards in unison. 'Happy birthday, Amanda.'

'It's the first time we've played without her,' Preston uttered plaintively, taking a sip.

'I miss her,' David said under his breath, twisting awkwardly as he realised everyone was looking at him. 'She was an outsider, like me. Suppose that's why . . . '

Marion placed a hand on his wrist, gently tightening her grip as he twitched and tried to pull away. 'We're all outsiders. That's why we have to stick together.'

The rain pattered against the window and a soft wind whistled through the street. It was warm and cosy inside the house and yet an undeniable darkness lingered.

'Well, let's get started,' Jessica said, gesturing to the board game in front of her, her eyes brimming. She picked up a tiny vile-looking gargoyle, one of the game's weapons, and stared at it thoughtfully.

Preston laughed, catching on. 'She *hated* that thing, didn't she.'

Maud chimed in. 'Yeah, she was convinced it could actually move.'

There was a lull in the conversation as, Marion presumed, each one of them walked their own private paths of mourning. Marion tried to picture Amanda sitting among them as they played, but it was hard to do so without recalling the last time she'd seen her – the look of terror etched into her cold, lifeless face.

'Goodness, have you seen this?' Jessica asked the group, breaking the quiet and smoothing out the latest copy of *The Times* during a short pause in the game. She read the front-page article out loud.

'Suspected murderer and Soviet spy Leonid Oblonsky (also known as the Florist of Moscow), who was apprehended by local constable for the Metropolitan Police, Marshal Redding,

*was found dead in his prison cell last night. Wardens on duty
are baffled as to how Oblonsky got hold of a tie, which he
used to hang himself. They claim the Russian was "restless
and anxious" following the announcement that his extradition
order had been denied and he wouldn't be allowed to return to
the Soviet Union. According to Constable Redding, because
Oblonsky was a member of the Russian state security police,
he might have avoided execution on counts of espionage against
Britain but would have "almost certainly faced death by
hanging" for two counts of murder in the first degree. Redding
went on to state that Oblonsky's timely suicide was "the last
act of a professional coward".'*

She folded the paper and pushed it away.

Bill and Kenny glanced briefly at Marion, frowning.
Oblonsky would surely have been convicted of murder, had
he stood trial. After all, it was his dagger that had killed Fraser
Henley and his Soviet service pistol – a Makarov – that had
killed Eddie Hopper. But would a trial have been in everyone's
best interests? Marion was starkly aware that the Russian knew
too much – about Miss Brickett's, about the supply chain of
gadgets from the Workshop to Hanslope Park. Indeed, if the
Florist had entered a court of law, his testimony would have
ruined the relationship Redding and Miss Brickett's had fostered
for nearly a decade.

Bill shrugged, muttered. 'Bit convenient, isn't it?'

Marion nodded. Oblonsky's death was certainly unexpected. And while it simplified things for Miss Brickett's, it
added to the tally of lies and secrets the agency concealed
within its walls. Would the price for such deception one day
be too much? Would Miss Brickett's cave in, crushed by the
weight of its past?

Hours later, after the group had opened their presents and filled their bellies, Marion found Kenny downstairs in the kitchen, staring vacantly across the room. It was eight months since he'd called things off with Kate, yet he and Marion were still in limbo, hovering somewhere between friends and lovers, surviving on stolen glances, a lingering touch. Were they both afraid of what came next? Or was it as Frank proclaimed – that true love takes time to be seen for what it is?

'Nice threads, by the way,' he said with a lopsided grin, turning to face her.

'Pardon?'

His eyes traced her collarbone, her neck, the dip of her shoulders. 'The dress. I like it.'

She swept her hands down her front, feeling the satin glide beneath her fingers. 'Oh, thanks. And thanks again for this . . . ' She held up a small silver screwdriver, engraved with her initials and the date: 24/12/59. She turned a dial on the handle several degrees clockwise and the screwdriver transformed into a pair of delicate tweezers. She turned it another notch clockwise and the tweezers changed into a miniature set of Allen keys. 'I've been playing with it for hours and I still haven't flicked through all the incarnations.'

'It was Bill and Jessica's idea, and all Professor Bal's mastery. He worked on it for a solid two months. At one point, I thought we'd have to tell him to give up. Not that he'd have listened.' He shook his head. 'Anyway, I'm glad you like it. Apparently, there're something like fifty-eight tools packed inside.'

'*Love* it,' she gushed.

Discarding her old leather roll of tools had been strangely cathartic. The collection she'd been given so many years ago was partly the reason she became a Miss Brickett's apprentice. But ever since she'd used them to unlock Swindlehurst's Holding Chamber, a shadow of unease seemed to follow her, as though Swindlehurst's ghost lingered nearby, always whispering: *I won't be the last.*

But now, as she flicked through her shiny new collection, marvelling at the myriad wondrous tools springing to life from their tiny silver roots, she found herself so enthralled that for a moment she forgot Kenny was standing in front of her. She flinched as his fingers encircled her wrist, pulling her hand towards his chest. She looked up. The air between them crackled and sparked. He pulled her chin towards him, pressed his lips to hers. They separated seconds later, though it felt like hours.

Kenny ruffled his flaxen hair, chewed his lip. 'I've tried so hard not to let this happen. I guess it's pointless now.'

'I think it always was,' she said as he trailed a finger along her jawline. 'But should we? I mean, you said . . . '

He pulled her towards him again, urgently this time, hand on the back of her neck, fingers knotted in her hair.

'I'll take that as a yes, then,' she laughed, taking a breath.

He looked over her shoulder. Someone was coming down the steps. 'Promise me you won't forget this tomorrow,' he whispered, though didn't wait for her reply. He picked up a beer from the counter and walked past her, touching the curve of her waist.

Jessica and Bill moseyed past seconds later, both grinning mischievously.

'What?' Marion said, patting down her ruffled hair.

'Smashing outfit, I must agree,' Jessica chirped.

'Threads, you mean,' Bill piped up, lips twitching with a suppressed smile, barely able to contain himself.

Marion gasped, swatting them away with a tea towel. 'You sneaky little—'

'We knew anyway,' Jessica said, stepping neatly out of the way. 'I mean, it's glaring, really.' She retrieved a steamed fruit pudding from the fridge and laid it on the counter. 'Bill, help me serve, won't you?'

'Yeah,' Bill agreed as he filled seven bowls with pudding and a helping of clotted cream. 'You'd have to be blind not to see it.'

'Or dead from the neck up,' Jessica added.

Marion crossed her arms but couldn't keep the smile from her face, which was now prickling and hot. 'See what, exactly?'

Jessica set the bowls on a serving tray, placed her hands on her hips. 'Oh, for heaven's sake, darling. You *are* stubborn, Marion Lane!'

Marion continued to feign confusion, her gaze fixed on Jessica's ivy-green eyes. Beautiful, intuitive, lovely Jess. And Bill, steadfast, gallant, forever at her side. Her chest swelled. It really *had* been the perfect Christmas, well, almost.

Jessica kissed her on the cheek. 'We love you, Mari. So much.'

Bill rapped her gently on the forehead. 'And in case it hasn't sunk in here yet, so does Kenny Hugo.'

'*And,*' Jessica added before Marion could object, 'you love us all back.'

'Fine,' Marion said with a playful sigh. She threaded her right arm through Bill's, her left through Jessica's. 'Guilty as charged.'

Jessica squealed with delight. 'Oh, at last! We're finally getting somewhere.'

Marion tipped her head onto Bill's shoulder. 'Anyway, Merry Christmas.'

Acknowledgements

Writing a book is a solitary experience. Publishing one requires an army. I have so many people to thank for *The Deadly Rose*, most of whom have worked tirelessly behind the scenes for months on end. I wish I could give you all a hug. Perhaps one day.

The brilliant team at the Madeleine Milburn Literary Agency – Giles and Madeleine Milburn, Liane-Louis Smith, Valentina Paulmichl, Emma Dawson – have been superb since day one. Thank you all for your continual enthusiasm and encouragement, primarily my agent, Hayley Steed. I tell people that signing with you was like winning the lottery. But actually, I suspect it's even better. Thank you for everything you've done to bring *Marion* into the world.

My gifted editors in England and America, Rachel Neely and Laura Brown, have cheered me on every step of the way. Thank you for filling in plot holes, sharpening sentences, enriching character arcs and turning my disorderly manuscript into something I can be proud of. Working with you makes everything easier.

To the long-suffering book wizards at Orion and the larger Hachette team, who have indulged my every query and concern without complaint, thank you for bringing this book into the world. Special mention to Ellen Turner, Lucy Cameron, Clarissa Sutherland and Claire Dean.

Micaela Alcaino, you are an incomparable talent. Thank you for *another* eye-popping cover design that perfectly captures the tone and essence of *The Deadly Rose*. I know readers will admire your work as much as I do.

As the winner of my character-naming competition, thank you to Keely Wagner. Ambrosia Clementine Quinn is your creation, and I do hope you like how she turned out.

Thank you to the ever-growing throng of fellow authors, booksellers, bloggers, librarians and readers who've gone out of their way to review, promote and shout about this book, even in the pandemic. I seriously considered listing all of your names here, then realised just how many of you there are (and how lucky I am to say that)!

I couldn't do any of this without the care, encouragement and love of the wonderful people who know me best. Mom, Dad, Ben, Willie (to whom this book is dedicated), the du Plessis family, Bridget R (the best godmother one could wish for), and all my lovely friends in South Africa and across the globe. I love you all.

Finally, to my lovely readers. Thank you for coming along on this adventure with me. I know that for most of you, the past two years have been long and difficult and uncertain. But I hope you were able to find an escape in Marion's world, and that the story helped you forget, just for a little while.

Credits

Orion Fiction would like to thank everyone at Orion who worked on the publication of *Marion Lane and the Deadly Rose*.

Agent
Hayley Steed

Editors
Rachel Neely
Francesca Pathak

Copy-editor
Claire Dean

Proofreader
Marian Reid

Editorial Management
Clarissa Sutherland
Jane Hughes
Charlie Panayiotou
Tamara Morriss
Claire Boyle

Audio
Paul Stark
Jake Alderson

Contracts
Anne Goddard

Design
Nick Shah
Rabab Adams
Charlotte Abrams Simpson
Debbie Holmes
Joanna Ridley
Nick May
Helen Ewing
Clare Sivell

Finance
Nick Gibson
Jasdip Nandra
Rabale Mustafa

Elizabeth Beaumont
Ibukun Ademefun
Afeera Ahmed
Levancia Clarendon
Tom Costello

Marketing
Lucy Cameron
Tanjiah Islam

Production
Claire Keep
Fiona McIntosh

Publicity
Will O'Mullane

Sales
Jen Wilson
Victoria Laws
Esther Waters
Frances Doyle
Ben Goddard
Georgina Cutler
Jack Hallam
Anna Egelstaff
Inês Figueira
Barbara Ronan
Andrew Hally
Dominic Smith
Deborah Deyong
Lauren Buck

Maggy Park
Linda McGregor
Sinead White
Jemimah James
Rachael Jones
Jack Dennison
Nigel Andrews
Ian Williamson
Julia Benson
Declan Kyle
Robert Mackenzie
Megan Smith
Charlotte Clay
Rebecca Cobbold

Operations
Jo Jacobs
Sharon Willis

Rights
Susan Howe
Krystyna Kujawinska
Jessica Purdue
Ayesha Kinley
Louise Henderson

About the Author

T.A. Willberg grew up on a small-holding in South Africa. At 27, she moved to Malta with her partner and wrote her debut novel, *Marion Lane and the Midnight Murder*. Though the novel is set in London, much of the inspiration for the story setting arose from the labyrinthine corridors beneath Malta's ancient capital, Valletta.

Willberg credits her father, a mechanical engineer from Germany, as the influence behind the novel's many wondrous gadgets and her mother, after whom the protagonist is named, as the architect of her love for books and storytelling.

When not writing, or dreaming up mystical subterranean worlds, Willberg is treating patients in her spinal therapy clinic or consuming unhealthy amounts of cake and wine.